Mercy Falls

by

Josie Grey

Mercy Falls

Contact Information: info@thewildrosepress.com

Cover Art by *The Wild Rose Press, Inc.*

The Wild Rose Press, Inc.
PO Box 708
Adams Basin, NY 14410-0708
Visit us at www.thewildrosepress.com

Publishing History
First Edition, 2024
Trade Paperback ISBN 978-1-5092-5439-2
Digital ISBN 978-1-5092-5440-8

Published in the United States of America

Dedication

To Liss Rose for being the absolute best.

Acknowledgements

First, a huge thank you to everyone who took the time to help me make this story better. Voss Editing, you are truly amazing for always making my work be the best it can be. Ellie Fredericks, you are responsible for making this story legible and I am eternally grateful. Brad Jensen, thank you for looking at so many drafts that I can't even count and bearing with me when I make the same mistakes hundreds (thousands?) of times. To my editor, Dianne Rich, I could not have done this without you and I thank you from the bottom of my heart.

Lastly, to all the readers who love this story like I do — thank you for making me want to keep writing.

Chapter One

Vee

Verity Taylor left the city like it was on fire.

The nervous energy that had her up since dawn coursed down her arms as she gripped the steering wheel and leaned into a turn. Her wheels hugged the edge of the on-ramp, catapulting her car onto the highway and away from the suffocating congestion of Boston. She reached up and adjusted the rearview mirror, ignoring the fear reflecting in the green eyes that stared back.

Freedom.

A ringtone blared through the car's speakers and her hand shot out, silencing the call. The guilt that would come from a conversation with her Aunt Rose might be enough to make her turn around, and there was nothing to go back to.

A voicemail notification chimed, and she pressed play before second-guessing it.

"Hi, Vee. Just wanted to wish you a good first day, Ms. Manager. I'm so proud of you."

Her shoulders slumped with the weight of what she was doing. Rose had taken Vee in with no reservations when her mom died twenty years ago. The truth was the least of what Vee owed her.

She took a deep breath as she tapped on her aunt's

name.

Rose's warm voice filled the car after only a few rings. "Hi, sweetie. You didn't have to call back. I'm sure you're busy."

A lump lodged in Vee's throat. She would've been busy if she'd accepted the promotion her ad agency had offered. But then her fifty-hour work weeks would have turned into seventy-hour ones, and the pressure of already impossible deadlines would have crushed her. She tightened her grip on the steering wheel and debated how to break the news that she'd given up her career, sublet her apartment, and was on her way to a job she could have qualified for in high school.

"Vee? Are you there?"

"Yes…" *Just having a quarter-life crisis.* She cleared her throat. "I'm here. Thanks for the message. It's a big change, but I'm excited." *Coward.*

"You'll do great. You worked so hard for this."

Vee flinched. She'd done the work, but Rose had used the better part of her savings to put Vee through school. A degree that meant nothing now. Her voice cracked. "I couldn't have done it without you."

"Nonsense. You can do anything. Except maybe mountain climbing."

A crack broke through Vee's self-loathing and one corner of her mouth tugged up. "I've only ended up on crutches once."

"True, but you also didn't make it past the parking lot that time." Her aunt's soft laugh came through the line. "I love you. Go have a great day."

The lump reformed, and Vee swallowed it down. "Thanks. Love you more."

Just breathe.

Her hold on the steering wheel loosened, color flooding back to her knuckles as the call ended. She'd tell her. Just not today. Preferably, not any day until she'd figured out what to do with the rest of her life.

****

Four hours later, Vee rolled down her window and took a deep breath. Tension had melted away with every mile she put behind her, and the breeze flowing into the car brought with it her first whiff of briny sea air. The car crested a hill, and she caught a view of the town below, wrapped around one side of a bay. Across the calm water, her destination waited, alone on a vast lawn, The Cliffside Inn.

She didn't have time to take more than a glance before her gaze was drawn up the cliff behind the inn. At the top, a slate gray mansion perched at the edge, its square tower rising five stories above the already dizzying height. A shiver of déjà vu slid up her spine but disappeared before she could latch onto the sensation.

A horn blared behind her, and her foot hit the gas too hard, jolting her car forward. She gripped the silver charm that hung around her neck and slid it back and forth on its thin chain, steadying her breathing as she wound downhill toward town.

When the road finally flattened out, she passed a "Welcome to Cliffside" sign, and the forest began to make room for houses. They clustered closer together the nearer she got to the center of town until there were only a few feet between each brightly painted or shingled façade. As soon as the tower house came back into view, she leaned over the steering wheel and squinted. The details were lost to the distance, and the sunny day had no effect on the house. Any light that touched it was swallowed up by the dark stone and shadowed windows.

A knot coiled in her stomach, and she forced herself to focus on the road as she passed a small beach nestled in the bay. Pavement gave way to dirt, and she bumped down the inn's driveway, second-guessing every choice she'd made in the past few weeks. The inn came into sight and the knot unwound. The cloud of doubt over her decision to uproot her life dissipated with the first glimpse of her home for the summer. The pictures on its website didn't do it justice. A three-story white colonial, its window boxes overflowed with yellow flowers tucked under blue shutters, and at the very top perched a cupola. Its warmth was a stark contrast to the cliff-top mansion looming overhead.

Vee pulled her car next to one of the few others in the lot and took a moment to stretch before tossing her sunglasses onto the passenger seat and stepping out. Tilting forward, she used the sideview mirror to smooth her windblown hair. The sunlight picked up the natural blonde and red highlights that ran through her otherwise chestnut brown waves. She straightened up and crunched across the gravel, silently thanking herself for choosing flats.

Inside, an empty reception desk sat under an impressive mahogany staircase. The inn's owner had warned her they wouldn't start filling up until the official beginning of summer in a few days. Her advice for Vee's arrival was to "poke around until you find me."

Vee followed a warm, buttery scent into the inn's dining room. Polished wooden tables gleamed in the sunlight that streamed through windows overlooking the lawn and ocean beyond. But the dining room was as empty as the entryway. She was about to backtrack when a painting above the fireplace caught her eye.

It was a boat's view of the inn from the bay at sunset, with breathtaking oranges and fiery reds erupting across the sky. The way the artist bled the colors together had Vee's fingers itching for her paintbrush, but just like on the road, everything faded away once her gaze landed on the tower house. She crossed the room and stepped up on the hearth, craning her neck to make out the details of the cliff-top manor.

A deep voice shattered the silence. "By the one and only Ruth Jacobs."

Vee slipped off the hearth and barely caught her balance on the back of the closest chair to keep from falling to the floor.

Heat rose to her cheeks. *Graceful as always.*

With her head tilted down, a pair of work boots were the first thing she saw. She lifted her chin and smoothed out her skirt, willing her hammering heart to slow.

A man's light blue eyes crinkled with an amused smile. "Sorry to startle you. I thought you were trying to make out the artist's name."

"Thanks." The shock subsided, and Vee took in his other features. About her age, he had dirty-blond hair, an untucked T-shirt, cargo pants, and was completely covered in paint splatters.

"Hi. I'm Damon. Resident handyman, dishwasher, and art historian May through September." He glanced at his paint-covered hands. His smile grew, sharpening his jawline and revealing a dimple on his left cheek.

"I'd offer to shake your hand, but this hasn't all dried yet."

"Nice to meet you. I'm Vee." His easygoing nature let her forget she'd almost fallen on her face in front of him. "Is Ruth Jacobs any relation to the owner of the inn, Meredith Jacobs?"

"As a matter of fact, she is. Ruth was Meredith's mom. And they both have the pleasure of being related to yours truly. Meredith is my aunt, entitling her to summers of my hard manual labor for almost no pay to take with me when I leave in the fall."

Behind him, a petite woman pushed her way through a swinging door and strode across the dining room. "Don't start filling her head with nonsense before I have a chance to warn her about you."

Despite her serious expression, affection filled her voice.

"Speak of the devil." Damon turned toward his aunt. "Don't worry, I was just telling her how lucky you are to have me."

Meredith was dressed in a crisp white blouse and pale blue capris with low-heeled sandals. Completely white hair, cut stylishly short, framed her tanned face. Despite the hair, she didn't look or move like she could be a day over forty.

She rolled her eyes and reached out a hand. "Welcome, you must be Vee. I've been expecting you and am so looking forward to having you with us this summer."

Damon shook his head. "She must really like you. All I got was a *do you know how late you are?* and two buckets of paint handed to me when I arrived this morning." His impression of Meredith's voice was spot on.

Meredith cocked her head. “Maybe that’s because you said you’d be here Monday, and it’s now Wednesday. Speaking of that, is the fence done?”

“Just about to finish up the last coat now.” With a wide smile, he mouthed to Vee, “Not even close.”

Meredith looked like she was suppressing her own grin as Damon backed toward the door. “Vee, it was nice to meet you. I’ll see you around.” He tipped an imaginary hat at Meredith. “Warden.”

He trotted down the back steps, and Meredith turned, shaking her head. “A real comedian.”

A short blonde stepped into the room, and Meredith waved her over. “Becca, this is Vee. She’s with us for the summer. Would you take her on a tour before I show her where she’s staying?”

“Sure.” Becca smiled at Vee. “I’m so glad you’re here. Last year’s summer hire didn’t show, and Memorial Day weekend was brutal.”

Classic rock blared from the cell phone in Meredith’s hand, and she jumped. She took a deep breath, answered, and asked the caller to hold for a moment. Turning to Vee, she said, “Come by the office when you’re done, and we’ll fill out the paperwork. By then, I should’ve found my nephew and properly thanked him for such an appropriate ringtone.”

Vee grinned as Meredith left, and Becca took over. “Here. I’ll show you where we put our stuff.” Off the kitchen, a small stock room had a row of cubbies and a couple folding chairs. Becca tossed her purse and the sweatshirt she’d been wearing into a cubby and pulled a short-sleeve button-up shirt monogrammed with *Cliffside Inn* from a rack in the corner.

She tugged it on over her tank top and yoga pants and looked at Vee as she pulled her hair into a messy bun. “We all take shifts in housekeeping, reception, and the dining room. I’m on housekeeping today, so I can look a little like crap.”

She led them back through the kitchen and into the dining room. “Breakfast is just for guests of the inn, but we’re open to the public for lunch and dinner.”

They crossed into the foyer, and Becca pointed to a door marked *Private*. “That’s Meredith’s living space, which is off-limits.” She didn’t slow on their way to the stairs.

Vee followed closely, trailing one hand on the smooth banister.

Becca led her through the second, then the third floor, pointing out which doors led to guest rooms and which were linen closets or full of cleaning supplies.

Near a sitting area on the third floor, Vee paused at the window. “This view is incredible.”

Becca’s eyes sparkled. “It’s not even the best one in the house. Come with me.”

Leading the way, Becca opened a small door next to one of the maids’ closets. Vee stepped in first and climbed the narrow stairs, emerging into the cupola. Windows lined all eight sides with heavily cushioned pillows occupying the seats below.

“Amazing, right?” Becca handed Vee one of the pairs of binoculars that rested on the window’s ledge. “Here. You can see the boats out to sea…or spy on people in town.” She raised her eyebrows and picked up another pair for herself.

Vee held hers up and adjusted the focus. It was true. She could make out boats rolling peacefully on waves so far out she wouldn't have known they existed. She made a slow circle, scanning the houses and shops that lined the point, continuing until she traced the hill upward to the house on the cliff behind them.

She adjusted the focus again to sharpen the image, her heart rate picking up. The house was stunning. Made of stone, it looked indestructible. Ivy snaked up the walls of the square tower, wrapping the hard stone in a soft embrace. Vee leaned toward the window, an overwhelming desire to get closer tugging her forward.

A flash of movement halfway up the tower caught her eye, and she squinted. A shirtless man peered through a set of curtains. Goosebumps trailed down Vee's spine as her gaze traced the path a jagged scar cut across his tanned, well-defined chest. She tilted her view up, but his face was obscured by shaggy, dark hair and his own set of binoculars. Pointed directly at the cupola.

Her grip on her binoculars slipped. When she pulled them back up, the window was empty.

"Ah, I see you've noticed our haunted house." Becca joined her, staring up the cliff.

"It's beautiful." Vee continued to search the darkened windows for signs of life. "Who lives there?"

In a mock English accent, Becca said, "It's the Dryer Residence." They both set down their binoculars, and Vee followed Becca back down to the third floor. "Their family has lived there for ages. It's owned by Eli Dryer currently and he's a real piece of work. Hopefully, you won't meet him. If he does come into town, you'll know it. He basically terrorizes everyone in his path."

"I think I saw him. It's only him up there?" Vee

shut the door to the stairs behind her.

"Him and a maid, or housekeeper, or whatever you want to call her. Gail. She has to be at least a hundred years old because she was already ancient when I was a kid. Eli also has a son, Blake. He's there on and off. He's gorgeous but takes being a jerk to a new level. Thankfully, both of them keep to themselves most of the time."

"Who keeps to themselves?" a female voice mumbled from behind a stack of towels coming up the stairs.

Becca pulled open the linen closet and took the towels, revealing a flawless porcelain face framed by short, dark hair. The girl's deep brown eyes looked Vee up and down.

Towels deposited, Becca turned back to them. "I was giving the newest addition to our Cliffside Inn family the rundown on the Dryer men. Vee, this is JJ."

JJ scowled. "Pair of assholes."

"And that's putting it lightly." Becca shoved the door of the linen closet shut.

"What got you on the Dryer history lesson?" JJ asked Vee.

"We were in the cupola, and I saw Eli shirtless in the window."

JJ's eyebrows rose. "Ugh. I'm sorry. A half-naked, pasty, old man with a beer belly isn't the most attractive sight to welcome you to town."

Becca giggled, and Vee shook her head. "It must have been Blake. I only saw him for a second, but he definitely didn't look pasty or fat. And that scar…" Vee's fingers grazed over her own scars on her right palm. The man's had looked much deeper.

Becca's laughter died. "What scar?"

Vee drew an imaginary line down her chest, tracing the path.

"No way," Becca whispered.

JJ's eyes narrowed at Vee. "You think you're funny?"

"No. Why?" A lead pit settled in Vee's stomach from her icy tone.

Becca turned toward JJ. "She just got here. She wouldn't know."

"So what do you think, Becca? It's a lucky guess?" JJ shot another glare at Vee before whipping around and storming down the stairs.

Vee raised her eyebrows. "Um, what just happened?"

"You really don't know?" Becca shifted her weight from foot to foot, avoiding eye contact. " 'Cause that would be messed up if you're playing some sort of joke on us."

"Know what?"

"Who you described doesn't sound like Eli or Blake." She bit her lip, her gaze flicking to the empty staircase. "It sounds more like Eli's older son, Luke."

"So? He never comes to visit?"

"That would be highly improbable." Becca met Vee's eye. "Luke Dryer is dead.

Chapter Two

Luke

Halfway up the tower, Luke Dryer turned on a tap in the bathroom, and a groan rose through the pipes. Judging by the layer of dust he'd found when he arrived last night, not even the cleaning staff had been in this part of the house since he'd been gone. Even back when he lived here full time, it was rare anyone would venture up the ancient stairs besides him.

He splashed water on his face and braced his hands on either side of the sink. Lifting his head, he stared at the empty space where a mirror used to hang. The reminder that he couldn't stand the sight of himself tore open something new in him each time it surfaced, and he turned away. He ran a towel over his face, ignoring the change in sensation when the material grazed his scars. Almost twenty years and the numbness still managed to feel raw.

He yanked his shirt off the towel rack and stepped out of the bathroom with it balled in his fist. *Fuck everything about this place.*

The loud caw of a raven came from the end of the hall, and he crossed the smooth stone floor, passing his bedroom. Outside the window, the bird leapt from its perch on the ledge, sunlight reflecting off its inky blue wings. Years ago, he'd whittled one just like it when he started to dabble in woodworking. He picked up a pair of binoculars that sat on the ledge and blew the dust off the lenses.

After adjusting the sight, he tracked the bird as it soared over the trees and down the hill. A flash from the cupola at the inn pulled his attention away from the raven, and he sharpened the focus to find a pair of binoculars aimed back at him.

The stranger holding them stared directly at the tower with no shame.

Probably trying to get a glimpse of the freakshow.

His heart pounded and an angry flush heated his cheeks. He'd been here less than twenty-four hours and the blatant gawking had already begun.

He closed his eyes and took a deep breath. The last thing he needed was to let insecurities bubble up and distract him from why he was here.

Let them look. This was as close as anyone would get.

He tossed down the binoculars and tugged on his shirt as he stepped away from the window.

The door to his bedroom stood open, his one-hundred-and-thirty-pound Newfoundland sprawled across the king-sized bed.

"Zeus, come."

The dog excitedly obeyed. Halfway down the worn stone stairs, he shoved by Luke.

"Damn, boy. Take it easy." Luke ducked to miss the low beam at the bottom of the stairs and found Zeus in the kitchen. His tail thumped on the deep-red tile floor where he sat, staring at the door that led to a small garden.

Luke pulled open the door but didn't bother closing

it after the dog shot out into the yard. Zeus would come back on his own timetable. He opened a cupboard and reached in for the dog food. The scent of freshly brewed coffee hit him, and his head dropped.

Someone else was here. He sighed and poured the kibble. So much for having a few weeks of peace.

A familiar female voice spoke from behind. “Please tell me you’re not just waking up now.”

A smile broke across his face, and he turned to where his family’s long-time housekeeper, Gail, entered the room with a bag full of groceries. Luke set the bag of dog food next to the bowl. “Here, let me help you.”

She twisted away. “Nonsense. I’m old, not infirm.”

Time was no match for Gail. She refused to divulge her age, but Luke guessed it as around seventy, although it was impossible to really tell. Her frail frame and severe gray bun hadn’t changed since he was a kid.

As happy as he was to see her, a twinge of dread snuck up on him. If she was here, his father had summoned her.

“So, they’re back?” He dropped onto a stool at the kitchen island.

“No. Both your dad and Blake landed safely in London days ago, but Eli told me you’d agreed to come. When I saw the lights up here last night, I figured it was you.” She placed the bag on the island in front of him. “I brought some groceries to stock you up.”

“You didn’t have to do that.”

She waved him off and reached into the bag. “And here’s a treat for my favorite pup. Where is he?” She pulled out a chew toy.

Zeus stepped back inside with his ears perked, then

bounded across the kitchen to Gail. She bent down as the dog slowed his approach. He tilted his head for her to scratch behind his ears. "There you are. Miss me?"

"He did. And so did I. After this is over, you should try to make it up our way more than once a year." Luke rubbed his forehead, careful to avoid touching the worst of the scars.

Gail raised her eyebrows. "After this is over, hopefully there'll be no reason for you to stay away." She pulled a carton of eggs from the bag and set a frying pan on the stove while Zeus gnawed on his chew toy at her feet.

"I can make my own breakfast." Luke stood when she turned on the burner.

"I know you can. I'm the one who taught you." She shot him a glance. "And I think this constitutes lunch since you've slept past noon."

"Burning the midnight oil." Luke reached inside the bag and pulled out the stuff that needed to go in the fridge.

"More like hiding." She cracked an egg in the pan and turned her back to him.

He didn't answer. They both knew she was right. After he put away the groceries, he folded the empty bag and poured two cups of coffee. Stepping around the island, he joined Gail at the hand-carved kitchen table. He slid one mug toward her and took a seat at the place she'd set for him.

One leg jittered under the table. Everything was about to become real. *If after all these years, the girl's no longer safe…* Luke shook his head to clear the thought and forced himself to look at Gail. "How bad is it?"

Gail cupped the warm mug in her hands and peered through the steam at him. “Not too bad, yet. Eli knows her birth name and age. It may be impossible for him to find more than that. There’s no paper trail.”

“I’m going to start leaving breadcrumbs today. Make it look like she’s living in San Diego.” Luke pushed eggs around on the plate, mentally taking inventory of his plans. Sign her up online for a gym membership, build a couple of fake social media accounts, add a not quite up-to-date resume to a job search site…it should keep his dad and brother convinced Luke was helping when he “found” each fake crumb. “Over the next few days, I’ll have enough to make them think I’ve got a solid lead on where she is.”

“Good. But temporary.”

“Temporary is fine. June fourteenth is only a few weeks away. Dad will give up when it passes and nothing happens.” Luke absently traced one of the patterns he’d carved into the table years ago, intricate vines wrapping around an oak tree. The whole thing was protected against time beneath a glass inlay. He looked up to meet Gail’s eye. “He’ll see there is no curse.”

Gail pushed back her chair and picked up her mug, setting it into the sink. “I hope you’re right.” She turned back to face him and crossed her arms, eyebrows knit together. “For now, at least she’s safe. She started a new job today, and that should keep her firmly in Boston until the danger has passed.”

Luke’s shoulders relaxed at the news. “If Dad and Blake catch on that something’s not adding up in San Diego, I’ll buy a plane ticket to somewhere in South

America in her name and have them follow an imaginary backpacking trip. They won't find her."

Silence hung between them until her voice broke the pause. "Thank you, Luke."

He looked down at his barely touched plate. "You never have to thank me for this."

The doorbell rang, and Gail raised her eyebrows. "Are you expecting anyone?"

Luke stood. "Yeah. I ordered some equipment, so I can work out of the barn while I'm here."

She waved her hand for him to sit back down. "Eat. I'll point them in the right direction."

He sank back into the chair as she started toward the door. "And Gail…"

She glanced back at him.

"Thanks for the groceries. I'll be fine on my own, though. Consider yourself off duty until my dad and Blake get back."

She nodded, then quietly left. He pushed the plate of eggs away but picked up his coffee. No one made coffee like Gail. She added a dash of cinnamon to the grounds, but whenever Luke tried it on his own, he got the proportions wrong and ended up with the taste of Thanksgiving on steroids.

He drank a second cup before dumping his uneaten eggs in the trash and heading to the front hall. One hand reached for the doorknob then paused and he sidestepped to a window instead. The delivery men were climbing back into their truck. He could wait another minute to go out. He gritted his teeth. *Coward.*

Through the window, the taillights of the truck disappeared down the driveway and he opened the door, sunlight warming his face.

The majority of the next two hours were spent setting up his woodworking tools in the barn and organizing a schedule for the orders he had waiting. It would be a little stuffy when the summer heat set in, but with the doors open, at least there'd be a breeze.

Satisfied it'd do while he was stuck here, he went back to the kitchen to grab lunch. Gail would be happy. He'd finally worked up an appetite.

The contents of the full fridge made him smile. No cold cuts or frozen meals. Everything in there would require some preparation.

Years earlier, she'd insisted on teaching him well beyond the basics in the kitchen. Her exact words had been, "If you're going to continue to be a broody mess, you'll need to make up for it somewhere if you have any hope of someone putting up with you long term."

His smile faded to a frown. Regardless of his culinary skills, plenty of girls were willing to put up with him once they realized how many zeros were attached to his name. There'd been only one who mattered, and the scars from that relationship ran deeper than any of his physical ones.

He reached into the fridge and pulled out thinly sliced chicken breast, eyeing the tomatoes on the counter. He toasted half a French baguette, rubbed a clove of garlic on the warm bread, then topped it with chicken, hot from the grill pan. Thickly sliced tomatoes, fresh basil, and a drizzle of balsamic completed the sandwich.

The first bite was better than anything he'd made in a long time. The past few months especially. He seldom left his small cabin in Novia Scotia if he could help it. That resulted in frequent meals of fish, complemented with canned soup. At times, for breakfast, lunch, and dinner.

A lifestyle he would have happily continued, until his father showed up last week unannounced.

Luke matched his dad at six feet tall with broad shoulders, but Eli's overstuffed presence filled the cabin as he'd poked around. "This is it? You trying to prove something by living like you're poor?"

"Yeah, Dad. You got me." Never mind that he could hear the ocean while he fell asleep and only had to walk steps to the beach to gather driftwood for projects. Or that it was a small corner of the world where he could relax, without worrying about anyone staring. The town was made up of locals who appreciated a good recluse.

"Well, maybe this won't be as difficult as I'd worried." Eli landed hard onto a chair at Luke's kitchen table. "You have any scotch?"

"Fresh out," Luke lied. It wouldn't benefit either of them to draw this visit out by making his dad comfortable.

"Then I'll just get to it. You need to come home." His eyes sparkled. "Luke, we found her."

Luke focused on keeping his breathing even while a wave of terror crashed over him. "Oh?"

"Practically. All these years sifting through old documents, and that blind idiot, Stu, finally earned his paycheck. He found a hospital record in Portland. A Jane Doe treated for lacerations on her right arm. Brought in on the night of June fourteenth, her fifth birthday, twenty years ago."

Luke swallowed, his throat bone dry. "So what?"

Eli shook his head. "So what? Don't you see what

this means? It's not a coincidence. The girl *survived.* I'm willing to bet my life that she's the key to ending the curse."

Through gritted teeth, Luke said slowly, "Dad, for the last time, there is no curse."

"Don't be stupid. Take a trip to your mother's grave." He pointed a thick finger toward Luke. "Or go look at your face and tell me that again."

Luke slammed his hands on the table. "You did this to my face!" As he said it, his skin tugged in an unnatural way along the edges of the jagged slashes marring his right forehead and cheek. Same as it always did when he had an exaggerated facial expression.

"Oh, please. You deserved the reminder, but you could have fixed it yourself once you turned eighteen. It's been your own choice to look like an extra in a horror movie since then."

"I'm not talking about you refusing to pay for reconstructive surgery."

"Enough." Eli's voice boomed in the small space. "You want to blame me for something set in motion almost two hundred years ago? Instead, you should be happy. I'm about to end it."

Luke leaned against the kitchen cabinets, not wanting to be an inch closer to his father than he had to. Debating pulling out the scotch after all, he fought to keep his voice disinterested. "Congrats. But I don't see what that has to do with me."

"We need your help. It's a long trail to follow, and you know we can't involve anyone else for obvious reasons."

"No one wants to be an accessory to murder?"

Eli narrowed his eyes. "Watch your mouth."

Luke stared at him until he steadied his breath. “I’m not interested. Sorry, you wasted a trip.”

“You should be sorry. For yourself.” Eli leaned forward, elbows resting on the table. “If you don’t help us, you’re cut off. Immediately.” Looking around the cabin, he added, “Although, by the look of things, that won’t change much.”

It wouldn’t. Luke hadn’t touched his family account in years. Even if he stopped living like a hermit, he’d be fine without his inheritance. The hand-carved pieces he made as a hobby sold for more than he’d ever dreamed. He’d started selling them when he’d run out of room. Now, his driftwood sculptures easily hit four figures. The custom furniture could tip into five, depending on the level of detail and the buyer’s specific requests.

Despite his father’s threat carrying no weight, an idea crept up. There’d be no better way to stop this insane quest than by misdirecting it. A second was all it took to decide how to play his hand.

He balled his fists, forcing his voice to rise. “You can’t disinherit me.”

Satisfaction spread across Eli’s face. “I can. And I will.”

“Fine. I’ll help.” Luke pointed toward a laptop tucked under a pile of papers on his kitchen counter. “But I can search for her here as easily as I can in Maine.”

“No. I want you home. All the files are there, and there could be something we missed.” Eli’s eyes widened. “Everything changes now that we know there’s a living descendant of the witch.”

Luke swallowed the urge to scream. His dad could

run multiple companies but somehow still believed the boogieman lived under his bed. Luke locked eyes with Eli. “Why can’t Blake do it?”

“I’m taking Blake to London to deal with an acquisition. Unlike you, he has an interest in learning the family business. We’ll be limited on time and there’s not a moment to waste. We’re really close, Luke, I feel it.”

“When do you and Blake leave?”

“Day after tomorrow.”

“I’ll be home by the end of the week.”

“Excellent.” Eli stood and twirled his car key around one finger. “I’ll make sure all the documents Stu found are waiting for you.”

And they had been when Luke arrived home last night. Neatly piled in a box on a desk in the office that his father had taken to calling The War Room since his obsession began.

The Dryer Family Curse was a tall tale Luke’s grandfather told them as kids. A joke when little mishaps occurred every June fourteenth. But when the same grandfather died on the supposed curse date, Eli stopped laughing.

Every year from then on, Eli scrutinized June fourteenth for any sign of misfortune. One year, Blake fell off his bike and broke his arm. The curse. Another, their vacation home in the Florida Keys was destroyed by a hurricane. The curse. Eli was sued for breach of contract. Obviously, the curse.

If a misfortune occurred on June fourteenth, it didn’t matter if it was an impulsive eight-year-old, an act of nature, or a completely justified lawsuit. Or a drunken mother, whom they hadn’t laid eyes on since

Blake was in diapers, crashing while driving into oncoming traffic. In Eli's eyes, it was proof.

Luke picked up his empty plate and washed it before heading deeper into the house, Zeus padding along beside him. They reached the office door, and Luke took a deep breath, flicking on the light.

Inside the room, insanity thickened the air. A massive whiteboard had been fastened to one wall. There, Eli or Blake had painstakingly listed every "curse" event they found going back the full two hundred years. Boxes were stacked wherever they fit, containing hundreds of newspaper clippings, death certificates, and other legal documents. All of it, the work of the historian Eli employed, a gentle old man named Stu, who had no idea what he was doing research for.

The back wall had two family trees sketched out side-by-side. One was topped with the name Jonathan Dryer, the ancestor involved in the curse's origin. The other tree's shorter limbs branched out from the supposed witch, Mercy Falls. Most names in both trees had been struck through with a thin line indicating they no longer lived. The Dryer side had three names remaining: Eli, Lucas, and Blake. Every name on the Falls' tree had a line through it except the last one. The last time Luke was here, the spot was blank except for a question mark. Now, the name was filled in and circled over and over in red maker: Verity Falls.

Luke turned his back on the family trees and powered on the lone computer in the room. Eli kept as much as possible in hard copy. A paper trail would be easier to erase once Eli found Verity and killed her. Just like he'd killed her mother twenty years ago.

Luke cracked his knuckles and sat down in front of the computer. Time to see how much damage he could do to his father's plan.

Chapter Three

Vee

After the encounter with JJ, Vee followed Becca outside to continue their tour. Somewhere between the outdoor grill and the gazebo, the friendliness in their conversation seeped back in. By the time Becca left Vee at Meredith's office, she'd almost forgotten anything had happened.

When Vee knocked on the open door, Meredith looked up from behind a tidy desk and waved her in. "How was the tour?"

"It was great. The inn's beautiful." Vee settled into the chair across from her.

"I'm glad you like it." Meredith beamed. "Now, I just need you to sign some paperwork, and I'll show you where you're staying."

Vee took the papers and breezed through the standard W-4, only to pause at the page asking for an emergency contact.

There wasn't a long list of options. Or any, really. Vee's father had never been in the picture, and after her mom died, the only one left was Rose. She'd be livid if the way she found out Vee was lying was through an emergency call. Vee tapped the pen on the paper.

With no one else coming to mind, Vee scrawled her aunt's contact info, resolving to not have any emergencies. She put the pen on the pages and slid them across the desk.

Meredith set them aside and took a set of keys from her desk drawer. “Great. Ready?”

Vee nodded and followed her out of the office, then through the front door. She glanced at her car as they walked past it. “When the ad said onsite housing, I thought I’d be staying at the inn?”

“Technically, you are. Last year, I was considering expanding the parking lot. When I had the property records examined, we found the land extends partway up the hill. That happens to include a beautiful stone cottage. It’s not one hundred percent ready for guests, but I think you’ll be comfortable there. Plus, you’ll have privacy while still being a short walk from the inn.”

This keeps getting better.

They walked down the driveway and crossed the street, stopping at the edge of the forest. Meredith pointed to a set of stone stairs that led down to the sandy beach. “The path’s a little overgrown at the moment, but the entrance is easy enough to find if you remember it’s directly across from those steps.” Meredith ducked under a low-hanging branch and Vee followed her into the woods.

The “short walk” turned out to be more of an actual hike. Meredith had to be part mountain goat from the way she expertly navigated the roots and rocks jutting up from the path while continually calling back details to Vee.

“I’ve had the cottage cleaned and furnished. The only downside is there’s no access by car—Whoops, sorry!” She paused as a tree branch swung back, catching Vee in the side of the head. "I'll have the grounds crew trim these back for you."

Vee brushed pine needles off her shoulder. "Thanks." Her calf muscles were happy for the break.

Meredith resumed her quick pace. "The land the inn's on used to belong to the Dryer's, so the only direct access by car is from their property. Eli was livid when he realized we'd made a few trips up his driveway with new furniture and equipment to clean up the yard. I'm trying to work out an arrangement with him, but so far, no luck." They stepped out of the woods at the edge of a small, well-manicured lawn. "See, that wasn't so bad of a walk."

Vee couldn't answer. The first glimpse of the cottage rooted her to the ground. It was the same gray stone as the house that towered above, but instead of dark and imposing, it glowed in the sunlight. The window frames were a royal blue, matching the front door. Somewhere, deep inside her, a key turned in a lock. *Home.*

"Come on. Take a look." Meredith started across the lawn. "We were going to use it for storage, but when I laid eyes on it, I knew it would be a waste not to turn it into a guest house."

Vee followed with quick steps, happiness settling over her like a second skin. This was the right choice. The inn, the town, the cottage…It was all perfect.

They passed a bench, shaded beneath the branches of an ancient elm tree. Vee stumbled to a stop. A curtain of misery descended over her, the deep ache of loss so overpowering, it robbed her of breath. The leaves above rustled as a warm breeze chased away the sensation, and just like swimming through a cold spot in a lake, the sorrow was gone. She stepped forward, glancing back to find nothing out of the ordinary on the patch of lawn behind her.

Adrenaline coursed down her limbs, tingling as she caught up to Meredith on the front steps, glancing back one more time. *What was that?*

Meredith turned the key, and the door swung open. “It’s come a long way, but it’s still a little rustic, I’m afraid.”

Vee stepped inside, catching the slightest scent of sage. A small but sturdy-looking staircase split the space between a cozy living room and a kitchen with a small dining area.

Meredith climbed the stairs, pointing at the fireplace in the living room. “Unfortunately, that isn’t usable until the chimney gets repaired, but I don’t think you’ll need it. I’m more worried about the lack of A/C but tell me either way. If the temperature’s unbearable, we can make other arrangements.”

“I’m sure I’ll be fine.” Vee’s hand paused above the banister, her palm tingling with the surety that it had done the same movement a thousand times. She grasped the smooth wood and exhaled. A pleasant chill ran up her spine.

A little hot or cold wouldn’t matter. This place was meant for her.

At the top of the stairs, Meredith pointed to the door straight ahead. “The bathroom’s in there and all in working order, thank God.” She opened a second door. “And here’s the bedroom.”

Following her in, Vee widened her eyes. The afternoon light filtered through lace curtains to make the soft yellow tones in the room glow. A patchwork quilt lay across a double bed and a window seat was tucked underneath a front-facing window. Vee hardly noticed any of it. The spectacular view of the beach and ocean below drew her in. From this angle, it looked like they must be at least halfway up the hill.

Meredith joined her at the window. "Makes the walk up worth it, doesn't it?"

"I'll say." The water in the bay glistened as if it was made of diamonds.

Moments later, Meredith cleared her throat. "Shall we head back down?"

"Yes. Sorry." Vee tore herself away from the view.

Meredith had started down the stairs when Vee stepped onto the landing and paused in front of a third door. "What's in here?"

Meredith glanced back. "Oh, it's the only room I haven't quite figured out what to do with yet. It's a little small for a second bedroom, so for now, it's not much of anything. Take a peek if you want, and I'll meet you outside."

Vee opened the door and found a room half the size of the bedroom, empty except for a shelf full of wood-carved animal figurines. She stepped inside and began mentally unpacking her art supplies. Everything she needed would fit easily and the light would be perfect for painting.

Turning to leave, the figurines on the shelf caught her eye. She leaned toward the closest one, an owl, small enough it could fit in the palm of her hand. Feathers so intricately carved, they looked like they'd be soft to the touch. She trailed one finger over its folded wing. Someone had poured their heart into these, only for them to sit forgotten. The front door slammed below, and she jogged downstairs, shaking her head free of the unexpected melancholy.

Silly. They're probably from a gift shop in town.

In the front yard, Meredith stared at her phone, frowning. "I don't seem to have service." She looked at Vee. "I can't have you stay up here with no way to reach out. Why don't we have you stay at the inn until I can get a landline installed?"

The thought of leaving the cottage behind made Vee's heart skip a beat. She pulled out her phone and glanced at the lack of bars. She forced a smile and tucked the phone away. "Weird, I have service."

"Oh, good." Meredith's shoulders relaxed and she held out the key. "So, if you're happy with it, it's yours."

Vee's fingers wrapped around the key, a gentle breeze bringing the scent of salt air up the hill. *Mine.*

She took the key, nodding. "I'm happy."

"Great. Let's head down."

Vee followed Meredith, already more surefooted on the path.

When they reached Vee's car, Meredith turned to her. "I stocked your cottage with the essentials, but the store in town is within walking distance. And the days you work, you're welcome to eat at the inn. Once a month, we close the dining room early and have a family dinner with all the staff. I'll let you know when we plan the next one."

"This is so much better than I expected." No one at Vee's last job would've used the word "family" to describe coworkers. "Competitors" would have been more accurate.

"I'm glad. It's shameful that cottage has been

empty for so long." Meredith stepped back. "I'll see you tomorrow morning at nine for your first official day."

"Sounds great."

"Good. I'll find Damon to help you with your bags. I'm sure he's somewhere around here, avoiding painting."

Vee shook her head. "I think I can manage, but thanks. I'll see you tomorrow."

As soon as Meredith set foot on the steps to the inn, Vee turned to her car and mentally planned how many trips it would take to get her bags up the hill. Confident she could do it in one, she slung a duffle over one shoulder, the case with her easel over the other, and dragged a suitcase behind her.

She'd only made it a couple dozen feet when Damon jogged up beside her. "Hey there, sherpa. You're in luck. I'm going your way and have two free hands."

"I'll take you up on that offer. Turns out wheels are not such an asset on gravel." She dropped the bags and pushed loose hair out of her eyes.

"Yeah. That looks heavy. Good luck with that one." Damon picked up the duffel and started down the driveway, leaving Vee staring at his back. He turned around, smiling. "Just kidding."

Vee laughed as he picked up the suitcase, leaving her with just the easel to carry.

"Thanks." She followed him down the driveway.

"So is Vee short for something?"

"Yes. My real name is—"

"Wait, wait. Don't tell me. Vanessa?"

She shook her head.

"Victoria?"

"Guess again."

"Velma?"

She huffed out a laugh. "Not even close."

"I'll get it. Just give me time." They crossed the road to the start of the trail and paused. Damon peered into the woods. "Meredith wanted me to take a look at how many branches need to be cut back. Looks like my answer will be, 'a lot.' "

"What good timing for me and my luggage." Vee smirked.

"Yeah, she's funny like that." Tires crunched on gravel behind them and his gaze shifted over Vee's shoulder. He waved, and Vee followed his eye line to where JJ's car turned from the inn's driveway onto the paved road to town.

JJ glanced at Vee, then cranked her radio as her car shot forward, spewing gravel in her wake.

Damon's gaze followed the car until it whipped around the curve and out of sight. "Wow. What's her problem today?"

Vee sighed. "Oh, I just seem to make friends everywhere I go."

He nodded, with a look of understanding. "JJ can be tough. She'll warm up."

"Yeah, well, I made a bad first impression. She pretty much lost it because I thought I saw a man with scars up in the tower house. She thinks I was messing with her about a guy that died."

Damon flinched. "Luke?"

"Apparently."

He let out a low whistle through his teeth. "Yeah, I can see that not going well."

“ ‘Not well’ is an understatement. We should start walking.” Vee stepped past him to take the lead. The conversation with JJ replayed in her mind with each step, and she fumed up the hill, fueled by frustration. She paused, panting, when they reached her new front door.

A few moments later, Damon stepped out of the woods and came up beside her, equally breathless. “Damn, you’re fast. Next time, you get the heavy bag.”

Her annoyance hadn’t lessened with the exertion and she frowned. “Sorry, it’s just the thing with JJ. I had no way of knowing what happened. Should I have a list of the town’s tragedies so I don’t bring another one up accidentally?”

“First, no need to apologize. Second, you don’t need a list. You hit the only sore spot. Particularly for JJ. Did Becca explain why she got so upset?”

“No.”

“Okay. Well, so you understand…Luke was in JJ’s class growing up. From what I’ve heard, he never had an easy time making friends. Classes here are small, so there wasn’t a lot of middle ground. You were either liked or excluded, and a lot of people were jealous of the Dryers.” He took a deep breath and nodded toward the house above them. “Something happened up there when they were in fifth grade. Police and an ambulance…but no official story in the paper. The rumor was that a woman and her kid fell off the cliff.”

Vee sucked in a breath, thinking about the dizzying drop.

“Luke was out of school for a few weeks, and when he came back, his face was all torn up. The rumor mill went wild, but the one that stuck was that Luke killed them, and his scars came from the struggle."

"That's a horrible rumor to make up."

"It is." Damon paused. "But apparently he never denied it."

Vee glanced to the top of the tower through the trees. "When did he die?"

"Both he and his brother Blake switched to private school shortly after the incident. The story I heard is that Luke kept to himself until he showed up to a party in high school. He didn't exactly get a warm welcome. The next day, Blake broke the news that Luke had gone back up the hill and jumped."

"Jumped? Off the cliff?" Goosebumps snaked up and down Vee's arms.

Damon nodded. "Kids can be cruel. Especially jealous kids. Kids like JJ."

Vee took a deep breath. "She was one of the kids picking on him? That's why she's so sensitive?"

"Bingo." Damon touched one finger to his nose.

"I really wish I'd never said anything." Vee slid the charm on her necklace back and forth. "Everyone's going to think I'm intentionally stirring things up, or that I'm a nut who thinks she sees ghosts."

"You saw his face?"

"No. Only his chest."

"I wouldn't worry about it. I doubt JJ or Becca will mention it to anyone. Plus, you said it was a grown man you saw, not a teenager. Unless ghosts grow, I think you can safely say you're not a nut. Blake's probably back. I'd bet that's who you saw."

"What about the scar?"

Damon shrugged. "It was far away. Maybe a shadow."

Vee let go of her necklace and looked up at him. "You're frighteningly rational, aren't you?"

"Terrifyingly." He offered a contagious smile, then nodded to her front door. "Want help getting the bags upstairs?"

"No, I can take it from here. Thanks, Damon."

He backed down the path with his hands in his front pockets. "Anytime. Vera."

She smirked and shook her head.

He shrugged. "I'll figure it out." With a last wave from the edge of the lawn, he ducked into the forest.

Vee carried her bags upstairs one at a time. After unpacking and setting up the spare room as an art studio, she took her time dusting off the animal figurines. Sitting down at her easel, she picked up a brush and the last of the tension in her shoulders melted away.

She tapped the end of the brush on her knee and frowned at the blank canvas. Usually, there were multiple projects fighting for attention in her mind. Now, when she actually had time, nothing.

Dipping the brush in paint, she held it a few inches from the canvas and closed her eyes. There it was. The image of a rowan tree growing out of the remains of a crumbling foundation filled her mind. Keeping her eyes closed, her hand trailed in slow arcs across the canvas, sketching the details. She could already picture the colors she'd need to blend to get the exact shade of crimson for the berries dripping from the tree's branches.

A grin spread across her face. She hadn't played this game with herself for years. Almost always, the painting would be salvageable even if it wasn't nearly as good as how she painted with her sight.

She opened her eyes and gasped. No sign of the tree, a thick line stretched down the canvas, thinner lines branching off until even smaller lines spread out from those. The fernlike patterns covered the page, radiating out from one another.

Leaning back, she crossed her arms. Her art ranged from landscapes, to dreamscapes, to an occasional portrait, but it'd never been abstract like this. She tilted her head. Weird or not, it was beautiful in its own way.

She checked the time on her otherwise useless phone. It was still early enough to explore the town. Leaving the painting to dry, she set off, careful to avoid walking beneath the elm tree as she crossed her yard toward the mouth of the path.

The sidewalk at the bottom of the hill followed the gentle curve of the bay, and the sun warmed her skin. Maybe she'd manage to get a tan this summer. She glanced down to her scar, which wrapped from the back of her right wrist to her palm. It was barely visible, but if her skin did have the opportunity to darken, it would make its presence known by staying a ghostly white.

A few minutes into the walk, the scenery changed from beach and trees to tidy wooden houses, set so close together they seemed to be elbowing each other for room. Vee passed a boutique clothing shop, a candy store promising saltwater taffy, and a coffee shop, before pausing at the steps to a library.

With no TV, internet, or phone, a few books would be a good idea to have around. She opened the door to a room with more dust than recent publications. An older gentleman perched on a stool behind a large desk. He hunched over an ancient ledger, leaning so close his nose almost touched the pages. Vee cleared her throat, but the man still didn't indicate any awareness of her presence.

Stepping a little closer, she tried again. "Hello?"

He jumped but looked up at her, smiling. "Oh, deary. I'm sorry I didn't see you there. Have you been waiting long?"

Surprised he could see anything at all through glasses thick enough to qualify as magnifying lenses, Vee returned his smile. "Not long at all. I'm here for the summer and was wondering if I could get a temporary library card." She eyed a spiral staircase that hopefully led to more books.

"Well, I'm Stu. And I'm the librarian in a manner of speaking, but I'm sorry to say we are not a borrowing library. This building is more of a storage facility for town records."

"Oh. Is there another library nearby?"

"Not exactly. But there is a lovely shop down the point called…" His bushy white eyebrows knit together. "Tied? No, that's not it. It's a funny name… Captured, maybe?" He shook his head. "Anyway, you'll know it when you see it. They have a wonderful selection of books."

"To borrow?"

"I believe they are for sale, but that's an excellent suggestion and you could certainly ask. I've been struck down many a time trying to convince Mr. Dryer to extend some of the funding here for a more traditional library."

"The Dryers control the library's funding?"

Stu's eyebrows raised above the rim of his glasses. "The Dryers *are* our funding. They started this library a few generations back with the sole focus on local history. All the town's records of births, deaths, marriages, and property are kept onsite." Stu took off his glasses to polish them on a cloth. He squinted until he returned them to his face and blinked a few times at her. "Well now, you've asked for the time, and I've told you how to build a clock, haven't I?"

Vee couldn't help but like him. "It must be an interesting job to comb through history."

"It's fascinating. But now, for you, if you walk down the point, about halfway, the shops on a side road branching off to the left."

"The point?"

"The bit of land that juts out into the bay."

"I only got here today and haven't done much exploring."

Stu held up a hand for a visual. "If you picture the point like a skinny mitten, the shop should be waiting for you at the tip of the thumb."

"Thank you, Stu. It was really nice meeting you."

"And you as well, Miss…"

"Taylor."

"Nice to meet you, Miss Taylor. Have a lovely day."

Once she reached the point, Vee stepped carefully along the cobblestone path, following Stu's directions. A shingled two-story house stood right where he'd said it would. Over the front door, a weather-beaten sign hung with a single word painted on it: *Bound.*

Inside, a teenage girl with short, purple hair and black nail polish sat at an ancient cash register, scrolling through her phone. When Vee the door swung shut behind Vee, the girl plucked an earbud out, a neutral expression on her face. “Can I help you?”

“I’m just looking.”

She shrugged and popped the headphone back in.

The building was old, with low ceilings, and Vee wound her way from one room to the next. She paused when she found a hall lined with bookcases and chose a few that looked promising. A cool breeze blew through a curtain at the end, exposing a doorway. She tucked the books under her arm and stepped through.

Inside was dim, the only light coming from open French doors. The small yard beyond was just big enough for the willow tree that resided there before the land gave way to the water. Across the bay, the inn could have been a picture on a postcard.

It didn’t have the same feel as the rest of the store and she turned, sure she’d stepped into a private area. A jewelry case stood open next to the door, and she froze. Arranged in neat rows, necklaces had intricately woven wire wrapped around a different colored stone. A jolt of recognition shot through Vee as her hand clenched the charm at her neck. The way the wire wrapped in an overlapping pattern, it was so similar.

A few years ago, Vee had taken hers to have it cleaned. The jeweler had told her the charm was made from a thin band of sterling silver wound around a black pearl. The silver overlapped and doubled back on itself so many times that, up until the jeweler pointed it out, Vee hadn’t known the pearl existed.

Vee stepped forward and gently lifted one of the necklaces to get a better look. These were lighter, made with looser knots, allowing glimpses of the different colored stones held within.

A soft voice spoke behind her. “Are you interested

in trying one on? The greens would look particularly beautiful with your hair."

Vee let the charm drop back into place and turned to face the woman. She stood unexpectedly close, and Vee stepped back, bumping the shelf. The woman had a smattering of gray strands running through her otherwise bright copper hair. Well-settled laugh lines creased the corners of her mouth, but she wasn't smiling as her sharp blue-green eyes homed in on Vee's neck.

"Ah, I see you have an older version." Her eyes trailed up to Vee's, gleaming. "I'm Ema."

"I'm Vee." Stepping to the side to make a little more space between them, Vee glanced at the rows of necklaces. "It looks like a popular design here."

"It's tied to a bit of a local legend. A curse, actually."

"That seems like a strange way to market your jewelry. Are many people interested in curses?"

Ema grinned, causing the lines around her mouth to deepen. "Not many. No. But the design itself isn't a curse. It's a binding knot, and one of the strongest. Once woven, it's almost impossible to undo, so whatever intention is captured inside stays protected." Her gaze tore away from Vee's as she picked up one of the necklaces. "What you see here are charms, not curses. This one has green quartz inside, for patience and understanding. This one"—she rested another against her palm—"is obsidian, for protection against anger and jealousy. The knot protects the stone, which holds the intention."

She returned the necklaces to their places and turned to Vee. "May I look closer at yours?"

Vee nodded and lifted it away from her neck to let Ema look without having to take it off. It was the only thing she had of her mother's. It never left her possession. "It's a black pearl."

Ema clasped it between her finger and thumb, and Vee instinctively pulled it back.

"So it is. Very well crafted. It takes an extraordinary amount of patience to craft silver into a binding knot. I've only ever seen it done once." Ema dropped the charm. "You're right to not trust strangers with it."

From the side of the room, an electric kettle whistled, and Ema walked toward the sound. "Why don't you choose a tea to sample while you wait for the storm to pass?"

Storm?

Vee's head swiveled toward the open French doors. The day had indeed darkened, and a steady rain blotted out the view of the inn. Her palms began to sweat, and she fought the urge to find a place to hide. Placing her books on the shelf, she took a deep breath. *Calm down. It's just rain.*

She picked up the closest tin and brought it to Ema.

"One of my favorite Oolongs. Excellent choice." Ema took it and prepared the tea.

Vee crossed to the open doors and poked her head out to scrutinize the sky. Rain brought the chance of thunder, which brought the chance of Vee having a panic attack. But these clouds were light, and the air held none of the humidity that came with the worst storms. Satisfied she wasn't about to embarrass herself, she backed away, mildly annoyed that at almost twenty-five her body still held onto the childhood fear.

Fear born from death.

A shiver crept up the back of her neck with the reminder and she wrapped her arms around herself. The few things she remembered from the stormy night that took her mom faded over time, but with a single clap of thunder, the terror always returned. The sound of footsteps pulled Vee away from the graveyard of memories that never fully let her back in. Ema brought two cups and a pot to the table and gestured to a chair. "Come, sit. I can do a reading for you while we wait for it to brew. Free of charge since you're stuck here."

Vee took a seat, the fresh scent of rain mingling with the earthy steam rising from the tea. "A reading?"

"Palm reading."

"You're a fortune teller?" Vee's eyebrows knit together as she glanced at Ema's cargo pants and short-sleeve button-up shirt.

"More of an interpreter. Here, let me see your hand."

Vee presented her left hand, palm up, familiar with the drill.

In high school, she and her friends had gone one at a time to a palm reader at the local carnival. Vee's reading had been empowering, about how she would overcome all her struggles, find the love of her life, and wind up rich and happy. All she had to do was buy a few shiny crystals and a book on meditation. The fifty-dollar price tag seemed worth the two Saturdays of babysitting it had taken to make that money. She and her friends had been euphoric, high on promises of happiness, and intoxicated by the scent of patchouli, until they realized they'd all received the same reading and there was a strict no-return policy.

Sitting with Ema, Vee was curious to know what the generic reading would be for a woman in her mid-twenties, so she sat patiently while Ema examined her hand much longer than seemed necessary to convince a willing audience.

Instead of launching into a confident speech, Ema released her and asked, "Can I see the other hand, please?"

Good luck to her. Vee turned over her other hand, and Ema frowned at the jagged scar that wound around her wrist, bisecting her palm. The scar probably interrupted the "your husband will be devastatingly handsome" line or the "you'll have a chauffeur" line.

Ema stayed silent, most likely trying to mentally work out the best reading to sell a bag of crystals.

Glancing from one of Vee's palms to the other, Ema gently pressed them together. She closed her eyes, taking a deep breath, and her cool, dry hands slid off Vee's. "Maybe a story instead of a reading. Would you like to hear about our knot there?" She nodded toward Vee's necklace.

Thrown off balance by the unexpected change in tactics, Vee glanced at the increasingly steady rain. A gust of wind brought the storm from a shower to a downpour, and she took the cup of tea Ema offered. "Sure. Why not?"

Ema poured her own cup and settled back in her chair, eyes sparkling. "This story will end here, in Cliffside, but it began farther away and a long time ago. It started in the early 1800s at a small settlement in what is now Western Massachusetts when Mercy Falls was sent away."

Chapter Four

Mercy
200 Years Ago

Mercy sat bolt upright in bed and focused on calming her breathing as the edges around her nightmare faded. It was the worst kind: a memory repeating itself. She'd had the same dream every night since arriving at her great aunt Siobhan's, almost ten weeks ago. It always started in the same place—Seth telling her he had no intention of marrying her and denying the child she carried was his. The ending varied, falling somewhere along the string of unpleasant events that had happened since that earthshattering moment. Tonight, she'd woken at the part where her parents told her to leave.

Mercy leaned over the edge of the cot Siobhan had provided and stared blurrily at the dying embers in the hearth, willing the hot tears not to fall as they threatened to do so often. Five months along and alone in this world, save for a distant relative who made it clear daily that taking Mercy in was a monumental act of charity on her part. At least when Mercy was under her parents' roof, she'd had far fewer chores and been free to indulge the fatigue and sickness that came along with the blessing.

And it was a blessing. She rested a palm against the

gentle curve of her abdomen. No one could tell her otherwise.

When Seth had filled her head with dreams of their future together, she'd easily fallen in love with the fantasy of being his wife, the promise of a big house, a stable future…Or at the very least, sharing a bed with only Seth, instead of her two sisters. The irony wasn't lost on her. Most nights now, she pulled the covers tight, wishing for their warmth and company.

But this was best for the baby. Here, no one questioned the story Siobhan created for her. Here, she was a widow who'd tragically lost her husband to the sea only weeks ago. Here, she wasn't a harlot, and her baby wouldn't be a mistake.

Upon Mercy's arrival, Siobhan had given her a cold welcome with an appraising look from head to toe. "I use the bedroom in the back. You can sleep in the loft overhead." She indicated with a nod to a small set of stairs. "I rise early, and you will too. You'll be expected to do your share of the housework as well as help me make the remedies I sell each week at the market in town. You'll need to be productive." She looked hard at Mercy's face before her eyes traveled to her stomach.

They'd been interrupted when a winded voice called from outside, "Hello? Siobhan? Are you home?"

A moment later, the door frame filled with the silhouette of a plump woman wiping her brow with a soiled kerchief. "Oh, thank goodness, you are. I swear that climb gets steeper each time." She collapsed into a groaning wooden chair at the table, panting. "Why on God's green earth do you not move closer to town?"

Her words mirrored Mercy's thoughts while

making the same climb just minutes earlier. Her legs still burned from the journey—a mile from town and mostly uphill.

"I'm used to it. And the hill invites privacy," Siobhan replied. "What brings you by?"

The woman ignored the question when her gaze finally landed on Mercy. "And who may this be?"

"My great niece Mercy. She'll be staying here with me. Mercy, this is Mrs. Blackwell." Before Mercy had a chance to open her mouth in greeting, her aunt lowered her voice to the woman. "Poor thing is recently a widow, and with child, nonetheless. She has no other family and I've taken her in."

The woman glanced in Mercy's direction and back to Siobhan with surprise in her eyes. "Bless your heart, taking on an extra mouth to feed, soon to be two at that."

Mercy covered her stomach when the woman's beady eyes rested on it.

"What do you need?" Siobhan turned her back on the woman to put another log on the fire.

"Mr. Blackwell's stomach has turned sour again. Three days now, all I've heard is his moaning and complaining. I can't take much more. I was hoping you'd trade me some of that tea that worked so well last time."

"And what do you have to trade?" Siobhan pulled a jar off a high shelf and took three sachets out. She laid them on a small cloth on the table and wrapped them with string.

Mrs. Blackwell reached into the folds of her skirt and retrieved a jar of honey. "I traded a traveler at the market two raisin loaves and a fresh-made cornbread for it."

Picking up the golden liquid, Siobhan appraised the jar and narrowed her eyes. "You'll want more than to simply ease a bellyache for this trade, I gather. What else are you after?"

"It's my legs." Mrs. Blackwell stretched the offending limbs out from under the hem of her skirt. "They've been paining me more and more, and I can't remember the last time my back let me sleep through the night."

With a quick nod, Siobhan picked up a tin from a lower shelf and removed an additional five sachets, wrapping them in a separate cloth.

"For your husband"—she handed over the first bundle—"put one bag in a kettle of boiling water first thing in the morning. Have him drink one cup morning, noon, and night for three days. For you"—she extended the second bundle—"empty one packet into the kettle and boil until it becomes fragrant. Drink one cup before bed for the next five nights. It will be bitter. Hopefully, you had the foresight to save some honey for yourself."

Mrs. Blackwell beamed as she heaved herself up, using the table for leverage. "My aching bones thank you, Siobhan. I will leave you to your day."

"Mrs. Blackwell," Siobhan called, turning her back to put the tins away.

"Aye?" The woman paused in the door frame.

"If that dram helps your pains, I'll have more at the market Saturday, and I remember your meat pies fondly."

"I will keep that in the forefront of my mind. Good day." Pulling the door closed, she left.

"That tea will cure her pain?" Mercy asked.

"The only thing that will cure her pain is to indulge less in her own baking. The human body is only built to sustain a certain amount of burden." Siobhan bent to retrieve a basket from under the table. "The tea will mask the pain and create a loyal customer. Now put your belongings upstairs and join me in the garden."

Mercy did as she was told, then found Siobhan by negotiating a complex series of pathways through a garden larger than any she'd seen before. It wrapped from the front of the house all the way to the back, with the boundaries marked by a stone wall.

"You have a use for all these plants?" Mercy asked her kneeling aunt.

"Even some of the weeds. Not this one, though." She pulled a handful out by the roots and held it up to show Mercy. "Have you tended a garden before?"

"Of course. We have a vegetable garden at home." She paused, struck by the sudden realization that she could no longer think of that place as home. Overhead, the gray clouds that had been present for days thickened.

Siobhan stopped weeding and turned to look at the sky, then at Mercy. Speaking in the gentlest voice she'd used since Mercy arrived, she said, "You have a place here, just as your child will. If you do good work, I'll teach you all I know so you'll have no need to depend on another." With that, she turned back to her work.

"I don't know what my mother told you, but I'm not a widow."

"Aye, you know that. As do I. And it will be your choice if your child is to know the truth, but you will have a right easier go of it here if the townspeople are unaware of your true situation. Look there. What do you see?" Siobhan stood and pointed to the town cowering in the valley below.

"The town."

"And what's at its center?"

The largest building stood out, stark white, the smaller homes radiating out from it. "The church."

"Exactly. These are people who put a great deal of stock in publicly demonstrating their beliefs, even if they don't live them," Siobhan said with clear distaste. "It would be no great task for them to believe you lost your young husband to the sea, most unfortunate." She glanced at Mercy with a glimmer in her eyes.

"Ouch!" Mercy slapped the crook of her elbow. "Something stung me."

Siobhan straightened Mercy's arm, studying the swollen spot. "Not stung. But whatever it was gave you a nasty bite. Here, come." She walked deeper into the garden.

She picked a green leaf off a nearby plant and handed it to Mercy. "Chew it for a few seconds, then put the pulp on the bite." Mercy hesitated, and Siobhan encouraged her. "Go on. It will help."

Mercy bit down on the leaf. A familiar sweet taste filled her mouth. Sure enough, when she put the chewed-up paste on her arm, the stinging faded. "That's amazing."

"No, that's basil. The primary ingredient in the tea I gave Mrs. Blackwell for her husband. As well as soothing bites and stings, it's a powerful digestive. He, like his wife, often overindulges—leading to his own discomfort. This is how you can tell it from similar plants…"

Day-to-day, Mercy learned the medicinal uses of

the plants by what remedies Siobhan happened to make. She followed Siobhan, helping more and more in collecting, drying, and combining herbs for teas, salves, and poultices to sell at the weekly market. By the time the baby was due, Mercy hardly needed to consult the small book of recipes Siobhan kept tucked in the pocket of her skirts for common requests.

Thomas was born as autumn claimed the leaves, turning them from deep green to vivid red, orange, and gold. When the baby was coming, Mercy looked out the window and, through the delirium of pain, mistook the brilliant red light through the oak trees for the world being on fire. Seconds later, the midwife handed Thomas to Mercy and the world no longer mattered.

Thomas was a happy baby. The first months flew by as autumn spiraled into winter. Unseasonably cold, that fall had the earliest snowfall anyone in the village could remember. On a particularly bitter night, Mercy and Siobhan sipped broth close to the fire they'd allowed themselves, with Thomas bundled between them. Business had slowed, and they were conserving in anticipation it might not improve. Mercy stood, trying to coax the dying flames back to life, when a booming knock on the front door interrupted her.

"Mrs. Falls, we are in need of your assistance." A masculine voice rumbled through the wood, piercing the sullen night.

Siobhan walked to the door, nodding to Mercy who stood next to the baby, fire poker still in hand.

"What brings you?" Siobhan called.

"Please. We were told in town that you have knowledge of healing and can aid our ailing friend."

Siobhan opened the door a crack, then wider,

ushering in a frigid blast of air. Two men, both breathing hard, held a third, unconscious man between them.

"Mercy, clear the table," Siobhan instructed, even as Mercy had already started to move the few things occupying the space. Siobhan turned to the men and pointed to the table. "Put him here."

Bending over him, Siobhan pulled up his eyelids and pressed a hand to his forehead. "When did the fever start?" She looked to the men who hovered close.

The tallest one ran a hand through his dark, unkempt curls. His gaze focused on the listless man on the table. "This morning. It came on quick. We went to town, but the doctor is away. They said you were our best hope." He turned to Siobhan. "Please, is he beyond help?"

Mercy held her breath, waiting for her aunt's answer. The man's gray-blue eyes held more than concern; there was a storm of pain behind his plea.

Straightening, Siobhan smoothed her skirt. "We'll do what we can. Mercy, boil water." The women sprang into action. Mercy filled a pot and added fresh wood to the fire, while Siobhan grabbed tins and jars from the cupboards.

"You." Siobhan set down the containers of herbs and plucked a basket from the wall. She handed it to one of the two men still standing near the door. "Gather some snow. Quick. We must bring his fever down if he's to have a chance."

By the time the man returned, Siobhan added the last of the herbs to the pot Mercy slowly stirred. Siobhan recited words spoken so low, only Mercy could hear what they were. When she finished, the shorter of the men mumbled, "Amen." Mercy and Siobhan's eyes met over the fire for the briefest of moments.

Mercy took the basket of snow from him. "What's his name?"

The man stood a little taller. "Jonathan. Jonathan Dryer."

"Jonathan." Mercy packed snow under his arms. "I'm going to try to cool your body temperature, then give you something to drink. It will help you."

Jonathan didn't make any sign he'd heard. Mercy wrapped a clean cloth around some snow and pressed it to his forehead, getting her first good look at him. Even with his face slack in sleep, he was handsome, with a strong bone structure and dark hair. Together, she and Siobhan spooned teaspoon after teaspoon of tea through his lips, being sure to tilt his head so he didn't breathe it in. They used their carefully rationed supply of wood to keep the fire strong. Once the worst of the danger passed, Jonathan's men ate the meager amount of food the women could spare and fell asleep, leaning against the cottage walls. Siobhan retired to bed with a promise to relieve Mercy at first light.

Lowering herself into one of the chairs, Mercy propped her elbows on the table and studied the man's face. Through a slight shadow of stubble, his color was returning to normal, and his breathing relaxed into the slow rhythm of sleep instead of the hurried cadence of a fever.

She didn't know she'd fallen asleep until her eyes shot open at a crackle from the dying fire. Immediately, her gaze rested on a pair of deep brown eyes looking intently into hers across the few inches they were separated.

It was a moment, or an hour, before the gaze was broken by one of Jonathan's men, speaking from behind Mercy. "Oi, you're awake. You gave us a scare last night."

Jonathan pushed himself up onto his elbows and cleared his throat. "I feel like I've been trampled by a horse."

He wavered as he sat up, and Mercy put her hand out to steady him, taking care to avoid meeting his gaze.

He shook his head, then looked to the man towering over them. "What happened, Roderick?"

"You mentioned you felt ill after the bad weather cleared yesterday afternoon. By nightfall, you couldn't sit upright. We'd taken a wrong turn in the storm, and it was sheer luck we happened on the lights from this here town. We rode in, only to find the doctor away. His wife directed us here, and"—he nodded toward Mercy—"because of their exceptional care, you're talking to us now instead of being fit for a box."

Jonathan's gaze bore into Mercy until she met his eye. "Thank you for your kindness. It seems certain you saved my life."

"It was nothing." Mercy's cheeks burned as hot as the fever that had recently released him.

Roderick's rough voice came from behind her. "It was something, miss. You pulled this one right from the devil's arms last night."

Siobhan entered the room, carrying Thomas. "Yes, surely something worthy of being repaid. Your life cost us most of our firewood as well as a hearty portion of our food stores." She nodded toward Jonathan's two companions.

Jonathan met her eye. “Of course you will be repaid. I owe a great debt to you both.”

Trying to push himself to his feet, he faltered and slumped into the chair Mercy vacated. He propped his head in his hands. “I may not yet be fit for travel. Roderick, take Sean and procure us lodging in town and replacement supplies for those we used.” He pulled a small leather bag from his pocket and tossed it to Roderick. “Use it all to repay the kindness.” He gave a subtle smile to Mercy before lowering his head to the table.

The men left, and Siobhan reheated then ladled the leftover tea into a cup for Jonathan. “Mercy, go collect the eggs. Our guest shouldn’t need spoon-feeding anymore.”

Jonathan and Siobhan appraised each other for a moment. He held her gaze while he smiled and reached for the cup. “No. Quite capable on my own, thank you.”

Mercy retrieved her cloak and stepped outside, taking deep breaths of the cold air. She found chores to occupy her time for the rest of the morning. Back in the house, she took care that the glances she stole toward Jonathan went unnoticed. He was indeed very handsome and much taller than she’d first thought. She shook her head at how silly she was, admiring a man so far from her reach.

A cry sprang from Thomas and she turned her attention to him, determined to not be distracted by fantasy.

The men returned from town too quickly. They left more than double the supplies they’d used and rode away with Jonathan.

Two days later, the weekly market was upon them. Up with the sun, Mercy and Siobhan packed their small cart with various teas, herbs, and salves. They bundled Thomas cozily into a basket and made their way into town. In front of the church, the market came to life. Townspeople trickled in until it bustled with men and women in thick cloaks walking quickly and exhaling little puffs of white as they went. Mrs. Blackwell let Mercy leave Thomas in the warmth of the bakery in exchange for a considerable discount on her order. Siobhan grumbled, but her rough edges were for show when it came to Thomas's wellbeing.

Mercy spotted Jonathan the moment he entered the marketplace, and her heart quickened. Improved health made a world of difference. Color returned to his face, and strength radiated from him. He strode toward Mercy and Siobhan's stall in a manner that had people alter their course.

"Good day." He nodded at each of the women, but his gaze lingered on Mercy, bringing a flush to her cheeks.

"Good day. You're looking well," Siobhan replied, forcing his gaze off Mercy.

"Quite well. I'm living proof that your reputation for potent cures is accurate." He gave the older woman a charming smile.

Siobhan didn't acknowledge the blatant compliment. "So, I take it you will be on your way soon."

"Soon enough." His eyes flicked toward Mercy, then returned to Siobhan. "I'm afraid I need your assistance one more time before I leave. There is a child in my town afflicted with a condition that, so far, no doctor or medicine has been able to relieve. He's never run and played like other children his age for lack of breath. Recently, he's suffered from unprovoked attacks where he cannot get enough air even when he's perfectly still. The attacks are increasing and getting quite severe. Would you have a remedy I could bring back for him?"

Siobhan frowned. "Aye, I know of something. I don't have any made at present, but if that's all that's keeping you here, stop on your way out of town. I will have it for you tomorrow afternoon."

"Excellent." He slapped an open palm on the women's cart with a spark of triumph in his eyes.

She named a price three times what they'd normally charge. Mercy started to say something, but Siobhan put a hand on her arm, silencing her.

"I'll have payment in full. Tomorrow then, ladies." He radiated happiness when he gave Mercy one last look before disappearing into the crowd.

Mercy turned to Siobhan. "Why are you charging him so much? He's helping a sick child."

Siobhan kept her head down, putting some of the items they'd brought into a satchel. "Did you not see the hunger in his eyes?"

"So, we're taking advantage? That's even worse." The thought didn't sit well. Siobhan had been harsh at times, but never cruel.

Siobhan snapped her head to face Mercy. "That man does not mean us well."

"How can you possibly know that? He's been nothing but grateful and kind."

"Because he sees something in us. Something he needs. If he wasn't desperate, he wouldn't have agreed so readily to the price. It's always good to know your value to others. Now, I'm going to deliver Mr. Sherman's order." With that, she picked up the satchel and left, ending the discussion.

Later that night, Siobhan spread the ingredients they needed on the table and described in detail what each component did and how much to use. Meticulous as always, Siobhan didn't waste a leaf and measured exact doses into neat piles that soon lined the table. Mercy followed her every move, needing far less instruction than when she first arrived.

When everything was ready to be wrapped into individual tea bags, Siobhan poured a small amount of fine yellow powder into Mercy's palm. She then repeated the same in her own hand.

Siobhan moved to the opposite side of the table. "Now, we give the child breath." Raising her palm toward her lips, Siobhan shocked Mercy by gently blowing on the powder while turning her body to let a fine dusting of the spice settle on the piles closest to her. No measuring or consistency to make sure all the piles got the same amount—reckless compared to her usual precision.

"Now you." She looked at Mercy. "Focus on our purpose."

Following her example, Mercy cleared her mind of everything but giving the unknown child breath and blew the powder across the table.

"Very good." The rare compliment from Siobhan came when Mercy opened her eyes. "Let's wrap these up."

After putting everything away, they sat at the bare table and Siobhan told Mercy to get her notebook. "The tea is preventative, but depending on the severity of the affliction, it may not stop the strongest of attacks. In the case of immediate distress, a salve can be used on the chest for relief." Siobhan opened her notebook to the page that listed the ingredients and preparation. She walked Mercy step-by-step through the completion of a small batch.

They were ready when the men came the next day, and Siobhan did not hide that she was eager for them to go. Jonathan took no notice and lingered, asking questions, making sure he remembered the correct instructions.

"I cannot fully express my gratitude for you saving my life, but for now, here is the payment we agreed upon yesterday." He slid a small bag toward Siobhan, who opened it but said nothing. He turned to Mercy. "Would you accompany me for a walk?"

Mercy looked at her aunt, who frowned but peered into the bag and gave a quick nod.

Outside, their steps crunched on the frozen ground as they made their way to the side of the house. Once out of sight, Jonathan stopped. While waiting for him to speak, Mercy pulled her cloak tighter against the chill.

"I have something for you so you won't forget me in my absence." He held a tiny, white object between two fingers and offered it to her.

She opened her palm to receive the gift. "It's beautiful." Mercy stared at the round, shimmering surface that reflected pink and yellow and blue all at once. "What is it?" she asked before she thought to be embarrassed by her ignorance.

"It's a pearl. Taken from the ocean near my home. It was formed from a single grain of sand that, with patience, evolved into something of beauty."

Roderick approached them, interrupting the moment. "We must go if we're to make Lynn by nightfall." His gaze traveled from Mercy's face to Jonathan's and he shook his head without waiting for an answer before turning back to where the horses waited.

Shame flushed her cheeks, and her gaze turned from Roderick's to the ground. *He knows I'm not worth this attention.*

Jonathan took her chin in his hand so she had to look him in the eyes. "Until I return," he whispered.

A spark of hope overrode the painful reality mirrored in Roderick's disapproval. She searched Jonathan's face. "You plan to come back?"

"That is a promise." Intensity burned behind his words.

Mercy stepped back. She had no need for promises. She'd had promises, and now she had Thomas. Still, it was a magical story for a grain of sand to transform in such a way, and Mercy had never owned anything so beautiful.

"Thank you." She clutched the pearl as they walked back. "I will cherish this."

Taking the reins to his horse from Roderick, Jonathan bowed his head to her. "Until next time." He swiftly mounted his horse and waved toward Siobhan in the doorway.

Mercy stood in the same spot, no longer cold. She watched their forms grow smaller until they disappeared over the next hill, the tiny white pearl clutched in her hand.

Chapter Five

Vee

Ema slid her chair back and picked up both empty teacups. "The rain's tapered off. You should go in case it starts again."

Vee shook her head, off-kilter from being jolted back into the present. "That's it? There wasn't even a hint of a curse in that story."

Ema carried the cups to a sink near the kettle, her back to Vee. "There's no need to rush the story, and it's best to end on a happy note when possible."

"That's a happy note? Jonathan leaving Mercy? Does he come back?"

"There wouldn't be more to the story if he didn't." Ema set the dishes on the counter and stepped toward a door at the back of the room. "But that's for another day. You should go soon if you want to buy those books. Amanda doesn't linger after she closes the shop at six."

Vee glanced at her phone—a few minutes before six. She reached to retrieve her books off the shelf then turned to thank Ema, but she'd already disappeared.

Vee's gaze fell on the necklaces as she walked past, and the slightest of chills ran down her arms. Dazed from the sudden rush to leave, she stepped through the curtained doorway into the bright light of the shop. She wound her way through the maze of rooms until she found herself back at the checkout counter.

Amanda glanced at a clock on the wall then back to Vee before keying in the prices on the cash register. "Twenty-three-fifty-three."

Vee slid a credit card from her phone case. "Here you go."

"Sorry. Machine's broken. Cash only."

"I don't have any on me."

Amanda let out a sigh and zeroed out the register. "I can hold them for you to come back." She glanced at the clock again. "*Another day*."

"Okay, thanks."

Ripping off a slip of receipt paper, Amanda picked up a pen. "What's your name?"

"Vee."

"V? Like the letter?"

"It's short for Verity."

Amanda stared blankly at her.

"Yes. Like the letter."

"Weird name. We're open every day, ten to six." She stacked Vee's books and tucked a note with a big letter V scrawled on it inside the cover of the first one, then set the pile to the side.

Amanda shut off the lights before Vee reached the front door.

****

Tossing and turning later that night, Vee kicked off the sheet tangled around her legs and sat up. She hadn't looked at the clock since midnight, when she'd started counting sheep in a vain attempt to bore herself to sleep. Well into triple digits, she gave up.

She got out of bed and walked to the window to stare at the full moon hanging over the bay. The lack of traffic and sirens only made her more restless. Maybe some fresh air would be the cure.

She tugged a fleece over the tank top and shorts she'd worn to bed and slid her feet into sneakers. On her way out, she took a flashlight out of the kitchen drawer. It had been dusk when she'd walked home from Ema's shop, but even with the last rays of sunlight filtering through the dense canopy of trees, she'd tripped more than once.

Negotiating the path was much easier with the aid of the light, and Vee made it down to the road with no major incidents. Out of the forest, the glow of the moon was bright and she pocketed her flashlight. She crossed the deserted road, jogged down the short set of stairs to the beach, then slipped off her shoes.

The sand was soft and cool as she walked to the water's edge. The first frigid wave lapped at her toes, and she gasped. This was a whole new level of cold compared to the lakes she swam in as a kid. Of course, that was also during the height of summer, not late May.

Not to be deterred, she waded out, following the glistening white path the moon laid on the water. After a few dozen steps, Vee looked down with curiosity. The water barely covered her ankles. Her feet were comfortably numb and the gentle lapping of the waves, along with the fresh air, helped her tense muscles uncoil. She kept going, paying attention to each step for a change in depth that would signal it was time to turn back. But the change didn't come, and she was at least a hundred feet out from shore. A breeze drifted by, and she paused. Facing out toward the never-ending black ocean, the air around her stilled.

A single, rumbling bark reverberated across the water, and Vee whipped around to scan the shoreline.

Where the sand met the water, a huge black dog paced back and forth, staring in her direction. Her heart raced. She hadn't even considered the risk of running into animals on her little nocturnal adventure, and she'd never been comfortable around dogs. Especially freakishly large ones, standing between her and dry land.

It barked again, a low, terrifying sound.

Instinctively putting more distance between them, Vee took a step back. In an instant, the night sky tilted, her foot finding nothing beneath it but water.

The fall didn't register until she plunged into the frigid sea. Taking in a mouthful of salt water, she kicked and clawed for an eternity before her head broke the surface. In a step, the bay had gone from less than six inches of water to a seemingly bottomless pit. She scrambled to keep her head above water while coughing out the gulp she'd inhaled.

Her hands fought for purchase to pull her back onto the ledge, but there was nothing to grip. Under the water, her feet sank into the side of a steep slope. The sand slipped away each frantic time she dug a foot into the soft wall.

Panic set in as the undertow pulled her backward. Exertion burned her lungs, her chest constricting from the cold and robbing her of the ability to scream. Already struggling to stay afloat, she was shoved under again when a wave rolled over her on its way to shore.

Dread circled with the imaginary sharks beneath

her. The dark water didn't relent in its effort to pull her out, and she had no choice but to wait for the next wave to roll in. Timing her kicks, she propelled herself with it when it came. But her arms and legs had already started to slow from the cold. Instead of launching forward, she slipped back under as it left her behind.

The panic dissolved to calmness and her thoughts turned inward. Who would find her?

After the next wave dragged her under, she broke the surface, eyes stinging from the salt water. Her fingertips lost their fragile hold on the ledge and she drifted out of reach, cold numbness seeping through her skin.

Fire shot through the ice in her veins as strong fingers circled her wrist.

"I've got you." A gravelly voice grunted as the iron grip found her other arm and heaved her back onto the safety of the ledge.

Vee landed on all fours, coughing and limbs stiff. The shallow water was like a warm bath compared to the freezing plunge. Her blurry vision fought to focus on the pair of running shoes in the water in front of her. They shifted and the man's rough voice came from overhead. "You need to get out of the water. Can you walk?"

Vee couldn't look up as another racking cough overtook her. She caught her breath and nodded, trying to stand. She pitched forward, doubling over. Her legs cramped and a shiver tore through her. Without another word, her rescuer scooped her up in warm arms and slung her over his shoulder in a fireman's carry.

"Hey—" She grabbed onto the back of his T-shirt, disoriented and upside down, jostling with each step he took. "Take it easy."

His words rumbled through his back. "Or what? You'll wait for someone else to rescue you?" The edge to his voice kept her from responding, but his pace slowed and the ride smoothed out considerably. When they reached the beach, he lowered her to the sand next to her discarded shoes.

He turned away, a tall silhouette, with the moon behind him. She swallowed the lump in her throat that his words had created. If he hadn't been there or had been one minute later…her toes and fingers began to burn.

He picked up a sweatshirt from the ground and tossed it at her. "Put this on."

Pulling off her soaked fleece, she looked up at his shadowed form. "Thank you so much. I don't know what I would have done…"

"You would've drowned." His statement was almost as chilling as the water had been.

"Well…" Vee swallowed a rising spark of annoyance at his harsh tone. *He saved you. Be nice.*

She narrowed her eyes at his shadowed form. "Like I said. Thank you." She pulled on the blissfully dry hoody and wrapped her arms around herself.

"What the fuck were you thinking?" Backlit by the moon, he towered over her.

A fire smoldered in her stomach and her voice rose. "Maybe I was thinking if there was a death trap, someone would have told me or thought to put up a sign."

He ran a hand through his hair and let out a humorless laugh. "There is a sign. A few, in fact. And buoys marking the edge of the drop. You probably would've seen them if you had the common sense to take a stroll into the Atlantic during the day instead of the dead of night." He turned away and brought his hands to the back of his head. "And maybe nobody thought to warn you because the water is fifty degrees, and no one in their right mind would be wandering out far enough to reach the shelf break."

Her seething response froze on her tongue when a flicker of movement beyond him caught her eye.

Anger forgotten, she pointed at the huge dog padding across the sand in their direction. "Look out!"

He turned with lightning speed, his head swiveling. "What?"

Fear collided with the cold to send her shivers into overdrive. "Right there! That's the dog I was trying to get away from when I fell."

With his body angled to face the dog, the moonlight illuminated the left side of his profile. The glimpse was enough to tell he had shaggy, dark hair and a sharp bone structure before he turned back to her, casting his face into darkness again.

He tilted his head toward where the dog had come to a stop next to him. "This is who you're worried about?" He reached down and scratched the dog behind the ears. "Zeus is scared of his own shadow. But that didn't stop him from saving your life tonight."

Edging herself a little farther away, she stared at the furry head that came up past his six-foot owner's waist. "What do you mean, he saved my life?"

"Sit, Zeus." The dog obeyed, earning another pat. "He barely ever barks. Tonight, we were on our way back from a run when he barked at you. That's what made me notice you standing out there, but when I blinked, you were gone." He paused. "I thought I imagined you…but he kept barking and ran into the water. I've had Zeus since he was a puppy, and it's a rare occasion when he voluntarily gets his paws wet." All the anger bled out of his voice, and it lowered to barely a whisper. "I knew you were really there."

Vee swallowed and took another glance at the dog. He could fit her entire head in his mouth.

The man cleared his throat. "Can you walk now?"

She pushed herself to stand, relieved that she could. "Yeah. I'm good." They started across the beach, her dripping and now sandy fleece in one hand.

"Are you staying at the inn?"

"Sort of. I'm staying in their cottage up the hill." *Good call, Vee. Tell the angry stranger your exact, secluded location.*

"I didn't know anyone lived in that house."

"I moved in today. I'm working at the inn for the summer." Vee pressed her lips together to keep any more unnecessary information from falling out.

At the base of the stairs to the road, she paused to tug on her shoes, acutely aware that Zeus stayed next to her while his owner passed by, disappearing in the shadows at the top of the steps. The second the shoes were on her feet, she rushed up the stairs, catching her toe on the top one in the process. The man's arm shot out and grabbed her hand, his palm warm in hers. A jolt tore through her, like a shock of a forgotten memory, but faded without locking into place. He pulled back like he'd been slapped and spun around, heading toward the tree line.

She followed, her hand tingling where his skin had met hers, and fished the flashlight out of her soaked fleece at the mouth of the path. "Okay, here we are. Thanks again."

She waved to the pair standing on the otherwise empty road, then turned to the path and clicked on the flashlight. Nothing happened. She shook it, sloshing the water inside. Clutching the useless light in her hand, she tried to project confidence as she stepped into the woods. A few feet in, the moonlight vanished, and she stubbed her toe on a root. Swearing under her breath, she slowed and began the painstaking process of carefully placing each foot, testing for uneven ground before putting down her full weight.

"We'll walk you. That path is dangerous enough in broad daylight." The man's footsteps were accompanied by the quiet tinkling of the dog's tags coming up behind her.

There was no way she wanted to tack on another forced favor. "I'll be fine. It's just a few roots and rocks." She took the next step, her foot landing on what felt like loose gravel.

"Yeah. Roots and rocks, and a sheer drop about halfway up."

She paused before taking another blind step. "I haven't noticed a drop."

"What a surprise. It's to the left of the path, and more overgrown than it used to be, but I promise it's there. For someone who's already fallen off one cliff tonight, do you really think it's smart to take your chances?"

"And you have a flashlight?" She bristled at his condescending tone.

"No. But I don't need one." He pointed to the darkened path ahead. "Zeus, go." The dog bounded forward, and the man's voice rumbled as he pushed past Vee on the narrow path. "Stay close."

She could make a fool of herself and go pound on the inn's door at what had to be well past one a.m. now. Her shoulders slumped. The thought of explaining why she was soaking wet and out in the middle of the night propelled her forward to where the man had stopped to wait for her.

As her eyes adjusted, she could make out the outline of the broad shoulders in front of her, but every step was blind faith. It was impossible to tell if she was staying on the path or veering off while she followed the commands he called back. "Step up, there's a rock. Root to the left." And finally, the one she'd been waiting for. "Stay close to the right, this is the drop."

His directions were annoyingly helpful, and Vee made it to the top, only tripping once at the tail end when the glow from the cottage's porch light distracted her. Tipping forward, she reached her arms out to brace herself against the fall. Except, instead of crashing to the ground, her palms met the warm, furry coat of Zeus, who stood patiently still until she righted herself.

Ahead, at the edge of the lawn, the man turned and walked back to her. "Think you can make it from here?" He didn't slow or wait for her answer before he continued past her and down the path.

She stared at his retreating back. "I'm sure I'll manage. Thanks." Reaching down, she tentatively petted Zeus's head. "And thank you for saving me twice." First from drowning, then from falling on her face. The massive dog leaned into her hand, panting after the climb.

Zeus trotted away, following his owner. The man's

deep voice called from the woods. “Try to be more careful.”

She swallowed her sharp reply when a quieter, more gentle voice trailed back. “Twice?”

Vee rushed toward the house, remembering a second too late to avoid the cold spot. Her limbs stiffened as soul-crushing misery encased her heart. A sob caught in her throat and she jolted herself forward, sprinting the last few yards to the door.

Triple checking the door was locked behind her, she wrapped her arms around herself, burrowing into the hoody and taking deep breaths. The scent of freshly cut wood and aftershave mixed with the sage from the cottage, slowly settling her frayed nerves. Her fingers found the charm around her neck and she climbed the stairs, ready to wash the night away in the shower.

Under a stream of hot water, it wasn’t the near-death experience on the beach or the freak spot on the lawn that dominated her thoughts. Instead, it was the interactions with the rude stranger she couldn’t shake. *How dare this man who barely met me judge me as some helpless idiot?*

She got out of the shower and yanked on the warmest sweats she owned.

Why did I let him get the last word?

She retraced her steps to pick up all the wet, discarded clothes she’d dropped on her way to the bathroom. Lifting his sweatshirt, she caught another whiff of his calming scent and flung it over the back of a chair.

Who jogs in the middle of the night?

She sat on the edge of her bed, staring at it and sliding her charm back and forth. She’d return it tomorrow. Hopefully, without having to see him.

She never asked his name, but she didn't have to. He knew her path like the back of his hand and when he left, he continued up, not down. He was handsome, and a clear-cut jerk. This was the man she'd seen in the window. Not a ghost. Blake Dryer had saved her.

Chapter Six

Luke

Dammit. The whole point of running at night was to avoid people. Especially people who made his chest ache when they looked at him.

What the fuck was that?

He'd gotten used to being deformed. There were times he even enjoyed the shocked looks he got when he faced people head-on, unabashedly inviting the comments that never came when provoked. But tonight, he'd regressed back to the uncomfortable kid who tried to hide his scars from the world.

Or at least from a girl.

All his old habits returned full force. The constant awareness of the light, the unnerving ability to know exactly how far he needed to turn to keep the right side of his face hidden, the screaming want of a hood to pull over his head after he'd given her his sweatshirt, his one layer of protection. She'd brought all his old, useless defenses back the second her head broke the surface of the water.

But why?

The question burned worse than her touch.

Luke shoved through an overgrown section of the path and emerged onto what used to be the cottage's driveway. Time and neglect had taken their toll on the pavement, and Luke crossed it carefully. The moon had slipped behind a cloud, keeping him from increasing his pace.

On the path in the woods, his muscle memory helped navigate the major turns, roots, and rocks. The slight changes that had come with his time away could be negotiated as long as he paid attention. The parking area was another story. No one had used that cottage in his lifetime, and the little offshoot of driveway from the main road up to the house had been left to deteriorate.

Zeus stalled behind him and whimpered toward the faint glow of the cottage through the woods.

"Come on, boy. She's fine." Luke patted his thigh to encourage the dog to move and stop making him feel bad for being such an asshole. He'd gone against his nature to leave before making sure she was safe inside the cottage, but it took everything he had to resist the magnetic pull yanking him in her direction.

He couldn't have let her drown, but he should have left the moment he set her safely on the beach. Maybe then he could've gotten out from under the crushing want to run toward someone he couldn't seem to face.

His breath caught when he thought about the heart-lurching moment when Zeus barked. He'd glimpsed her standing in the ocean, pale and ethereal, glowing in the moonlight like he'd imagined her into existence. He'd stopped in his tracks with an instant desire to know who she was. The searing panic that followed when she fell should've been a blaring alarm to protect himself.

Instead of heeding that warning, he tortured himself by staying once she was safe on shore, painfully aware the entire time that he'd reverted to instinctively hiding his scars. Even fully conscious of doing it, he couldn't stop. He didn't want this beautiful stranger to see his flaws. The muscles in his jaw clenched. *As if she could miss them.*

His hand still tingled from the electricity that shot through him when she grabbed his hand on the stairs. He rubbed his palm on his pants as he glanced over his shoulder to where Zeus hadn't made a move.

"Zeus. Now." His yell echoed through the night, and the dog finally followed.

Luke stepped around one last pothole before reentering the woods for the final leg of the path. It was steep but would get him home faster than the meandering driveway. The sand that had made its way into his wet sneakers ground into his skin, giving him something to focus on besides the thoughts that had been pummeling him the entire climb.

Zeus caught up by the time Luke stepped into the Dryer's side yard. Together, they entered the house through the kitchen door. Luke kicked off his soaked sneakers and filled Zeus's water bowl, then took the tower stairs two at a time. He passed the floor with his bedroom and continued up the remaining flights.

The large, open room at the top had windows on all four sides, which provided spectacular views of the ocean, town, or forest.

Luke panted from the climb and walked to the windows facing the ocean. He pressed his forehead against the cool glass and gazed down.

The house was close enough to the cliff's edge that this position gave the impression of being suspended above the black water crashing against the rocks below. The surreal sensation used to settle his mind, but not tonight.

Over a year had passed since his last, and only, relationship ended. Before then, he'd only had casual flings, mostly with women he met on the rare nights he'd join his father and brother at company functions. None resulted in real connections. Some were drawn to his family's money, others tried to get closer to Blake through him. Worst were the ones who thought dating him was an act of kindness. Poor-mangled-rich-boy pity fucks were never fulfilling.

Then there was Kay.

After Luke left Maine, he moved to Florida. His father set him up with a tutor to finish high school at home there, under the condition that he'd work for Eli when he graduated. Luke reluctantly agreed and wasted away the years he would've spent at college learning the family business of venture capitalism from the Florida branch of Dryer Global.

Kay came into his life when Luke was at his most vulnerable. He'd stepped down from his position to take a break and clear his head. Eli's never-ending quest for more was exhausting. More money, more property, more success. The last straw had been when Eli shifted his drive and resources to tracking down the descendants of Mercy Falls. Eli's paranoia crept more and more into Luke's job duties until he finally had enough.

Convinced he could find his own way, he toyed with the idea of being a paramedic, but after a few weeks' worth of horrified looks from patients, that fell apart. Beaten down, he fled Florida, landing in New Orleans. A local woodworker needed an apprentice and Luke started to find his way.

Work wasn't all he fell in love with. The food, the

music, and, most importantly, people's attitudes drew him in. He'd gotten less sensitive about his scars over the years, but New Orleans was the first place where people either didn't look or didn't make it weird that they were looking.

And then he lost Zeus.

Usually, Zeus would meander in and out of the woodshop as Luke worked and learned. He'd never go far, but one night, he didn't come back. Almost twenty-four hours of searching on foot and reaching out to local vets resulted in nothing before a woman called, saying she'd found him.

Luke barely looked at her when she showed up at his house with Zeus an hour later. His whole mind was occupied with making sure his friend was in one piece.

"I'm so sorry I lost you, buddy. I should've paid better attention." He'd crouched down to wrap his arms around the dog's furry neck, and Zeus licked the side of his face.

A soft female voice broke the spell. "Looks like he forgives you."

Still crouching, Luke turned his head up toward her. She was tall and fit, and a breezy dress showed off her sun-kissed skin. Luke stood and cleared his throat. "Hopefully. Where'd you find him?"

"He found me." She cocked her head to the side, letting long, black hair drape over one shoulder. "He was walking alongside the road last night on my way home." She held out a hand for Zeus, and he crossed to her for a pat, his face pure contentment when she scratched behind his ears. "He was too handsome to be a stray, so I called the local vets to see if they knew who he belonged to. One got back to me with your info right before I called you. And, hi. I'm Kay."

Luke clasped the hand that she extended. "Luke. I called all the local vets and shelters to see if he turned up."

"Great minds think alike." She leaned down, and Zeus nuzzled her. "He's so sweet."

"He is. Luckily, he doesn't take after me." A smile tugged at the corners of his mouth when she laughed. He reached for his wallet in his back pocket. "Can I offer you a reward?"

"No. It was nothing." She stood, and Zeus lumbered back over to Luke's side. He was about to thank her and take him in when she added, "I wouldn't say no to a coffee, though."

Luke rubbed a hand through his shaggy hair, his smile growing. "That can be arranged. Come on in."

They'd hit it off. She was beautiful, smart, and their conversations flowed like they were made for each other. It was easy to let his guard down. To trust her. To want to trust her.

The end of summer approached quickly, and Luke decided to stay in New Orleans permanently the second Kay agreed to move in with him. Then, on one particularly beautiful Friday afternoon, he left the woodshop early, planning on going home to surprise her with a night out. He entered the house and his eyes zeroed in on a man's suit coat, neatly folded on the banister.

Blood rushed to his ears as he fought to hold onto the hope that things weren't about to go to shit.

That hope disintegrated when Kay's raised voice traveled down the hall from the kitchen. "…this is what Luke wants."

"I don't care. You're not going to continue living together." Eli's voice was strained, but firm.

Oh, hell no.

Two days ago, Eli had balked when Luke told him he wasn't coming back to work, then he'd berated him when he found out the reason was a girl. Luke should've anticipated that the angry phone call wouldn't have been the end, but in no way did he think he'd show up unannounced.

Seething, Luke rushed down the hall. He needed to save Kay from whatever twisted shit Eli was filling her head with. He was steps from the open office door when Eli's next words made him freeze in his tracks.

"I'm not giving you any more money. End of story. You want to keep dating him, it's no longer at my expense."

The sweet voice Luke had gotten used to went cold. "If the money stops, I'll have no choice but to come clean to Luke, and how do you think he'd feel knowing you paid me to go out with him? He's in love with me."

"He's not in love with you. He's in love with Kay. Who I created, by the way. He wouldn't have looked twice at you if I hadn't thought to lure him in with that mutt. And it's your own fault that you let this go on too long. You were supposed to nudge him in the direction of coming back to work for me, not convince him to stay in this swamp and play house."

"You agreed to keep it going," she shrieked.

"I thought you meant for another week, maybe a month…but this has gotten ridiculous. Don't you want a real boyfriend? That's got to be hard to get when you're fucking someone else for money." Eli huffed out a dry laugh.

"I can make things work with Luke. Now that I know him, I can see myself with him."

"Oh, I bet you can. What's your plan? I keep you on salary until he pops the question and starts bankrolling you himself? And suddenly you're okay with the scars? You're the one who asked for double the money once you saw his face."

"You won't have to pay anymore. Just leave us alone."

Eli didn't respond, but Luke had heard more than enough.

The familiar numbness that had protected him from his feelings for years settled over him as he spun around, heading straight upstairs. In his room, he threw whatever could fit into a duffle bag and called for Zeus to follow him. He'd just pulled open the front door when both Eli and Kay came down the hallway.

"Oh, hey, sweetie," she called. "I'm glad you're home early. Look who's here!"

He turned and met her glowing smile. She was good. Even now, for a moment, he could've been fooled into thinking she was genuinely happy to see him.

His gaze flicked over her shoulder, a wave of nausea rolling in his gut. "Here to drop off a housewarming gift, Dad?"

Eli glared and opened his mouth, but Kay stepped between them, closer to Luke. "Actually, he offered to help me get a job if we move to Florida and you go back to work. It's so generous of him."

Luke shook his head and scoffed. "You can both go fuck yourselves." He turned and shut the door behind him and Zeus. Moments later, it creaked back open and heels clicked across the pavement.

"Luke. Luke, wait!"

She reached him as he yanked open the car door and let Zeus climb in before tossing his bag into the back seat.

She put a hand on his arm. "Luke, stop. What's going on?"

"Don't touch me." He shook her off.

"Come on, don't be like that. I know you don't get along with your dad, but he's really happy for us. Come inside."

He whipped toward her. Whatever emotion was in his eyes made her flinch, and he spat out a single question. "What's your name?"

Pure shock registered on her face, and she paled.

He slapped his palm on the roof of the car. "What's your fucking name?"

Cowering, she took a step back. "Rachel."

He bit his bottom lip and looked to the door of the house where his father stood. Luke shook his head and flung himself into the front seat, jamming the key into the ignition.

That had been the last time he'd seen her. And the last time he'd seen his father until Eli showed up in Nova Scotia last month.

Luke had met girls since and gone out with a few. He was more cautious and much more guarded, but he'd never had such a visceral reaction as the one on the beach tonight. The potential for pain rained down, and Luke couldn't shake the feeling that, like Kay, this clumsy, beautiful girl, had been purposely placed in his life.

Chapter Seven

Vee

Sleep should've been elusive after the intense night, but exhaustion overtook Vee as soon as she climbed into bed and she fell into a dreamless void. She woke late the next morning and barely had time to splash water on her face without risking being late for her first day.

Taking her time on the path, Vee slowed to a stop when she reached the place Blake had called "a drop" last night. Sure enough, peering through the branches, she noted the ground fell away only a few feet from the path. She swore under her breath. A bit of overgrowth obscured it, but not enough that she wouldn't have noticed if she'd paid any attention. In Boston, her radar was always up for threats—footsteps behind her at night, overly friendly drunken guys at the bar, insane cab drivers… She wasn't used to watching her back around Mother Nature.

She made it to work in one piece and found Meredith in the front flower bed of the hotel. Her boss pulled out a handful of weeds despite being dressed in a freshly pressed skirt and top.

"Vee, good. You're early." She reached her hand out for Vee to steady her as she climbed out of the mulch, teetering on heels. "I can't stand this crabgrass trying to choke my azaleas." She tossed the handful of offending weeds to the side of the stairs. "Come with me. You'll be my shadow this morning."

Vee followed her into the inn and spent the next few hours learning the basics of daily operations.

She'd grasped the procedures well enough that Meredith left her at the front desk and she checked in two guests on her own. As she handed the second couple a set of keys and directed them to their room, Meredith strolled out of her office.

She leaned against the reception desk. "I think that was the last check-in for today. Why don't you go get some lunch?"

"Okay, thanks." Vee didn't waste any time following the divine smell that had been trickling into the reception area for the past hour.

In the kitchen, a plump woman was pulling a tray of biscuits from the oven. The woman turned, giving Vee a chance to read her apron's advice to "never trust a skinny cook" before she noticed Vee. "You must be our summer hire. Welcome, I'm Maria. You look hungry." She held out a basket of biscuits.

"Hi, I'm Vee. Thank you." She reached in and took one with a napkin. The first bite of buttery pastry melted on her tongue. "These are amazing."

Maria beamed. "My mother's recipe. She had a gift."

The door swung open, and Becca entered with an older woman. Becca plucked a biscuit off the tray. "Yeah, a gift for making me not fit into my bathing suit."

Not missing a beat, Maria handed Vee a bowl of soup and shot a look at Becca. "No one's forcing them down your throat, deary."

The older woman who'd come in with Becca pulled up a seat at the prep table where Vee had settled to eat. "Hi, I'm Peg. I make all the desserts here."

"I'm Vee. I'm the summer hire. Nice to meet you."

Peg pointed toward the back of the kitchen. "You see that rack back there with the mixer?"

Vee twisted in that direction. "Yes."

"That's my baking supplies and they are never to be touched. Don't borrow anything, don't move anything, and God help you, don't try to organize it. We'll get along just fine if you can do that."

"I can," Vee said, smirking at the woman's straightforwardness.

"Good. Well then, Vee, you're from Boston, I hear?"

"Not originally. I'm from Seattle, but I went to school in Boston and worked there since I graduated."

"Seattle to Boston? That's a haul." Peg's eyebrows rose. "Your family doesn't mind you being so far away?"

"It's just my aunt, but yes, she minds." *Hates it, actually.*

"What happened to your parents?" Peg stared at Vee with curiosity.

"Peggy. For God's sake, stop interrogating the girl," Maria yelled from near the stove.

Vee broke in, "It's fine. I don't mind. My dad was never around, and my mother died in a car accident when I was four."

"Oh, I'm sorry." Peg's frown deepened.

Vee shrugged. "I was lucky, and my mom's sister took me in. She didn't have anyone and neither did I, so we had each other."

Peg pursed her lips, then gave a sly grin and said, "Wow, you're really trying to make lemonade out of those lemons, aren't you?"

"Peggy!" Maria shouted a second time, making Vee laugh.

Peg ignored her and stood up with her empty plate. "Well, welcome. Now you have us, too."

The red in Maria's face faded and she turned back to the stove but kept her head angled in Peg's direction, on guard until she left the kitchen.

Vee spent the next hour making sure the unoccupied rooms were ready for the guests that would arrive over the next few days. The work didn't keep her busy enough to block out thoughts of Blake. No matter how many times his sarcastic comments replayed in her mind, they couldn't override the stir of butterflies she got each time she thought about seeing him.

She finished smoothing the bedspread and stepped to the window. Ahead, the water reflected gray, mirroring the sky, and she leaned on the sill. The smart thing would be to toss the sweatshirt and forget Blake existed. She rubbed her palm, unable to not remember the feel of his rough skin against hers. She took a deep breath and watched the clouds part. Sun caught on the water, transforming the ocean into a sea of diamonds. She wasn't going to be smart.

Tearing herself from the view, she'd just come down the stairs when Meredith stepped out of her office.

Vee paused. "I think everything looks good."

"Excellent." Meredith shut her office door. "Memorial Day's this weekend and we'll be packed from then on. Why don't you take advantage of our slow day and head out?"

"Really? It's not even three." At her advertising job, it had been rare to get out on time, let alone early.

Meredith called over her shoulder as she headed into the dining room, "Trust me. Take advantage of the downtime now."

Vee didn't give her a chance to change her mind. She grabbed her bag and started down the driveway where a group of workers filled in potholes.

A familiar face stood out and Vee paused when she reached Damon. "No fences left to paint?"

"Ha. Yeah. It seems I've been demoted." He leaned on his shovel. "You're out early. You get time off for good behavior?"

"Something like that. Hey, I solved my ghost mystery and you were right. It was Blake I saw in the window."

The grin faded from Damon's mouth. "Ugh. That means he's back. How'd you figure it out?"

"I ran into him and his dog on the beach last night."

"A dog?" Damon raised his eyebrows. "Blake doesn't strike me as an animal lover. You sure it was him?"

Doubt crept in. "I thought so from how you guys described him. He wasn't the nicest. Do you know anyone else in town with a big black dog named Zeus?"

"I don't. It could be a tourist."

"No, I'm pretty sure he's a local. He seemed to know his way around." *And could hike through the woods blindfolded.* Her certainty returned. It had to be Blake.

Damon straightened and lifted the shovel in one hand. "Be careful. It's a ghost town here at night. No one's usually around if you run into trouble."

Boy, did she know it. "Thanks. I should let you get back to work before there's a mutiny." Vee nodded her chin toward the other guys who were still working but casting occasional annoyed looks in Damon's direction.

"I suppose." He rolled his eyes lightheartedly. "Your path's on our list for tomorrow. No low-hanging branch will survive. And hey," His expression was uncharacteristically serious. "If it was Blake, my advice is to steer clear."

She nodded, turning before he caught the flush rising to her cheeks. At the end of the driveway, instead of crossing the street and heading up her path, she took a left and walked toward town.

The beach was practically empty, with only seagulls, a few sunbathers, and a woman building sandcastles with two toddlers. Out in the bay, there was a clear line of buoys topped with red flags a few feet from where the light blue water turned dark. Vee shook her head. How could she have missed that? It didn't make it any better that there was also a huge sign at the entrance to the beach: *Caution: Shelf Break 100 Yards Offshore*.

"Pay better attention, Vee," she mumbled to herself and kept walking until she reached Ema's shop.

The little bell over the door chimed as she stepped through. Approaching the front desk, she pulled her wallet out of her bag. "Hi, I'm back for my books."

Amanda was hunched over her phone. The only thing that moved were her eyes. Rimmed by electric blue eyeliner today, they flicked from her screen to

Vee. "Books?"

"Yeah, the pile I left last night. You said you'd hold them for me?"

Amanda slid off her stool. "Name?"

"Vee…for Verity." Vee paused at her blank look. "Like the letter."

Amanda shook her head but ducked under the counter, coming up a moment later. "There's nothing here. You sure it wasn't a different store?"

"No…it was here. Last night, right at closing?"

"Sorry. I closed last night and I'm the only one on today. I think you must have been in a different shop."

"I'm sure I wasn't… You really don't remember me?"

Amanda just raised her eyebrows. Vee narrowed hers. "Fine. I'll pick out some new ones."

"You do that."

Vee walked away, determined not to react to Amanda's monotone taunt. *She's just a bored teenager messing with a tourist. Let it go.*

The maze of rooms was more familiar this time, but the books she'd chosen yesterday were missing. Scowling, she plucked up the first ones that caught her eye then poked her head into the room with the necklaces. Ema was there, setting a teapot on the table by the open French doors. Today, bright sunlight streamed in.

"Vee. What perfect timing. I just brewed a fresh pot. Can I pour you a cup of tea?"

Vee stepped through the curtained doorway, enticed by a warm, earthy smell. "Sure."

Ema pointed to the table. "Come. Sit."

Vee settled into a chair and set her books on the

table next to her. Ema poured steaming gold liquid into Vee's cup. "Lavender Sage. It's good for settling the soul."

Vee glanced away from her piercing gaze and accepted the cup. "Thanks."

Across the table, Ema took a seat and pulled one foot up on her chair, wrapping her arm around her knee. "Ready for more of Mercy's story?"

Vee nodded and picked up her cup, the image of Ema shimmering through the steam.

Chapter Eight

Mercy
Two Hundred Years Ago

As weeks turned into months with no sign of Jonathan returning, the winter grew harsher. Still, Mercy always kept the pearl on her, even taking the time to sew a special pocket into her gowns so it wouldn't be lost. Young Thomas thrived, growing stronger as each day passed. And although the weather limited their trips into town, with Mercy's help, Siobhan now had more to sell, making each trip more lucrative.

By mid-January, Siobhan had been ill for a few weeks and was resting in her bedroom. Mercy had just finished feeding Thomas breakfast when a booming knock on the door startled them both. Wary, Mercy stood and smoothed her skirt, the tiny bump of the pearl offering reassurance as her fingers brushed over it.

She pulled open the door and caught her breath, unprepared for the sight that greeted her. Jonathan's man, Roderick, filled the doorway, a near-bursting sack slung over one shoulder. Behind him, warm rays of golden sunlight caressed the blanket of snow that lay over the surrounding hills and valleys.

He didn't wait for an invitation and stepped around her, lowering the sack to the table with a grunt.

"Provisions. In gratitude for your kind hospitality from our last trip."

"Mr. Dryer has paid us twice over already." She stared at the overflowing bag.

"I've made him fully aware of that fact, but he insisted."

Mercy narrowed her eyes at his scowl. *I'm certain you did.*

Roderick smoothed a hand through his untamed hair and lowered his voice. "He also wants to know if you would be amenable to a visit from him this afternoon."

He's here.

Mercy's heart swelled and she pinched the pearl through the fabric hard enough that its shape indented into her fingers. Thomas's cry broke through her daze and she scooped him up, soothing him with soft words until he quieted and nuzzled into her shoulder. It would be nothing but selfish to indulge the fantasy surrounding Jonathan.

"I won't be able to spare the time. My aunt has been unwell." Mercy looked away. The strain of caring for both Siobhan and the baby was taking a greater toll than she wanted to admit.

Roderick let out a breath, his shoulders relaxing with the exhale. "I'll give him the message." He turned and left, pulling the door shut firmly behind him.

Mercy didn't dare embrace the hope that was circling her thoughts.

It wasn't until hoofbeats approached in the late afternoon that she let a glimmer of excitement surge through her.

She stepped outside where Jonathan was

dismounting, snowflakes softly drifting around him. He turned to face her and stilled. “My dear Miss Falls. You are lovelier than I remembered.” He strode toward her and took her hand to gently place a kiss while his warm brown eyes bore into hers.

Mercy fought to control her heart as it beat wildly against her ribs. “Hello again, Mr. Dryer.” She stepped back and held the door open. “Please, come in from the cold.”

A gust of frigid wind blew in before Mercy could close the door, causing Thomas to shriek in his bassinet. She bent over and tucked his blanket a little tighter. “Shhh, there now,” she cooed then straightened up and gasped, finding Jonathan right behind her.

He made no move to step away and instead peered down into the bassinet. “A beautiful child.” His gaze trailed up to Mercy’s face. “And a beautiful mother.”

She drew in a sharp breath, and he lowered his voice. “I haven’t stopped thinking about you since I left.”

“Neither have I.” The words had barely passed her lips when a racking cough sounded from the back room.

“Mercy? Was someone at the door?” Siobhan entered the kitchen, breathing hard and leaning on a walking stick. Her eyes flicked from Mercy to Jonathan, but she didn’t break her slow stride. “You’re back,” she stated in a hoarse voice and collapsed into the nearest chair.

He stepped away from Mercy and turned his attention to Siobhan. “Indeed, I am. And I have come to sing your praises.” He shrugged off his coat and took a seat at the head of the table. Mercy busied herself pulling out some of the cheese and bread that Roderick had left. Jonathan took a large bite from the portion she set in front of him and closed his eyes. “This cheese is exquisite. This town is full of surprises.” His gaze flicked to Mercy, causing her to blush.

“The tea helped the boy, I take it.” Siobhan waved away the plate of food that Mercy slid toward her.

“Helped is an understatement. He was up and running within a week of taking it. He was doing marvelous, in fact, until the supply I purchased was exhausted. His symptoms immediately returned, even though every attempt was made to replicate your recipe. Our town’s apothecary is quite dismayed as he is certain he identified all the ingredients, but he must be mistaken.”

Siobhan coughed into a handkerchief, then cleared her throat. “It’s a lot of trouble for you to come all this way for someone else’s suffering.”

Jonathan’s eyes narrowed. “It is. But then again, the one suffering is a child.” He scooped up the last of the crumbs on his plate and leaned his elbows on the table. “I’ve come to offer you a generous sum for the recipe.”

“It’s not for sale.”

“You haven’t heard the amount.”

“There’s no amount that would change that fact.”

“What about—”

“No amount,” Siobhan said with finality.

He took a deep breath in and out through his nose. “I see. Well then, would you see fit to work out an arrangement for a schedule of sorts. We travel close to here every few months, and I’d be happy to provide you with any supplies you may need.”

Siobhan paused as another coughing fit shook her

shoulders. “An arrangement would work.”

“Wonderful. We will be passing back through this area in one week’s time. Will you have a three-month supply ready by then?”

“That should be no trouble.”

He stood and swung his traveling coat on. “In that case, I’ll be counting the days until we meet again.” He winked at Mercy before he let himself out.

Siobhan all but collapsed in the next coughing fit and Mercy helped her back to bed. “The fits are getting worse. I’ll bring you a eucalyptus salve for your chest.”

“Thank you.” Siobhan sank back into the pillows. “Will you be able to start on the tea order for Mr. Dryer?”

“Yes. I remember it well and have my notebook to consult. I’ll start tonight.”

“Good child. It will be dependable income, and if it’s ready when they arrive, there will be no excuse for him to dawdle.”

“If you don’t want him around, why not sell the recipe?”

“Because it’s not the kind of recipe that can be followed. It has to be taught. And it has to be in your blood. If I sell him the recipe, the child may get some relief, but not nearly as much as when it’s crafted by our hands.” Siobhan placed one of her cold, dry palms on top of Mercy’s warmer one. “Yours or mine.”

Her eyes fluttered closed, and Mercy drew away to the kitchen with furrowed brows. Siobhan not putting up a fight to being fussed over was more concerning than the cough.

****

Mercy followed the instructions precisely, and the

order was complete when Jonathan returned. If he had any thought of lingering, Siobhan had no trouble making his decision for him by ordering Mercy to start a brew of fever-reducing tea to be delivered to Mrs. Blackwell.

Mercy walked Jonathan back to his horse to say goodbye. "You will be back for more of the child's tea?"

"Among other things, I hope," he said with a look that set a fire in Mercy's stomach. He stepped toward her, angling his face down. She was certain he was about to kiss her, here, in the light of day where anyone could see. Marking her as his. Her heart fluttered erratically. Instead, he paused, his lips close enough to her ear that she could feel his breath. "I will return in the first days of spring."

This time, she didn't doubt the promise, and the memory of that moment made the rest of the harsh winter months pass in a blur. With hope as a distraction as well as caring for the house, Thomas, and Siobhan, Mercy was barely aware of the whispers in town. The illness there afflicted more and more each day and ran a long course. No cure Mercy or the doctor provided seemed to tame the wild fever that progressed. Mrs. Blackwell had finally recovered, after weeks of being confined to her bed when her husband showed the first signs. That's how it spread, delicately, like a spider weaving a deceivingly fragile web, one family and one person at a time.

By the last few weeks of winter, not a home in town had been spared, most suffering at least one death. Mercy's remedies had little effect on the symptoms, which kept her tucked away in the house on the hill caring for her small family. Thomas continued to grow stronger as Siobhan grew more fragile. Siobhan's affliction was not the same illness as the one burning through the town below. Instead, she was slowly being robbed of her breath. Her cheeks were sunken, and Mercy knew she was losing her fight when the handkerchiefs came from her lips stained red after bad coughing fits.

Once the snow melted, Mercy began the task of reviving the garden alone. One particularly gray day, she glanced up to find a lone rider on the horizon. Straightening from where she knelt, she raised her hand over her eyes to block the sun and squinted, hoping to make out the form of Jonathan. The first days of spring were only a week away.

Maybe he couldn't wait.

She watched the form eagerly. It was him. His broad shoulders were unmistakable. The rider reached the fork in the road at the bottom of her hill that would decide if they would continue to town or turn toward her. She was sure he was slowing…then no, he went on to town.

She frowned. It had looked so much like him. Maybe he had business in town and would come later? She half-heartedly returned to her work.

The first day of spring came and went. Then another week. Mercy fell fully clothed into bed at the end of the day, disappointed and exhausted. She'd been woken up twice the night before with Thomas breaking his first teeth. Now, she tried to steal a few hours of sleep before the spicy-scented oil she'd rubbed on his gums wore off.

She'd come to the edge of release into sleep when

light danced across her closed eyelids. Sitting bolt upright, she flung off her covers. *Fire.*

She peered down the stairs and her panic wavered. The light came from outside the house. Fully awake, dread crept up her spine at the sound of multiple voices. She scooped Thomas out of his cradle and took him downstairs. A window in the kitchen framed their front yard, full of people, their torches piercing the night.

"What's is it?" Siobhan called from where she leaned on the door frame to her room.

"I don't know," Mercy said, placing her hand to open the door. "Something must have happened in town."

Something had happened. The magistrate's oldest child had succumbed to the illness that very afternoon, despite the doctor's best attempts to save him. The town had been building to a frenzy for weeks and only needed a slight nudge for the hushed whispers to become shouts of accusations.

Witchcraft.

What else could set a plague so destructive on an innocent town?

Mercy went with mild resistance when the magistrate led her roughly to a waiting wagon, his hand clamped on her arm.

Behind her, Siobhan's cries cut through the stillness of the air as two men dragged her to follow. "You weren't crying *witch* when you knocked on my door with your complaints of restlessness, Mr. Smith. Or when you begged for relief from your child's hives, Mr. Miller." The fire from the torches paled in comparison to the fire in her eyes when she turned them from face to face in the crowd. They landed on the magistrate's wife and Siobhan's voice turned to a scathing hiss. "Or when you wanted to rid yourself of the proof of your infidelity, growing in your womb, Mrs. Henley."

The magistrate's fingers crushed Mercy's arm and she cried out over the gasps from the crowd.

He thrust her into the wagon and turned to Siobhan, his voice booming. "Enough with your lies! We've tolerated your presence for far too many years and this is our penance, but it ends tonight."

He stepped aside and the men holding Siobhan lifted her into the wagon, securing its gate behind her as she landed hard on the floor. The rough treatment didn't silence her condemnations and she pulled herself onto her knees, leaning over the side of the wagon as it drove off. Her voice was raw, as if her words were being torn from her throat. "Your God is watching! You will never rid yourself of this stain on your souls."

Mercy couldn't bring herself to release even one arm from the iron-clad hold she had on Thomas, but she leaned against Siobhan's thin frame, hoping to provide reassurance. "Don't strain yourself. Surely, they will come to their senses."

The crowd followed the wagon, their heads down, while Siobhan's cries continued. "What page of your good book allows for such crime? Hypocrites and liars condemning—"

Siobhan's words died on her lips and Mercy gasped as flames began to lick the edges of the cottage's roof.

A yell escaped Mercy, setting off a new burst of cries from Thomas. Beside them, the silence from Siobhan rang louder than her screams.

****

The night passed with the women huddled together in an old root cellar. The faint scent of smoke filtered through the air as their home burned to the ground in the distance. A numbing fog clouded Mercy's thoughts since the moment Thomas had been pried from her, his cries coming from farther and farther away while she and Siobhan were left alone in the dark.

There had been no trial, just the pronouncement by the magistrate that their hanging would take place at dawn.

Mercy had never known a cold so bitter. It seeped into her bones, and Siobhan's breaths rattled in her chest, followed by racking coughs that left her too exhausted to sit upright. Mercy's arms ached where they longed to feel the weight of Thomas. After Siobhan fell into a wheezing sleep, Mercy prayed through her tears over and over for him to be warm and taken care of, wherever they'd taken him.

Before first light, the sound of the door being unchained reached Mercy's ears. She helped Siobhan to her feet to meet their soon-to-be-murderers with chins held high.

Light from a torch pierced the darkness and Mercy squinted against it. She couldn't make out the man coming toward her, but every inch of her recognized his voice. "Good lord, Mercy, what have they done to you?"

Her dress was filthy, bruises stuck out on her pale skin where she had been mistreated, and her wrists were scraped raw where the rope she'd been restrained with had bitten into her skin. She thought she'd exhausted her lifetime's supply of tears overnight, but new tears stung her eyes as she threw herself at Jonathan, praying her imagination wasn't playing tricks on her. His solid form and strong arms enveloped her and his torch fell to the ground, where it sputtered out. He was there. Her mind raced to the only other thing that mattered.

"Thomas," she choked out. "They have Thomas."

"He's right outside. Safe and sound. Come quickly. We must leave at once." He smoothed her hair back.

Safe. The relief that came with the word was enough to make her lightheaded.

Wiping her face, Mercy nodded and reached for Siobhan's hand to help her through the dim cellar, but a harsh voice stopped her. "The deal was only for the girl and the child. And you're lucky I agreed to that." The magistrate spat in Mercy's direction from where he stood in the door. "The town will forgive letting one escape, and the child would have been a burden, but we must have a witch to hang come full dawn."

"We can't leave her. I won't." Mercy reached back and grabbed both Siobhan's stiffened hands in her own. She turned her face, panicked, toward Jonathan.

"You can and you must, child," Siobhan said in a scratchy voice. "I've got but a few more days of breath in me at best." A deep cough bent her double and produced a mouthful of blood that she spat out, emphasizing her point. "You are going to learn all your lessons the hard way, but at least you'll live to learn them. Now, go quickly and leave an old woman to her fate."

Mercy still clutched her hands, as if she could hold onto her forever that way. "But it's not fair."

"This world doesn't owe you fairness." Siobhan's gaze flicked to the men behind Mercy before returning to her.

"But I can't..." Mercy started but was cut off by Siobhan.

"Never forget what I taught you. Take this, Mercy Falls." She pulled her own tattered recipe book from her skirts and leaned against the closest wall. Mercy looked down at the book Siobhan had given her, along with her last name, and couldn't bring herself to look up again when Siobhan said to Jonathan, "Take her quickly."

Jonathan did just that, steering Mercy toward the door held open by his man, Roderick.

Inside her chest, her heart shattered and a sob escaped her.

The magistrate slapped her across the face, shocking her into silence. "Quiet girl. If anyone sees us, the deal is off and you will hang as sure as the sun will rise."

As quick as a bolt of lightning, Roderick had a blade at his throat. "You should count yourself lucky if I don't kill you where you stand," he warned as a rooster crowed in the distance, marking the approach of dawn.

"Roderick, let him go. We need to leave." Jonathan led Mercy toward the waiting carriage a few steps away.

With a final glare, Roderick pocketed the knife and the carriage door opened. Mrs. Blackwell stepped down, bouncing Thomas against her chest.

Her eyes brimmed with tears. "You have to understand, there was nothing I could do. If I spoke up when they decided to go up the hill, they would have damned me as well. One voice wouldn't have mattered against so many," she pleaded, handing Thomas over.

Resigned to her powerlessness, Mercy went numb. She no longer felt the cold, or the pain from her wrists, or the joy in seeing Jonathan, or the sting from the Magistrate's hand. The only reason she climbed into the carriage was the child in her arms.

"Please, you must forgive me," Mrs. Blackwell continued, with the urgency of someone who thought hearing the words would make a difference.

Mercy looked deep into her eyes. "I'll weep for your soul." She entered the carriage, leaving Mrs. Blackwell, for once, with nothing to say.

Resting her head against the seat, Mercy listened to the men outside.

"Best not to forget your end of the deal," the magistrate threatened. "One yell from me and a dozen able-bodied men will be here to stop your departure."

Jonathan's voice came in a harsh whisper. "Here is the amount we agreed upon. And, before you look too proud of yourself, you should know I would have paid a great deal more." Moments later, he joined Mercy and Thomas.

The carriage was off before he'd fully settled himself in the seat next to her and despite his warmth, she did not sleep. She stared silently through the window as the sun gently rose above the horizon, the cold light of a new day touching things one by one.

There was a moment right after it had fully risen that the briefest pain tugged at her heart and she closed her eyes. A gentle rain began to fall on the roof of the carriage like tears from heaven itself, and Mercy opened her eyes to a world forever changed.

Chapter Nine

Vee

A gentle breeze toyed with the branches of the willow tree in the yard while Vee stared at Ema in shock. “Siobhan died?”

“She did.”

The breeze drifted through the doors, fluttering Vee’s hair. “But she was only trying to help people. She wasn’t a witch.”

Perfectly still, Ema stared at her. “What she was or wasn’t is irrelevant. It’s human nature to assign blame.”

“So, what happened to Mercy? Jonathan brought her here?”

“He did. But I’m afraid that will have to wait for another day.”

Vee bit back the urge to argue. “Of course. Thanks, Ema.”

She reached to help clear her cup but Ema waved her hand away. “Come back when you can and we’ll get to more of Mercy’s story.”

Vee thanked her again and paid for her new selection of books before stepping outside onto the cobblestoned lane. She stopped at the market to get dinner supplies and a new flashlight, then started up the hill. The sun was setting as she placed the bag on her kitchen counter. Keeping out the salmon and garlic,

Vee turned on the stove.

After finishing her meal, she sat down at her easel and picked up a brush. Forcing her hand to outline the Rowan tree that was so clear in her mind, she struggled with every stroke. She took a deep breath and closed her eyes, turning inward.

Stop fighting it.

Opening her eyes, she stopped resisting the current inside herself and let go. Hours later, she stood in the middle of her art studio and surveyed her work. Four new paintings leaned against the wall. Each one was a more intricate version of the same pattern she'd painted the other day.

She flipped off the light and went into her bedroom, stopping when she reached the window. The moon hung high overhead in a cloudless sky, but her attention gravitated to the beach below. In the moonlight, the sand glowed white, with no sign of a human or dog. She glanced toward the hoody still hanging on her chair. It wouldn't hurt to take a walk down there, just in case. Her heart raced with anticipation while she pulled on jeans, then headed out the front door with the replacement flashlight.

The beach was deserted, and her heart sank with her as she dropped down on the sand, keeping her distance from the dark water. After a few minutes of listening to the gentle waves, Vee was about to get up when the hairs on the back of her neck prickled. She held her breath until quiet panting broke the night's silence.

A large, furry shape came up next to her and butterflies took off in her stomach. "Hi, Zeus."

He inclined his head toward her for a pat. When

she obliged, he dropped down next to her, resting his huge head on her knee.

His owner strode into view, staring out at the water instead of at her. “Looks like you made a friend.”

“He isn’t so bad for a monster.” On her lap, Zeus let out a contented sigh. She looked up to study the man’s profile again. Instead of jogging clothes, tonight he had on well-worn jeans and an untucked flannel shirt. What stood out the most was the hardness of his features. His stillness was unnatural, and Vee had the urge to touch him to make sure he hadn’t turned to stone.

His lips parted, breaking the illusion. “You down here planning another swim?” His tone was flat, not giving a clue as to if he was joking, or he really thought she was that dumb.

“Hardly. Actually, I was looking for you.” Vee smiled at the small triumph when his stone face registered a flicker of surprise.

“You found me.” His voice turned back to ice. “What do you want?”

“I wanted to return your hoody today, but realized you never told me your name. I thought you might come down here again.” She eased Zeus off her lap and stood holding the sweatshirt out. “I’m Vee, by the way.”

He didn’t move to take it. “It’s not very bright to seek out strangers in the middle of the night.”

“You’re the one choosing to remain strangers.” Enough of this game. No one was forcing him to stay and talk to her. “Here, take it.” She thrust it closer to him.

The side of his face she could see twisted in anger,

but he made no move to turn toward her. "You expect me to believe you don't know who I am?" He spat out the words with venom. "After last night, no one helped you figure it out?"

Heat flooded her cheeks. *Such a jerk.* "I don't need anyone to figure it out for me." Around them, the air stilled. Dread crept in through the fire in her veins, but she went on. "You're Blake Dryer."

He shook his head and let out a huff of a laugh, then finally turned to face her. "Sorry to disappoint you."

His icy blue eyes met hers with a concentration of anger and pain that struck her like a lightning bolt. Involuntarily, she stepped back and gasped. He looked down, breaking the hold on her focus and she took in the jagged scar running from his forehead, through his right eyebrow, continuing down his face and neck until it disappeared into his shirt.

Luke.

A moment of hurt crossed his features before he stepped closer to her and gritted his teeth. "Unfortunately, I'm the other Dryer. Take a good look. I'm sure your friends will want details." He yanked the hoody out of her hand and stormed across the beach toward the woods.

Vee stood frozen in shock while Zeus jumped up and trotted through the sand after his owner. The way he never faced her, how he angled himself to keep the moon at his back, the scars…oh, no. He thought she'd gasped at the scars. The pieces clicking into place propelled her forward.

She reached the road as Zeus's tail disappeared into the darkness of the forest. "Wait!" She pulled out her flashlight and snapped it on, then followed them as fast as she dared. Even with the aid of the light, Luke stayed well ahead of her, and she didn't catch so much as a glimpse of him or Zeus as she climbed. Once she passed the drop, she quickened her pace to a near run and vaulted over the last bundle of roots to land in her yard, panting. There was no sign of them. Immediately, she whipped around and started back down the path. It must branch off somewhere to continue up to his house.

They couldn't have gotten too far. She jogged down, scanning the edge of the woods for a break in the trees. Her foot snagged on a rock, and she crashed to the ground. Bracing herself with her arms didn't stop her from crying out or from hitting her head on one of the roots sticking up.

She slowly sat up and assessed the damage. Bruised palms, but nothing seemed broken. It was mostly scrapes.

The spot on her head that had hit the root was tender and swelling, but it was under her hair, which may have cushioned the blow. After years of being accident-prone, she knew better than to stand up too fast. Instead, she used her hands to feel around in the dark for the flashlight.

Her fingers wrapped around the cracked plastic and its insides rattled as she lifted it. She pressed the button, not surprised when it didn't turn on. "I'm going to have to start buying these in bulk," she said under her breath.

Across from her, the leaves rustled, and Zeus's head poked through the foliage, followed by his lumbering body. He walked to her side and let out a whimper of concern.

Luke's angry voice preceded him crashing through

the woods. “Zeus! Dammit. Tonight’s not the night to play games!”

He broke through onto the path, breathing heavily, and halted, facing Vee.

“Oh, Jesus.” He took quick steps to get to her. “What have you done now?”

“Nothing. I tripped. I’m fine.” Vee started to get up and swayed.

His arm shot out to steady her and he frowned. “Easy. You hit your head?”

“Just a little. I’ve had worse.” She reached up to touch the tender spot under her hair.

“You need to see a doctor. You could have a concussion.” Strong fingers tightened on her arm, and he steered her toward the cottage, missing the cold spot by only a few inches.

“No way.” Insurance was one of the benefits she’d left behind with her old job. She rubbed her forehead. “I had a concussion once. This isn’t that bad.”

“Of course you have,” he muttered as he opened her front door.

He told Zeus to stay outside, and they entered her kitchen, where she sank into a chair. Vee flipped her hands up to examine her palms.

Luke glanced down. “Those cuts need to be cleaned. Do you have a first aid kit?”

“Yeah, upstairs in the bathroom medicine cabinet.” She started to stand, but he shook his head.

“I’ll get it.” He started toward the stairs and pointed to the kitchen sink. “Wash your hands.”

A minute later, he set the kit on the kitchen table next to where Vee gingerly toweled off her hands. He pulled out a chair and sat facing her, staring at her eyes.

"Follow my finger." He traced out a 't' in the air followed by an 'x' then asked her, "Any dizziness now?"

"No."

"Headache? Nausea?'

"No. Are you a doctor?"

"No." He turned his head down to rummage through the first aid kit, pulling out supplies. "Let me see your hands."

Vee stretched her left one out, palm up and he took it, surprisingly gentle. Using gauze, he dabbed at the cuts to dry the area. Vee took advantage of his concentration to study him in the full light of the kitchen.

The thick scar running down his face split his eyebrow, but it wasn't the only scar. Smaller ones also marked his skin, one cutting into his top lip. Even with the scars, he was handsome, in a rugged, clenched sort of way. His eyes were a deep blue and they turned on her now, bringing forth another gasp from her at their intensity. He flinched and looked back down.

"It's not the scars," she said quickly. "It's your eyes…they're…" She trailed off, wishing she could sink through her chair. *Breathtaking.*

"This is going to sting." He dabbed a damp cotton ball across the scratches.

She sucked air through her teeth.

"Sorry," he mumbled, finishing and taping a bandage over her palm. "Other hand."

She turned up her right one and he paused, cotton ball mid-air.

Vee followed his gaze to her own scar running from her forearm to her palm. "You're not the only one with scars."

His eyes snapped up and she made a point not to react as they bore into hers. One of his eyebrows twitched. "You're hilarious."

"Maybe it's the head injury."

His lips curved up and he shook his head. Releasing the hold his gaze had on her, he turned his attention back to her palm. "This one's not so bad."

"The flashlight took the brunt of the damage." Vee glanced to where it rested on the table, bulb cracked open.

His fingertips grazed her scar as he smoothed the next bandage into place. "How'd it happen?"

"Car accident." She pulled her arm back.

He got up and opened the freezer, taking out a bag of frozen vegetables and handing it to her. "Hold this on your head."

She took the bag and watched as he cleaned up and put the supplies back in the kit.

"Take those bandages off in the morning and let some air at the scrapes. It's all superficial and should heal fast."

"Luke, it wasn't the scars that surprised me."

He took a step toward the door then turned to face her. "You expect me to believe that instead of a face full of scars, you noticed my eyes?"

"I don't know…Yes?" She hesitated before adding, "That…And for the briefest second, I thought you might be a ghost."

"What?" His face twisted, a cross between confusion and annoyance.

"My first day here, the girls at the inn told me you'd died as a teenager." Her voice lowered. "They all think you killed yourself."

His jaw clenched and he shook his head. "I'm guessing my brother didn't bother to correct them."

She cringed. "It sounds like he may have been the one to start the rumor."

His head tipped up to the ceiling and he sighed.

Half of her hated herself for prying, but the other half couldn't stop. "So, you've been locking yourself in that house since high school?"

"Of course not. I'm only here to deal with a family…issue. I live in Canada."

She shamelessly fished for more details. "And work in a hospital?"

"Please." He scoffed. "I took a few entry-level EMT courses a long time ago when I thought I might want to go down that path."

"What made you stop?"

His gaze flicked to her bandaged hands, then trailed up her scar and settled there, unfocused. "They made us go for ride-alongs. One of our calls was for an elderly woman with dementia who'd broken her arm. She wouldn't let the paramedics near her until I left. She kept screaming that I was a devil, come to take her away."

"Oh, Luke. She was mentally impaired and in pain. She probably had no idea what she was saying."

"She knew." He pulled open the front door and stepped out.

Through the window, Vee watched as Zeus fell into step next to him. They faded into the shadows at the mouth of the path.

****

Work went by in a blur the next day. Guests filled

the inn, and the staff functioned as a true team, seamlessly interchanging jobs. It was a great feeling to be part of it and when Vee left at the end of her shift, she was tired, but not drained.

The afternoon was warm and the whole way up the hill her thoughts circled back to the previous night.

Luke.

Not dead. Not aloof. Just trying to hide. A pulse of sympathy grew at the way he'd known exactly how to position himself to keep his scars from being seen.

She passed the place she'd fallen last night and stepped into her yard.

It must have taken years of practice for him to control the way he moved with such precision. The pain that twisted his features when he finally faced her—

She gasped, almost falling, her legs threatened to give out as a sudden wave of sorrow pummeled her. Her eyes squeezed shut but couldn't block out the hollow well of loss that filled her. Forcing her feet to move, she stepped out from the shadow of the elm tree, her heart hammering.

The sensation disappeared as fast as it'd come. Turning, she held out a shaking hand and swiped through the air where she'd just stood. Nothing.

She dropped to her knees, resting one palm on the soft grass and slid it forward along the earth. Her fingertips dipped into an icy pool of air and her lungs constricted on an involuntary sob.

Yanking her hand back, she clutched it to her chest and rocked back to stand. Maybe there was some type of underground vent. *That makes you feel like you're losing yourself?*

A soft whimper came from the tree line and Zeus

limped into her yard, keeping his front right paw off the ground.

She cautiously approached him, talking in what she hoped was a soothing voice. They were on the road to becoming friends, but he was still a wounded animal. She reached him and scratched behind his ears while she angled her head to look for signs of blood.

Finding nothing obviously wrong, Vee stood, debating how to get him inside. She couldn't pick him up, but maybe if she brought a blanket out, she could tip him onto it and drag him. He saved her from having to figure it out by standing and continuing his uneven walk to her front door, where he stopped and waited to be let in.

She got him settled in her living room, a bowl of water near enough that he wouldn't have to get up if he wanted some, then she glanced at the stairs. The last thing she wanted was for him to hurt himself more by attempting them while she was gone. She took a few minutes to build a makeshift fence by balancing her kitchen chairs on one another. After promising him she'd be back soon, she left, hoping he wasn't the type of dog that would tear up a couch, given the opportunity.

Between remembering where she fell the night before and having the benefit of daylight, Vee found the continuation of the path and crossed through to the driveway on the other side. She kept a fast pace, hopping over potholes. The pavement smoothed when it joined the road uphill to the Dryer Manor and shortly after, Vee faced the towering house.

Up close, it was even more imposing. Dark tendrils of ivy clung to the walls and snaked up the tower. The windows reflected the sky like possessive mirrors, unwilling to give a glimpse inside. Directly behind the house, the earth disappeared over the edge of the cliff. Her mouth went dry. The only barrier between solid ground and the sea below was a thin railing.

The faint beat of music pulled her in the other direction, toward a barn set far from the house and the cliff. Large doors stood wide open, the music drowning out her footsteps as she approached. Inside, the warm air glowed with sawdust drifting like fine snow. Luke stood over a worktable in the middle of the room, the blade of a saw screaming over blaring music.

Vee paused, not wanting to surprise someone with a power tool in his hands. He was fully engrossed in his project, a mask of concentration on the small part of his face she glimpsed as he worked with his back to her. He'd taken his shirt off, exposing a broad, tan back. His muscles tightened as he stood upright and put down the saw, then brushed wood shavings out of the way as he inspected his work.

"Hello?" she called.

He whipped around. "What are you doing here?" Three long scars ran across his torso.

"I'm sorry. I didn't mean to startle you, I heard the music and—"

"And decided to wander around on someone else's property? That's called trespassing."

"I didn't come here for myself," Vee snapped back, heat creeping up her neck. "Zeus hurt his leg."

Luke took the slightest step back and narrowed his eyes. "You just happened to find Zeus injured?"

"I didn't find him. He limped into my yard about half an hour ago. I left him in my house and came to get you."

A flash of vulnerability crossed his face. "He's really hurt?"

"I don't know. I didn't see anything obvious, but he isn't putting weight on one of his front paws."

"Okay, I'll get my keys." He strode across the barn, grabbed his shirt off a hook, and slipped it on without slowing. "Come on."

Vee followed him across the lawn and through the front door of the house. He led her through a maze of hallways, passing closed doors as they went. Finally, they stepped into a bright kitchen that was either well cleaned or rarely used. Luke called back, "Wait here," and disappeared up a stone staircase in the corner of the room.

Vee let out a deep breath and turned in a circle. The room was a cross between old and new, with ruby red tiles making up the countertops, cabinets that looked well-made but ancient, and top-of-the-line appliances. Vee slowed, the window above the farmhouse-style kitchen sink catching her eye.

It faced out to sea, and she took a tentative step toward it, then another, until she was gripping the sink's edge and standing on her tiptoes, leaning forward to see if she could find where the ground came back into view. No matter how far she leaned, it didn't. She stepped back, bumping into a solidness that hadn't been there a minute ago.

"Careful," Luke said in a rough voice, putting a hand on her arm to steady her. "Don't you have enough trouble walking forward?"

"Oh, he jokes." Vee stepped away, keeping her voice even despite her heart thundering against her ribs.

"Let's go." He led the way out of the room.

"There's the monosyllabic Luke I know."

He angled his head back with the slightest hint of amusement and shoved his hands in his pockets.

She followed him to a black pick-up truck that looked like it had been around for a while. They drove down the bumpy driveway in silence, her awareness of his proximity growing larger in the confined space. Tension radiated off him, mixed with the scent of sawdust and aftershave. When he slid the gear shift into park, Vee was already opening her door, hating how much she wished the ride was longer.

Luke's concern for Zeus showed with the urgency he crossed her yard. He took the most direct path and it wasn't until he'd stepped under the elm tree that Vee thought to warn him.

"Wait," she called.

He turned, standing in the spot that usually affected her. "What?"

She met his concerned gaze, no hint of anything abnormal in his voice or appearance. "Nothing. Sorry."

Keeping her distance from the spot, she walked beside him to the front door. The knob turned easily in her hand, and she pushed it open for him to go in.

"You should lock your door." He frowned.

"You don't."

"*You* should." He stopped short, looking at her chair barricade. "What the hell?"

Vee lifted the first chair and pulled it down. "He's through here. I didn't want to chance him going upstairs and hurting himself worse."

Luke took the chair from her with one hand and shook his head, grinning.

"What?" She crossed her arms.

"Nothing."

His smile grew and she continued to stare at him. "What?"

He shrugged. "It's just funny. You thought a couple of chairs would deter Zeus from doing anything he wanted. I didn't pick that name out of a hat."

Vee looked from him to the rickety tangle of chairs and the massive dog on the other side. She bit back a smile, mumbling, "Shut up. I had to think fast."

She couldn't help sneaking glances at Luke while they deconstructed the rest of the blockade. His face transformed when he smiled. Little crinkles formed at the edges of his eyes and the sadness that seemed etched in stone faded away.

As soon as it was down, Luke kneeled next to Zeus. "Which paw?"

"Right front."

He gently took Zeus's foot and looked it over with the same mask of concentration as when he'd bandaged her hands. "Ah-ha." He hunched forward, holding Zeus's paw with one hand and used the other to pluck something out. He leaned back on his heels and held it up. "A thorn."

Zeus stood and wagged his tail, all four feet on the floor.

"Thank God," Vee said. "I thought something was seriously wrong."

Luke stood, looking relieved. He paused and turned to Vee. "You have rose bushes down here?"

"I haven't seen any. Why?"

He crossed his arms and glared. "We do up in the garden. And it strikes me as a little odd that he'd limp all the way down here for help."

"What are you implying?" Nothing got to her faster than being accused of something she didn't do.

All the humor left his voice and his eyes narrowed, laugh lines gone. "I'm not implying anything. Should I be?"

"You should be going, that's for sure." *Last time I try to help.*

"Gladly." He shook his head and breezed by. Zeus trailed behind with a sympathetic look to Vee as he passed.

The evening air turned cool, and Vee rubbed her arms after shutting the door forcefully behind them. *This guy and his mood swings...*

In the kitchen, Luke's sweatshirt rested on the table, where he'd forgotten it last night. She grabbed it and put it on, the scent of aftershave and sawdust wrapping around her on her way upstairs. *Infuriating.*

Chapter Ten

Luke

Luke barely made it a few steps from Vee's front door before he bent down and scooped up the huge dog. It was only a thorn, and Zeus was walking fine, but better safe than sorry on the short trek through the woods to the truck. He placed Zeus in the passenger seat and got in, rolling down the windows to get the lingering scent of vanilla and cinnamon out.

It had been pure torture driving down here with her. Worry for Zeus kept him from thinking straight and it never crossed his mind to grab another hoody to hide his face. Instead, he'd endured the drive, his scars on full display mere inches from her. It was shocking he hadn't burst into flames from the heat rising to his face. All the while, her calming scent surrounded him, making him not want to care.

He gunned the truck's engine and shot forward, only to slam on the brakes to negotiate the minefield of potholes. His shocks didn't deserve to have his frustration taken out on them.

At home, he retreated to the tower room. Luke crossed to a neglected bookshelf and reached behind the row on the top shelf, his fingers clasping cold glass. He'd swiped the bottle of twenty-one-year-old whiskey from his dad as a teenager, and it was still half full. He uncorked it and took a long drink, shuddering as the smokey liquid burned on its way down. He took it to the couch and sank into the cushions. The image of the chair gate Vee constructed flashed behind his closed eyes and he couldn't help but laugh, the smile quickly turning to a grimace. If only he could believe she was what she seemed. Taking another drink, he settled in, praying the alcohol could quiet his flailing mind.

It had the opposite effect. With each sip, a new detail popped into his head to torture him. The way she didn't back down when he tried to push her away. The way her eyes held secrets that he wanted to know. How those same eyes looked at him like he was worth seeing.

The empty bottle slid to the floor, and he gave up fighting. Her face was the last thing to flash through his mind before sleep released him from his misery.

The next morning, he woke to a blissfully overcast sky, saving him the pain of blinding sun piercing his hungover brain. His head pounded, and his tongue was thick when he sat up and dragged himself downstairs.

Gail stood at the kitchen sink, rinsing out a coffee cup. "Good morning, Luke."

"Morning." He squinted. "Is there more coffee?"

She nodded and poured a mug for him. "You look a little rough around the edges."

"Yeah. Apparently, I still can't handle my whiskey." He took the carton of milk she offered and poured a splash. "Thanks."

"Bad habit to start, drinking alone."

"It's not a habit." He took a sip of coffee. *Fucking cinnamon.*

He laughed and put his head in his hands.

Drunk…hungover…she was still so in his head. *I can't take this.*

Gail narrowed her eyes, appraising him. "Tell me."

He sighed and everything that'd happened since he'd pulled Vee out of the ocean poured out.

When he finished talking, Gail took a deep breath and shook her head with a disapproving look.

He grimaced. "I know. I'm just going to stay away from her. The more I think about it, the more I'm sure my dad's behind it. She even used Zeus, like Kay…Rachel did."

"You're not stupid, Luke. Stop acting like you are." She snapped a dishtowel, folding it into a perfect square.

"Talk about insult to injury, Gail."

"It sounds like you're scared and looking for an excuse."

Luke looked down at his coffee. He should've never said anything.

Gail went on. "First, you're here. What incentive would Eli have? You're doing what he wants already."

Good point.

"Second, you said this girl almost died the night you met her. You don't think Eli could have come up with something less risky or at least simpler to catch your attention? I think you're looking for something that isn't there."

Another sip of coffee went down with Gail's words.

"Third." She took a deep breath. "When I heard about what happened in New Orleans, I made your father swear on his life that he would never do something that despicable to you again." Her lips pressed into a thin line. "My point is, if you like this girl, give her a chance."

Luke smiled at the thought of this tiny, but terrifying, woman threatening his father. "Thanks, Gail."

She waved his gratitude away. "That was a truly disappointing moment."

"One of many." Luke scoffed. He glanced at the lines that had deepened on her face since the last time he saw her. "What makes you stay here? Don't you want to retire and spend time with your family?" Anytime she'd mentioned her daughter in the past, her face lit up.

She swallowed. "They have their own lives. This is my place. For better or worse." She cleared her throat and smoothed the front of her dress. "I have a cleaning crew coming in shortly to give the place a once-over."

Recognizing that he'd touched a nerve, he went with a subject change. "Are Dad and Blake coming back soon?"

"Not as far as they've told me. But there's no reason for you to be living under a blanket of dust."

"I'm fine."

"Good. Now, you'll be fine and breathing clean air."

Gail turned to leave, and Luke called to her retreating back, "Thanks for the advice."

She acknowledged him with a nod. He poured another cup of coffee and navigated his way to Eli's War Room.

Once inside, he closed the door and dropped into a rolling chair. Swiveling, he turned to face the back wall and the insanity written in thick black marker from floor to ceiling.

Eli had written out a timeline going back two hundred years, to the supposed start of the curse. Next to most years, there was an event listed that occurred on the fourteenth of June. The closer it got to present time, the more filled in it was, but some were a real stretch. A handyman breaking a leg on their property, the year Blake and Luke both got chicken pox for the second time, Eli even included the time he'd driven home drunk and crashed into their front gate.

Then there were the more serious ones. The fire that had burned through their vacation home in Florida. *June fourteenth.* The day Luke's mom left. *June fourteenth.* And the one that had started Eli's crusade, the day his brother died of a sudden heart attack at the age of forty. *June fourteenth.* The day that Verity Falls was born.

It was Eli's smoking gun. A schizophrenic's proof that the voices weren't just in his head. Luke's anger grew the longer he looked at it. He was rocking in the chair, contemplating getting a bucket of paint to white the whole thing out when he stilled. He stood and picked up a marker. Ignoring the minor events, he went through and circled the years that listed actual deaths or life-altering tragedies. Stepping back, he frowned, a chill tracing icy fingers up his spine.

All the major events were evenly spaced apart by five years. That was a heck of a coincidence. Luke threw down the black marker and picked up its red twin. He double circled the worst of the worst. His grandfather's death, twenty-five years ago. The car accident that killed both of Eli's sisters, fifty years ago. His great aunt's catastrophic stroke, seventy-five. One hundred years back simply said, "The Massacre."

A heavy pit formed in Luke's stomach, and he spent the next hour ripping tops off the file boxes and flicking through the folders they contained. Finally, he found the right one. He sank to the floor and opened the file. Inside were three articles, each from a different town, but all nearly identical stories. Three separate families, all found dead the morning of June fifteenth from presumed gas leaks in their homes.

Luke shot to his feet and crossed to the family trees sprawled across a different wall. One hundred years ago, there were four branches to the Dryers. Three of those limbs ended there with the three families who died in their homes. The fourth was the line that led directly to Eli, Blake, and Luke, the last surviving members of the Dryer line.

Shaking his head in disbelief, Luke sat down and read the articles from start to finish. The last one contained an interview with his great-grandfather. It explained that he'd been a teenager at the time and had snuck out to spend the night with the woman who would eventually become Luke's great-grandmother. He'd returned in the morning to the overpowering smell of gas, and the bodies. All three articles stated that no gas leak was found in any of the homes.

A knock on the office door startled Luke. *The cleaning people.*

"Not this room," he yelled, with more force than he meant. Rushed apologies came from the other side of the door.

He scowled and propped his elbows on the desk in front of him, rubbing his face with both hands. This was insane. He couldn't fall down the same rabbit hole his dad and brother had lodged themselves in. Picking any random date, he could probably find an equal amount of bad stuff, if he dug deep enough.

And a massacre?

He slapped his hands on the desk and stood. He needed to get out of this room and clear his head. Luke locked the office behind him, found Zeus in the kitchen, and went to the barn. He had a couple of projects going and chose the one that he'd need to think about the least. It was a good call. His thoughts wandered almost immediately.

Gail's advice rolled around his head as he worked. It was true, Vee had been in real danger the night they met. If he'd been a few seconds slower, she would've been pulled too far out for him to reach. The reminder of how close she'd come to death made his breath hitch.

He tossed down the block of wood in his hand and picked up his phone. If a curse was going to claim him in two weeks, he should at least make an effort to enjoy the time he had left. He frowned at his own sarcastic thought. He had to stay out of that office. The lunacy was contagious.

He scrolled through a couple of websites, found what he was looking for, and checked out with expedited shipping. Fuck flowers. If he was going to apologize, he was going to do it right.

Chapter Eleven

Vee

Memorial Day weekend was as crazy as the inn's staff had warned her. By the time Vee had got out on Saturday, she was exhausted. Tomorrow would be her last shift before she got two days off, and boy was she ready.

She trekked up the hill to find a blue gift bag waiting on her stoop. A blank, white envelope was propped up against its side. Vee picked it up and slid out the card. It was a black-and-white photo of a full moon over the ocean and her heart sped up. Inside, elegant handwriting scrawled across the page.

I'm sorry I was so rude. Let me thank you for helping Zeus by taking you to dinner Monday night. – Luke P.S. I thought you could use this.

Vee tucked the card back in its envelope. Butterflies battered her ribcage and she reached into the bag. A laugh bubbled up when she pulled out a tactical flashlight with a tag proclaiming it both waterproof and indestructible. Vee took the gift and invitation inside, already thinking about what she'd wear.

****

The next day, work was equally busy. Vee checked out the guests leaving, welcomed the new ones, and served mimosas and Bloody Marys when Damon took his break from manning the brunch bar. Her shift ended at seven, but she hung around to restock housekeeping supplies, wanting something to keep her busy so that tomorrow would come faster. When she'd checked and re-checked the housekeeping closets on all the floors, she made her way to the kitchen.

Peg stirred a wide mixing bowl full of something thick and chocolatey. "Still smiling after today, huh? You'll do just fine here," she said when Vee passed by.

"Of course she'll be okay. She fits right in," Maria interjected then turned to Vee. "Have a good couple of days off. And don't forget family dinner Tuesday."

"I won't." A dinner with her coworkers at any of her past jobs would have verged on torture, but this felt different. Possibly even fun.

She stepped out of the inn into twilight and found Damon on the porch.

He turned his head toward her. "Hey there. You're here later than usual."

"Yeah, I stayed to help Becca. It was crazy today."

"Just wait, this is only the start. You okay getting home? It's pretty dark."

She reached into her bag and pulled out her gift. "I've got a flashlight."

"I'll say you do." He let out a low whistle as he stepped closer and examined it. "What are you? A Navy SEAL on the weekends?"

She laughed. "No, just a klutz. Supposedly, I can't break this one."

"I would hope not. That's a Marauder. It's at least a few hundred dollars. I've only ever seen them in video games."

Vee opened her mouth, shock robbing her of words

as JJ stuck her head out the door. “Damon, Meredith’s looking for you. Either come in or find a better hiding spot. She’s coming this way.”

“I’ll face the pain.” He smirked and followed JJ inside, calling back through the screen door, “Good night, Valerie.”

Vee mumbled something incoherent back. The light in her hand felt heavier as she walked down the driveway. *A few hundred dollars is a lot to spend on a joke gift.* Then again, it’s from Luke Dryer. He probably had flashlights like this stuffed in drawers all over his mansion.

At the tree line, she pointed it up the dark path and clicked it on. It was worth every penny and illuminated a good fifty feet ahead. She made better time up the hill than she usually did in daylight.

She came around the last bend in the path, the beam swinging in front of her and right into Luke’s face.

“Jesus, point that thing down, will you?” He shielded his eyes with his hands.

“Sorry.” She pointed it to the ground. “Are you okay?”

“Yeah, I’m sure it’s normal for your corneas to bleed.” He rubbed his eyes. “What do you have it set to? Stun?” He reached out and she handed it over. A few twists and the beam dispersed wider, decreasing the intensity.

“You know, you’re funny when you’re not hostile.” She took the flashlight when he offered it, trying to ignore the backflip her heart did when their fingers brushed. “And thank you. It’s a really thoughtful gift.”

"I'm just trying to keep you alive till tomorrow night." The corner of his mouth tugged up.

"And just what should I be prepared for? Casual dress? Fancy? Drive-thru?"

"Now who has jokes?" His grin faded to a more serious look. "That's actually why I came down here. To see if you've decided to accept my invitation."

She tilted her head, not wanting to give in to him or her own screaming desire to say yes without thinking it through. "That depends. Do you promise you're not going to storm off and leave me stranded somewhere?"

"I know my track record there isn't great, but yes. I promise." He stepped forward so they were inches apart. His rough voice rumbled, "I'm dealing with a lot of family stuff that's putting me on edge. None of it's your fault, and I'm sorry for how I've behaved."

She met his gaze and held her breath. The ocean of pain in his eyes parted, making way for a tidal wave of longing to crash through. Around her, the air took on weight, anchoring her to the moment.

This is where I belong. She shifted toward him and he stepped back, breaking the spell.

He looked down, both hands clenched into fists. "Say you'll come."

She took a shaky breath, her whole body tingling. "I will."

His eyes crinkled into a smile. "I'll be in your driveway at seven. Be careful until then." He moved toward the path that would take him to his house, then paused and looked back at her. "Oh, and drive-thru attire is perfect."

****

It was torture waiting for Monday night to come.

She'd given up on painting again when all she'd produced were two more canvases' worth of the same weaving pattern of lines branching off of one another. Mid-morning, Vee was ready to climb the walls. Instead, she tugged on her sneakers and set out on her first run in over a year. Before she found herself devoid of free time, running had been a good stress relief, and today, she needed the heart-pounding, rhythmic meditation it provided.

She got as far as her yard when she had to backtrack to get her phone. It hadn't even been a week with no service and she'd already found herself forgetting it existed. Retracing her steps, she made sure to avoid the elm tree and started down the hill.

For not running in almost a year, Vee made great time. It felt so good she added on a little more than she'd planned, regretting that decision once she reached the end of town and looped back. Fatigue set in and slowed her pace considerably.

A sudden blast from a horn sent her stumbling over her feet. She regained her balance and shot an angry glare over her shoulder as the truck pulled up next to her and slowed.

"Sorry," Damon yelled. "I was just trying to say hi. I didn't mean to knock you off your feet."

Vee slowed to a walk, panting. "I startle easy," she said when she caught her breath.

Damon inched his truck along next to her. "There're some nice trails in the nature preserve. Less assholes in trucks. I mean, there's still some, but less." His wide grin lit up his face. "They have maps at the visitors center down the point."

"Thanks. This may be my last run for a while. I

don't know what I was thinking." Her left hamstring threatened to cramp with each step.

"I'd offer you a lift if I wasn't overflowing with precious cargo here." He pointed to the potted flowers filling the seat next to him. "I can drop them off and swing back if you want?"

"That's all right. I'll make it." Sneaking a glance in his side-view mirror, Vee confirmed her suspicion that she looked like death. *Great.*

"Okay then. See you tomorrow night."

"See ya." She kept a smile on her face until his truck rounded the corner. A wave of nausea hit and she took a deep breath. *Too much. This was way too much.*

She pulled out her phone and clicked open the app she had running to track her time and speed. Less than two miles. *For the love of God. I used to run that far as a warm-up.*

Vee walked the rest of the way home and slipped into a hot bath, coming out half an hour later a new person. Any possibility of exhaustion burned away from the nervous energy coursing through her. By a few minutes before seven, she was done second-guessing the sundress and strappy sandal combination that she'd settled on and walked out the door.

Luke was already in her driveway and came around to open the passenger side door for her.

Taking in the baggy hooded sweatshirt and jeans he wore, anxiety stirred to life. "Am I overdressed?"

He held out a hand to help her into the truck. "You look perfect."

He climbed into the driver's side and flipped up his hood, hiding his face. Vee settled back and they bumped up her driveway. At the end, he turned toward the Dryer manor instead of heading down the hill and into town. He parked and shut off the engine.

She glanced from the house to him. "I thought we were going to dinner?"

"We are. Come on."

The overcast sky blotted out the sunset as she followed him from the truck into the dark house.

"Sorry, I should have left on some lights out here." He pulled off his sweatshirt and tossed it on a bench by the door, revealing an untucked, white, button-up shirt.

The doors that had been closed the other day now stood open, and Vee caught glimpses of furniture and artwork. A soft glow and an enticing smell led them to the kitchen. Luke went directly to the oven. He cracked it open to peek inside, allowing more of the delicious aroma to escape.

Zeus padded into the room and stopped for a pat from Vee before continuing on. She turned and watched as he headed out a propped open door that led into a garden.

Luke stood and turned to her with a pleased look. "Wine?"

"We're eating here?" She raised one eyebrow, glancing around the kitchen. The lights were dimmed and a single candle was lit in the middle of the table, which was set for two.

"It's not quite ready, but yes, we are." He picked up an open bottle of red and nodded toward the waiting glasses.

"Wine would be great."

He poured two glasses and handed her one. "Here, take a seat." He gestured to the stools next to the island.

She slid onto one and took a sip of wine. As soon

as it hit her lips, she slipped into heaven and closed her eyes. It was like drinking velvet. There was an immediate earthiness followed by a touch of sweetness before peppery notes kicked in. Opening her eyes, she found Luke staring at her.

"You like it?" he asked.

"It's incredible."

He smiled and took a sip from his glass, keeping his attention on the liquid inside instead of her. "I didn't know if you'd come."

"I didn't know if you'd change your mind."

"I'm not good at this." He gestured between them.

She raised her eyebrows and smiled. "And what is *this*?"

He opened his mouth to speak, but the timer sounded. "Saved by the bell." He put down his glass. "I hope you're hungry."

"Starving." Even if she wasn't, she would have eaten whatever came out of the oven. It smelled that good.

Luke carried a deep baking dish to the table, set it on top of a waiting potholder, and pulled out a chair for her.

"Thanks." She took the seat and unfolded her napkin. "I would have thought in a house this big, you'd have a stuffy dining room."

"We do. I like here better." He served them from the pan of roast chicken and vegetables, then sat. "Bon appetit."

The first bite exploded in her mouth. Garlic and herbs, a touch of wine, and a smooth buttery finish. "Wow," was all she could get out before scooping up her next forkful. "Where did you learn to cook like this?"

He nodded toward a shelf of cookbooks. "Betty Crocker."

"Is that so?"

"Nah. Our housekeeper taught me a few recipes." Candlelight flickered between them, the shadows deepening the lines of his scars.

"Woodworking, first aid expert, and you can cook? You seem to be a man of many talents."

He lifted his wine glass and peered over the top. "Jack of all trades, master of none." He sipped, then set the glass down and picked up his fork. "What about you? What brought you to the inn?"

"Honestly? I don't know. I hated my job, my career really, and I needed somewhere to clear my head."

"How's that working out?"

She took another sip of wine, unsure how to answer. The sense of belonging that came in waves since she arrived was at war with the feeling she'd never been so lost every time she sat down to paint. "I don't know. After so many years of going through life one foot in front of the other with nothing feeling quite right, I guess I was hoping to find a path I could be sure was for me." She blushed and glanced at him. "That probably sounds stupid."

He caught her gaze and held it. "Not at all. Sometimes, to change you have to burn everything to the ground. That's not a simple process."

A lump caught in her throat at the unexpected ease of being understood. "Maybe that's what's happening." As she said it, the truth in his words sank in and another coil inside her unwound. She cleared her throat. "At least I'm in a place I love while I figure it out."

"You do? Love it, I mean."

"So far. I'm already dreading when it's over at the end of summer."

Zeus wandered back inside and headed up the stairs.

"What happens when it's over?" Luke got up to shut the side door as a gust of wind blew through the room.

"I have no idea. When my aunt finds out I've burned my bridges in the ad world, I'm sure she'll want me to move back west."

"You're close with your aunt?" Before he sat, he refilled her wine, then his own.

"She raised me after my mom died." Vee involuntarily rubbed her scar.

His eyes followed her hand and he frowned. "I'm sorry."

"It was a long time ago." She took the glass from him. "But thank you. So, what about you? You don't seem too happy to be here. What made you come back?"

He settled into his chair. "My dad needs help with a project. It wasn't something I could say no to."

"I see. So, you're trapped here?" The wine was taking effect, warming Vee from the inside out.

One corner of his mouth lifted. "Basically, a prisoner."

"Maybe it's the curse." Vee looked at her plate and slid the remaining piece of chicken across it to pick up every possible bit of sauce. She savored the last bite, then put her fork down and picked up her glass. "I'd say this was at least a step above drive-thru."

Her gaze returned to Luke across the table and the

grin faded. All the color had drained from his face, his jaw clenched, and the flickering flame from the candle mirrored the fire in his eyes.

"Luke?" she said, quietly. The intensity of his stare sent goosebumps down her arms.

His lips barely moved. "What did you just say?"

"I…I don't know. About what?" She racked her brain for where she'd misstepped in their playful conversation.

"About a curse." The words came out a growl. "What did you say about a curse?"

"I don't know, I was making a joke about you being trapped here—"

His voice rose over hers. "What do you know about the curse?"

"Nothing. I mean, I just heard there was one." The way Ema told the story, Vee'd assumed it was local folklore. *Shit.* "I'm sorry, it was a stupid joke."

"Yeah. It was. You shouldn't know anything about my family."

"I don't." Her voice was firmer. Obviously, she'd hit a nerve, but he was overreacting.

Finally, he looked away and ran a hand through his hair. "This is too much for one day. I need to go…to take you home."

"Because of one comment?"

"Yes. Because of *that* one comment," he snapped.

Vee bit the inside of her lip and stood, furious at herself for trusting him to not run hot and cold on her again, and even more furious at the tears pricking at the back of her eyes. "You know what? I'll save you the trouble. I can walk."

She turned her back on Luke and went to the door

that Zeus had used.

He called after her, “No, wait. Please, listen—”

“Bye, Luke.” Vee reached for the door without looking back.

The moment she touched the knob, a blinding flash was accompanied by an ear-splitting crash of thunder that shook the stone floor underneath them. The hair on her arms stood up from the electricity in the air. She froze as the first wave of overwhelming panic shot through her. Her breathing stuttered as she struggled to find enough air. The terror sent her heart galloping into an unsteady rhythm as she remained rooted to the spot while her mind screamed at her to move.

A second crack of thunder reverberated through the house, releasing Vee from her silent prison.

Run.

She turned, launching herself forward, and slammed right into Luke. Strong arms wrapped around her and her shaking legs gave out. She sank to the floor, taking him down with her.

Chapter Twelve

Luke

Rumbles of thunder echoed farther away with each passing minute since Vee had collapsed into Luke's arms.

They sat on the cold stone floor, her face burrowed into his chest. She kept shaking, no matter how tightly he held her. His heart pounded from the pure terror radiating off her. Fear was something he knew too well. He squeezed his eyes shut and pulled her closer, not knowing what else to do.

When she finally lifted her head, her face was tear-streaked, pain twisting her features. "I'm so sorry. Oh, my God, I'm so sorry." She pushed back from him and scrambled to her feet, burying her head in her hands. "It's the storm. I didn't know it was going to rain tonight."

It wasn't. He'd checked the forecast not long before he left to pick her up. Those weather sites didn't work half as well as a window. Luke stood and wrapped his arms around her again. "Shhh. It's okay."

He relaxed when she leaned into him. Her words came out muffled. "This is so embarrassing."

"You think this is bad? You should see me when a spider's around."

She started to laugh, but another rumble sounded in

the distance, and she tensed.

He rested his chin on the top of her head and breathed in her soft scent. “This house has been through thousands of storms. You’re safe here.”

She let out a long exhale and pulled away from him. “Thanks.” She stilled as another rumble echoed in the distance but steadied herself and met his eyes. “It’s always worse when I’m caught off guard.”

I know the feeling. Everything about her caught him off guard. Before the thunder, the certainty that he was overreacting settled over him the second she stood to leave. He didn’t blame her for wanting to go after the way he’d acted, but he couldn’t let her leave the way she looked right now, terrified and vulnerable. The night may have been doomed from the start, but he’d ruined it by putting his baggage on her before the lightning struck. And God help him, he wanted to fix it. “Can I show you something instead?”

She paused and looked at him nervously. “What?”

“My favorite place to watch storms.”

“I’m really hoping it’s the basement or a lightning-proof bunker.”

“Not quite. But I promise I’m not going to let anything happen to you.”

She bit her bottom lip but nodded.

“Come on.” He led her up the dimly lit staircase to the tower.

They reached the top and a flash in the distance briefly illuminated the room. She grabbed onto his forearm and hesitated to go farther. “Is this some type of immersion therapy?”

“No.” He laughed. “The storm is miles away out over the ocean. Come look.”

He gently pulled her farther into the room to face the windows. Far across the water, a crackle of lightning broke across the sky, tendrils snaking out in a jagged spiderweb. She gasped and clutched his arm tighter.

"See? It's not too bad, right?"

"It's beautiful," she said, as another pattern split the sky.

He turned to look at her and exhaled slowly, relieved that the terror was gone from her eyes. "Beautiful," he echoed quietly, then pulled his arm from her grasp. "You want to sit?"

He gestured toward the couch and she joined him there, still staring out the windows. Her eyes were wide now, searching for the next strike.

"I think it's from the accident. My fear." She tucked her feet up underneath her. "I don't remember much from the night my mom died, but I think there must have been a storm. It's probably why we crashed."

"You were in the car with her?" His gaze traveled to the scar on her arm.

"Yes." A distant rumble reached them, and she shifted closer to him.

End it, Luke. She'd been through enough. Pulling her into his messed-up world would be selfish.

Ignoring his conscience, he leaned forward and lifted the hinged top of the trunk used as a coffee table. He pulled out a thick, soft blanket and passed it to her. "It gets drafty up here."

"Thanks." She wrapped it around herself.

He settled back and stretched one arm along the couch behind her. She inched closer with each distant rumble. He closed his eyes and inhaled, not noticing when his hand slid from the back of the couch to her arm.

The storm gradually rolled away until the only sign of it was the occasional flicker of light behind the clouds. Next to Luke, Vee had drifted off to sleep, his arm wrapped securely around her.

He rested his head against the back of the couch. This was so stupid. She could be playing him, like Kay, or she could be perfect but would run when she realized how damaged he was. Either way, this wasn't going to end well. Still, there was no getting away from the fact that he wanted it to begin.

****

The steady drum of rain on the window woke Luke to the first hints of daylight behind the clouds. Vee was tucked under his arm, her head on his chest. She shifted and he froze, hoping she wouldn't wake up and end the moment yet. He'd thought for hours about what to do before he fell asleep, and he still had no idea.

With Kay, a part of him deep down had known something was wrong. He never doubted his decision to leave without giving her a chance to explain. But doubting Vee's intentions didn't feel right. What did feel right was this moment, being with her.

She shifted again, this time turning her face up to him and opening her eyes.

"Hey." Her voice was barely above a whisper.

His own voice was gravelly from sleep. "Hey, yourself."

She cleared her throat and sat up. "What time is it?"

He forced his arms to let her go, and she slid away. He rested his elbows on his knees and squinted at the overcast sky. "I don't know. Really early or really, really late, depending on how you look at it."

She pushed back her hair, then covered her face with both hands. "I'm sorry about last night. Getting so angry and trying to leave, then breaking down like I did. I'm a mess."

Luke reached over and pulled her hands away from her face. She turned to look at him, and he rubbed the back of her hand with his thumb as he spoke. "You're not the mess here. I ruined the night first. You wouldn't have been angry or trying to leave if I wasn't being such a jackass. I get alarm bells when people know too much about my family, and the whole curse thing is a sensitive subject."

"I won't bring it up again." She looked down at their hands as he entwined his fingers with hers. She turned her face back to him with a trace of the same vulnerability he'd seen last night. "Still, nothing screams red flag like a girl having a panic attack on the first date. I must seem like so much trouble."

"Well, yeah. But to be fair, you've seemed like trouble since I fished you out of the ocean." A laugh escaped her and her hair fell forward, hiding her face. He let go of her hand and softly tucked it behind her ear. "Besides, if you hadn't had that panic attack, you'd have left and whatever's between us would have ended before it started."

Her head tilted up, green eyes piercing through the last of his resolve as she asked, "So, have we started something then?"

"God, I hope so." He leaned down and pressed his lips to hers, and the world fell away. She responded with a ferocity that ignited a fire in his chest. Without breaking the kiss, he pivoted, using one arm to lower her onto the couch beneath him. Her hands wound around his shoulders, pulling him closer.

He propped himself up on his elbows and broke the kiss to slowly trail his lips up her jawline toward her ear, where he whispered, "I've been wanting to do that since I first saw you." Under him, she inhaled a shaky breath that turned to a gasp when his mouth found its way to her neck.

A small whimper from the stairway broke the spell, and Luke closed his eyes, resting his forehead on hers to catch his breath. A moment later, a cold nose nudged his elbow and he sighed. "Can you hold it, boy?" He turned to look at Zeus, who cocked his head and let out another pitiful whimper.

Angling his head back to Vee, he pulled himself off her. "Sorry, he needs to go out."

She sat up next to him and smoothed her hair. Standing, she quirked an eyebrow. "It's okay. I should go while we're still on speaking terms."

He stood and swooped her into his arms with one more passionate kiss. "I think we're on better than speaking terms."

When they broke apart, she was smiling. "Good."

Zeus urged them on with another whimper from the top of the stairs and they followed him down. Luke opened the side door of the kitchen and Zeus tore out.

"Come on. I'll give you a ride home." He left the door open for Zeus to return and led Vee through the house, picking up his keys on the way.

As they drove, he ran a hand over his face, bumping across the scars, a twinge of vulnerability making him want to cover them. *Stop. She's seen them plenty.*

He lowered his hand. No matter how hard she looked, the scars wouldn't betray him. His secret would be safe, hidden in the internal wounds. He clenched the wheel, shame pressing in on him from all sides.

They slowed to a stop when they reached the end of her driveway. He got out of the truck and came around to her side to help her down. Even rumpled from sleeping on a couch, she was so beautiful. He took a deep breath and faced her. "You should know I'm not good at this sort of thing. Dating."

"I don't know. As far as first dates go, I've had worse."

His face relaxed into a grin. "Can I see you again tonight?"

"I have a dinner to go to at work. But tomorrow?"

"Sure. Come up to the house whenever you finish at the inn."

"I can't wait." She stepped closer and tilted her face up. "Thanks for the wonderful night. Even if I was terrified for part of it." She raised on tiptoes and he bent to meet her kiss.

"Likewise," he said as she pulled away.

She began to walk toward the path that led to her cottage, too far away to hear him mumble, "Completely terrified."

Chapter Thirteen

Vee

Vee's day passed in a haze, her mind replaying the night over and over. She tried to occupy her time with a trip to Ema's shop, but it was closed and provided no distraction.

By the time eight o'clock rolled around and she headed to the inn for their family dinner, she was practically bouncing off the walls. Waiting another whole day to see Luke seemed an eternity.

She rushed down the hill and entered the inn, going straight to the dining room. Tables had been pushed together to make a single large one. Around the room, staff members clustered in groups of two or three, with drinks in hand. Meredith made quick work of introducing Vee to the few employees she hadn't met yet, then sent her to get a drink.

Damon smiled from behind the bar as she approached. "What's your poison?"

Before she could answer, JJ walked over, placed an empty glass on the bar, and faced Vee. "Stick to simple." She turned to Damon. "Another Jack and Coke."

"Hey, be nice to the bartender," Damon said with a wounded expression. He poured JJ a fresh drink. "I learn as I go."

"Yeah, well, whatever you put in that monstrosity you called a margarita last time still haunts my dreams."

"Ouch." Damon clutched his chest over his heart. "I had three of those before I served you one, and I can assure you, they only got more delicious."

JJ raised her eyebrows at him and her cool demeanor cracked with the hint of a smile. She took her drink. "Thanks, Damon."

"You're welcome." He raised his eyebrows and shook his head at Vee after JJ left. "She's right. It was horrific. What can I get you?"

Vee chose a glass of wine and joined the group Becca was talking to. Shortly after, Maria announced dinner was ready, and everyone helped ferry platters from the kitchen to the table. Vee carried a bowl of salad over and took a seat, surveying the other dishes. Hand-made pasta in a sweet-smelling red sauce, sausage and peppers, escarole with garlic, stuffed portobello mushrooms, and fresh bread were spread down the middle of the table.

She took a seat between Peg and Becca as Damon raised his glass. "To new co-workers. May we not scare you away."

Vee toasted with the others, taking a sip of her wine.

Before she'd set her glass down, Becca had raised hers again. "To guests who clean up after themselves."

Next to Vee, Peg mumbled, "Oh, here we go."

"What?" Vee whispered.

JJ called out, "To big tippers."

A louder round of cheers rang out and Peg leaned toward Vee, sighing. "It's a tradition, once someone gives a toast, we all take a turn. We should fill you up." She reached across the table for one of the open wine bottles and topped off both their glasses.

By the time everyone had gone, Vee was well into her second glass of wine. For her turn, she'd blurted out something about making new friends and grinned like an idiot when JJ clinked glasses with her. She happily dug into a full plate of food. Maybe JJ could forget their rough start.

Vee was the only new employee, and the others entertained her by reminiscing about summers past. One of the stories involved two guests who stole everything not nailed down.

Becca pushed her plate away, laughing. "It was insane. The bedspread, the blow-dryer, they even took the lightbulbs from the lamps. That was how I learned about the Ban List."

"What's the Ban List?" Vee asked.

"The list of people who aren't allowed to set foot here." Becca settled back in her chair with her wine. "But it's only that couple and Eli Dryer."

"Why's Eli on it?" Vee asked, causing a round of groans from the others.

"Why wasn't he on it sooner would be a better question." JJ set down her fork. "Before Meredith banned him, he used to come in once a week when he was in town and complain about everything."

"The service," Becca said.

"The temperature of the food." Maria scoffed.

Peg slapped the table next to Vee. "The fucking cheesecake."

"The awarded-winning cheesecake." Damon tilted his glass at them from across the table.

"Thank you." The smile lines around Peg's mouth deepened. "Seriously though, that guy's a monster."

"Him and his offspring." Becca took another drink and looked at JJ with a scowl. "I still can't believe Blake had the nerve to cheat on you."

Vee's head snapped toward JJ. *She dated Blake?*

"Becca," JJ warned. At the same time, Peg exchanged Becca's wine for a glass of water.

Not paying attention to either of them, Becca's face took on a look of disgust. "And with more than one skank."

"Becca!" JJ shouted.

"What? I hate him. You deserve much better. I hope there really is a curse on them." Becca crossed her arms.

Vee broke in before the murderous look JJ was giving Becca turned into action. "A curse?" *The curse?* Maybe she wouldn't have to wait for Ema to hear the rest of the story.

Meredith shook her head. "That's a silly rumor that's gone around for years. There's a lot of bad blood between the Dryers and this town. No one really believes it."

"Eli believes it." JJ frowned, her eyes focused on the tablecloth. No one spoke and she glanced up, toying with the edge of her napkin. "That's what they have Stu doing in that dust museum. Eli's been looking for a way to break a curse on his family. Blake told me. It's true." She pushed back from the table. "I'm gonna get some air."

Next to Vee, Peg sat up straight in her seat. "Well, this is fun." She tossed her napkin on the table. "And speaking of the Devil, if you guys start clearing the table, I'll bring out the worst cheesecake Eli Dryer's ever tasted."

The mood lightened considerably over the absolute best cheesecake Vee had ever tasted, but she couldn't get her thoughts off Luke. If what JJ said was true about Eli and Stu, then the curse wasn't some ancient folktale for the Dryers. Eli believing in something so insane had to be hard to watch. No wonder Luke got so upset when she brought it up.

JJ returned, snapping Vee out of her thoughts. Around her, the table had been mostly cleared and people started to filter out the back door to the lawn.

Vee stood as Becca grabbed JJ's arm. "I'm so sorry. Just, I really hate Blake for how he treated you."

"It's fine." JJ shrugged, but her frown stayed. "Are we doing a fire?"

Becca's face relaxed into a smile. "Me and Damon set it up before dinner." She turned to Vee. "You're coming, right? We're going to have a little after-party at the firepit out back."

Vee glanced out the window at a sunken seating area and the inviting glow at its center. "Sure."

JJ was already on her way outside and they trailed after her.

When they reached the fire, someone waved Becca over and Vee settled onto one of the stone seats built into the sunken patio.

Damon walked over. "Now it's the official start of summer."

She looked to the sky. The first thing she'd done when she got to the inn was use the internet to look up the weather. Possible chance of a shower, but nothing even close to a storm for at least the next few days.

Overhead, patches of stars came in and out of view between a scattering of clouds. “This is perfect.”

He grinned. “I mean, it’s no fancy, big-city party. But it gets the job done.” His attention drifted across the fire.

Vee followed his gaze and landed on JJ, who was standing with a small group. Instead of joining in their conversation, she stared into the flames.

Vee frowned. “JJ still looks upset.”

“Yeah, Blake’s a real piece of shit. But I think she’s okay. Her baseline demeanor is pretty dark and moody.” His eyes hadn’t left JJ, but the corner of his mouth rose and his gaze flicked to Vee. “Exactly my type.”

She laughed. “Well, maybe we should start a support group. I think I gravitate to the volatile myself.”

Damon turned to her and held out a hand. “Hi. I’m Damon. Welcome to the club.”

Vee took his hand and shook it. “Verity. Pleased to be your first member.”

Damon laughed and took a long drink from his bottle. “Verity, huh? I’d never have guessed that.”

“Yep. Verity Taylor. I could have gone with something a little more mainstream. I remember a solid period of time when my aunt first adopted me that she tried to get me to change my name, but I wholeheartedly refused to go by anything besides the full and archaic, Verity.”

“Really? Why’d she want to change it?”

“I don’t know. I think she must have had a premonition that such a unique name wouldn’t be the advantage my five-year-old self thought it would be once I hit grade school.”

"Ahhh, you got yourself some nicknames, did you?"

"Oh, did I. And they were not clever, 'Vomity' was a memorable one, but my favorite was when I developed early and was known as 'Verititty.' "

Damon burst out laughing. "Sorry. I'm sorry."

Vee nodded, smiling. "Yeah, so it's been Vee since fifth grade."

"That's rough," he said, still chuckling. "I'll take that secret to my grave for you."

"Please."

A fat raindrop landed on Vee's arm, and she brushed it off as a second one took its place.

Damon tilted his head up. "Uh oh. I think the party's over. Do you have an umbrella?"

"No, but I'll be fine." She stood. The air held none of the electricity or humidity that would set her nerves on edge.

Next to her, Damon mirrored her movement. "It's late. I'll walk you."

"You don't have to. I'm getting pretty fast on the path."

He pounded the rest of his beer and flashed her a wide grin. "A race then?"

She smiled and shook her head. "No, really—"

"One, two, three, go." His words tumbled out on top of one another and he sprung forward.

Laughing, she followed him around the side of the inn to the driveway. Catching up, she matched the jog he'd settled into as the rain picked up.

Chapter Fourteen

Luke

Up in the tower, Luke stared out the window toward the inn. A slow patter of rain drummed on the glass, becoming steadier and blurring the image.

The dinner had to be over by now. He stepped back and ran a hand over his face. *Stop thinking about her.*

Zeus padded to his side and cocked his head.

Luke reached down and scratched behind his ears. "She's fine. Yeah, she's a disaster on that path when it's not slippery, but she probably made it home hours ago."

Zeus pushed his head harder into Luke's hand when the scratching slowed.

A gust of wind drove more rain against the glass and Luke sighed. "Or she's sliding halfway down the drop right now. Fuck."

Decision made, he jogged down the stairs. He stepped into the rain, arguing with himself as he made his way down the path to the cottage.

This was stupid. She was a grown woman who could take care of herself. *Unless she's cracked her head open.* He picked up his pace until he reached the edge of the cottage's lawn and the sound of laughter came up the trail, stopping him in his tracks.

Moments later, Vee raced across her lawn,

followed closely by a guy. Luke stepped back deeper into the woods. A surge of jealousy lit his blood on fire.

They paused under the overhang of her front porch and she laughed again, breathless. "Thanks for making sure I got here safely, even though I'm the more sober one. I feel like I should be worried about getting you home now."

Luke's fists clenched at the sudden fear she was about to invite him inside, and he held his breath until her next words reached him. "Want to borrow my flashlight?"

"Nah. I've got one on my keychain that will do the job. Plus, I'd need to take out a loan if something happened to yours in my custody."

"And it has sentimental value, so you'd have to deal with my wrath." Warmth spread through Luke's chest, only to be doused in ice as she said, "Do you want to wait inside for the rain to let up a little, at least?"

"Absolutely not. No offense, but it would probably damage my chances with JJ if she heard I set foot in your house in the middle of the night."

"Well, she has nothing to worry about. I'm sort of seeing someone."

"Oh yeah? Flashlight guy?"

"Flashlight guy," she confirmed, sending Luke's pulse skyrocketing.

"Does the mystery man have a name?"

"Not one I'm going to tell you tonight."

"All right, all right. Big secret. I get it, you're not ready to bring him home to meet the family."

"Ha. I couldn't if I wanted to. My aunt doesn't even know I'm here."

"Why not?"

"For one, I quit my job with essentially no plan for the rest of my life. And second, she has some special hate-filled place in her heart for Maine."

"What? That's oddly specific."

Vee nodded. "Once, she won a weekend trip to York Beach in a raffle at my school. The second we left, she ripped up the voucher. She said neither of us was ever to set foot in Maine. You should've seen the fight we had before I got her to agree I could go to school in Boston. She apparently has a hip-hop-level feud with the East Coast."

The guy with her laughed. "Hopefully, she'll get over it." He reached a hand out from under the overhang. "Looks like the rain's letting up. That's my cue. I'll see you tomorrow, Vivian. Damn, sorry, force of habit. 'Night, Vee."

"Thanks for walking me home," Vee said, as he stepped off her front stoop.

Luke stayed perfectly still as the guy passed by, only a few feet from where he was hidden in the woods.

Vivian. "Vee" fit her so well he'd never considered it was short for something. He could check it off the list of things he didn't know about her. A list he hoped would only grow shorter.

His clothes hung heavy from the rain and Luke let out a long breath. *What the fuck am I doing?*

He'd look like a stalker if he showed up now. She was safe. That was enough.

He turned and made his way back home.

****

Harsh sunlight streamed through Luke's window when his eyes popped open to the sound of yelling from downstairs.

"Dammit. Get out of the way." The deep voice was unmistakably Eli's.

Luke shut his eyes again. *Not today.*

"I said move!" This shout was followed by a yelp from Zeus and Luke shot out of bed.

He thundered downstairs, his gaze landing on Zeus as soon as his feet hit the kitchen floor. The dog's eyes were wide and he cowered under the kitchen table, staring at Eli.

Luke's head snapped toward his father. "What did you do to him?"

"Nothing he didn't deserve. Stupid mutt. How long do dogs live anyway?"

Blood pounded in Luke's ears, but Zeus crept from under the table to his side. His tongue lolled and tail wagged, calming Luke slightly. He bent and ran his hands over the dog to make sure there were no apparent injuries.

Eli rolled his eyes. "Oh, relax. I barely nudged him. And I'm not even wearing shoes."

Luke stood and clenched his teeth. "Why are you even here?"

"Why am I here? In my own house?" The redness across Eli's cheeks inflamed more than usual. "Because I damn well want to be. That's why."

"How long are you staying?"

"Until I'm sure you're pulling your weight." Eli set down an empty coffee cup. "You've been here over a week and I haven't gotten so much as a text from you with something useful."

Shit.

Luke forced his voice to keep its angry edge. "I

didn't know you needed daily reports, Sir, Drill Sergeant, Sir."

"Don't be a smartass. I see you've wasted no time taking over my barn. My guess is you're fucking around out there more often than doing something to actually help this family."

Yeah, fucking around making six-figures a year without taking advantage of a single person in the process.

"You're right, Dad. It was my master plan to get you to trap me here so I could work in your shitty barn."

Fire roared behind Eli's eyes, but he stayed outwardly calm. A sure sign he was losing control. "It's too bad you choose to be a sarcastic little shit instead of taking some initiative like your brother. We just got here and he's already in the War Room working. Meanwhile, you have nothing to show for yourself."

Luke took a deep breath and focused on why he really was here. *The girl.* "Listen. I have made progress. I didn't want to send you anything until I was sure."

Some of the flames died down and Eli raised his chin. "Sure of what?"

"I found a lead." A cold sweat dampened Luke's brow. He'd created the lead for a situation like this, but he never thought he'd have to use it so soon.

"What kind of lead?" Eagerness crept into Eli's voice.

"I searched her birthday on a few websites where people who were adopted look for their birth families. I found six possibilities so far."

Some of the angry flush bled from Eli's complexion, but his frown stayed in place. "Six isn't one." He met Luke's eyes. "Still, that's a smart angle."

A knot of tension released in Luke's gut. "I'm working on finding them on social media." And he would find them. He'd already created the profiles, each designed to take off on its own wild goose chase.

Eli nodded. "All right then. Get to it." He eyed Zeus. "And keep that dog with you or put him in a kennel."

Luke gave Zeus another pat and sneered at his father's back as he left. "Wish I could put you in a kennel," he mumbled.

Zeus licked his hand and Luke passed his friend a dog biscuit before leading him upstairs. "Come on, boy."

He set out water and shut Zeus in his room, then went back downstairs, determined to keep Eli from succeeding.

In the War Room, a slightly younger and more polished, brown-eyed version of Luke sat at one of the desks. Blake's gaze flicked from his computer screen to Luke. " 'Sup."

Luke circled behind him and glanced at the screen. "Solitaire? Really?"

"Whatever. The old man is happy thinking I'm helping. Besides, this is insane. What's he going to do if he even finds this chick? Beg her to unhex us?" He clicked the mouse and the cards jumped across the screen.

Luke reached toward the power strip on the desk and reset it, sending the screen instantly blank.

Blake shot to his feet. "What the fuck?"

Luke growled and stepped forward. "What the fuck is right. You can't seriously pretend you don't know he's going to try to kill her if he finds her."

"Pft." Blake flopped back down into the chair and rolled it to another desk, where he picked up a stress ball and started tossing it into the air. "He won't actually do it."

The start of a tension headache tightened at Luke's temples. "He's done it already. He killed that girl's mom."

"Shut up, dude. She fell. He told me he wasn't even conscious when it happened."

The memory threatened to resurface and Luke forced it down, slamming his fist on the desk. "She should have never been on that cliff in the first place. He brought her here, chased her out there…he's responsible for that death."

"Is he? 'Cause the way I see it, he's not the one who was close enough to get maimed for life." Blake traced a finger down his face, miming the track of Luke's most prominent scar.

Luke swallowed the urge to yank him to his feet. It's what Blake wanted. To get under his skin. "That's what you told people? That I killed her, then killed myself."

Blake stopped tossing the ball and laughed. "I didn't start the rumor you killed anyone. That was all the police chief's daughter."

JJ.

Blake leaned forward in the chair. "All I did was add on the suggestion that you hadn't been able to live with the guilt. I can't believe it finally got back to you. I'd forgotten about it until last year when I partied with that townie and she confessed that all this time, she thought it was her fault you'd killed yourself."

I shouldn't have been able to live with the guilt. Luke swallowed, willing himself to not go down that path.

Blake threw the ball up again. "Don't worry. I forgave her. And boy, was she grateful to be absolved. Three months of grateful if I remember right. I wonder if I still have her number…"

"Nice. Lying about a tragedy to get in a girl's pants. She's one lucky lady." He'd never been the biggest fan of JJ, but no one deserved this shit.

"At least I know Dad's not paying her." Blake shot up out of the chair and jogged from the room before Luke had the chance to lunge at him. He called back, "I'm taking a break."

"A break from what?"

"Trying to keep my inheritance."

Blake disappeared down the hall and Luke rubbed his forehead. *And Dad thinks I'm the one fucking around.*

Luke collapsed into a chair. Even if he didn't show it, Blake had succeeded and was fully under his skin with his last comments. The memory of what happened the last time he tried to have a relationship with Kay… It was still too fresh. What was he thinking starting something with Vee?

Shit, Vee.

He glanced at the time. Over four hours before she got out of work. That left plenty of time for him to smooth out the edges of his plan to distract Eli. He'd make sure to be waiting for her at the cottage. There was no way he could risk her coming up to the house and meeting the walking nightmares that passed as his family.

Just before five, he stopped at his room to free Zeus and together they jogged down the path.

At the cottage, he knocked with no answer. *Good.* He settled onto the worn bench under an elm tree to wait and closed his eyes.

Chapter Fifteen

Vee

The door to the inn shut behind Vee as she left for the night and she pulled out her phone. *One new message.* She didn't listen to it before returning the call to her aunt. Even if she had service at the cottage, there was no way she could carry on a conversation walking up the hill and not give away she was out of breath.

"Hello?"

"Hi, Aunt Rose. I saw you called."

"Just wanted to see how things are going." Rustling came through the line, along with a muttered curse word.

"Things are good." *Not a lie.* "What are you doing?"

"Digging out my suitcase. I still can't believe Joan convinced me to go on another wellness retreat."

Vee smiled against the phone. Joan lived in the house next door and her lifelong mission was trying to get Rose to relax. "You guys will have a great time. When do you leave?"

A crash prompted another swear before her aunt answered. "Day after tomorrow. Then it'll be two weeks dodging rattlesnakes in the middle of the Mohave desert."

Vee's smile grew. "Yeah, with daily spa treatments

followed by gourmet meals. Poor you."

"All right, all right. There are some perks. I emailed you the resort's main number for the second week since we'll be glamping technology-free."

"It's not so bad. I haven't had reliable service since I got—" Vee choked on the words about to leave her mouth: *Since I got to Maine.* A cold sweat broke out across her forehead as her mind searched for a way to finish the sentence. "Since I got my new office."

She tilted her head back and blew through pursed lips. *The worst liar ever.*

"Really? That's weird." More rustling ended with a sigh. "I should let you go. I think I'm going to need a shovel to free this thing."

A seagull cawed and Vee cringed, hoping her aunt didn't catch the sound. "Okay. Love you."

"Love you more. And when I get back, I was thinking of planning a trip to Boston to see you."

Vee clenched her teeth. "Sounds good. Have a great time."

She started up the hill, trying to put the call behind her. A lot could change in two weeks. By the time Rose got back, maybe she'd have figured out what to do with her life. She glanced at the phone still clenched in her hand. Almost six.

Too early to go to Luke's without seeming eager. She took a deep breath of the cool forest air. She'd burned her career to the ground and her future was shaky at best, but she'd never felt like she belonged anywhere as much as she did last night in the tower with him.

Stepping into her yard, she paused. He was on the bench, Zeus asleep at his feet. A well of warmth bubbled in her core. *He's eager, too.*

The sensation faded as she approached and he stood. He angled the scars away from her, but it didn't hide the hard set of his jaw or the hurricane of unrest raging in his eyes.

He rubbed his hands on the front of his jeans. "Sorry for showing up like this."

"It's fine." *I was about to do the same to you.* Except she wouldn't have looked like her world was crumbling. She fought the urge to touch him, not sure where they were on the casual contact scale of relationships. "Is everything okay?"

"No. I came to ask you to stay away from the house." She held her breath until he went on. "My dad and brother came home."

She exhaled. "Oh. So, no more dinner dates?"

"Not up there." His head tilted toward the towering house overhead and a muscle in his jaw twitched.

The sun dipped behind a cloud and an icy chill ran up Vee's neck when his gaze didn't leave the clifftop. "Luke?"

He faced her, no longer hiding the scars. "I'm sorry. It's not pleasant with either of them around."

"You can hide here for dinner, if you want. I may not have half the skills you have in the kitchen, but I can boil a mean pasta." The words came out light, but her stomach clenched, waiting for his response. He'd just started letting down his guard and now the undercurrent of tension drifting off him hinted the wall was on its way back up. *Say yes.*

The storm raging across his features dulled and one eyebrow raised. "I may have a better idea. It's Wednesday, right?"

“Yes.” She drew the word out, not sure where his mind was going.

He pulled out his phone and flicked his thumb over the screen, frowning. His eyes shot to hers. “There’s no service here?”

“No. I think the cliff must block it.”

The frown lines deepened. “I don’t like that. What if something happens?”

“Luckily, I lead a quiet life.”

He cocked his head. “In the week I’ve known you, you’ve almost drowned, gotten a head injury, and had a panic attack.”

She bit her lip, holding back a grin. “It sounds bad when you say it like that.”

“It is bad.” He shook his head. “I’ll figure something out. For now, I’ll make the call from the house and come back to pick you up.”

“For dinner?”

“Yes. Nothing fancy, but it’ll be a…unique experience.” He reached down, entwining their fingers.

The icy blue of his eyes met hers, fire shooting to her core as he bent at the elbow to press his lips against the back of her hand without looking away.

His Adam’s apple rose and fell when he let go and stepped toward the woods. “I’ll be back soon.”

She opened her mouth, closing it again when she couldn’t find her voice. This didn’t seem like what people described as falling in love. This seemed more like plummeting through space, burning in a blaze of uncertainty with the ground a million miles away.

****

Half an hour later, Vee kept her ears perked for the sound of his truck returning and started across the yard as soon as the low rumble reached her. She met him in the cottage's driveway and climbed in as Luke ushered Zeus from the passenger side to the back seat.

The dog's head poked through to the front seat and she scratched the soft fur behind his ears. "So where are we going?"

"Some old friends throw a clambake on a beach up the coast every few Wednesdays in the summer. Lucky for us, it's on tonight."

"A clambake?" *With friends?*

He glanced at her, half his mouth tugging up. "You'll see."

Zeus settled behind them as they turned onto the road that led out of town.

Luke leaned an elbow on the door, one hand on the wheel. "So, how'd you end up in our quiet town?"

Vee took a deep breath and decided on the truth. "It seemed like a good place to hide while I ruin my life."

He raised an eyebrow and smirked. "I know I'm not the best date, but damn, that's cold."

She slapped his shoulder, biting back a laugh. "Not everything's about you, Mr. Self-obsessed."

He cracked up. "Oh, you nailed me. But go on, tell me about the bad decisions you've made besides hanging out with a ghost from a cursed family."

A hint of his aftershave drifted to her and she inhaled, relaxing into the seat. "I got offered a promotion at one of the best ad agencies in the country and instead of accepting it, I quit. I've been with them since I graduated, so it basically destroyed every professional relationship I'd built."

"Not expecting a glowing recommendation?"

She huffed out a laugh and shook her head.

"Definitely not. I didn't exactly give notice. I already felt like I was suffocating from the workload. Once I realized I hated it enough that more than double my salary wouldn't make me happy, I couldn't stand to be there one more minute. I found the ad for the summer job at the inn in a coffee shop the next morning, and it seemed like a good place to try to figure out what to do with my life."

He'd pulled his bottom lip in between his teeth while she talked. In the silence, he released it but didn't say anything.

She cringed. "You think I'm a flake now."

He turned onto the highway, the engine roaring with the increase in speed. "I think you're brave."

"Right. Very brave to hide from my problems at the beach."

He shrugged. "It would be less brave to stay at a job you're miserable at because you're scared what will happen if you leave. Knowing what you don't want is the best way to find what you do want."

"You say that like you've learned from experience."

The hard edge returned to his voice. "I've been especially lucky in learning what I don't want."

He took the next exit. They drove through a town even smaller than Cliffside, leaving it behind as the sunset began to turn the clouds a soft pink. The road followed the coastline until Luke slowed and pulled his truck to the side, parking behind a line of other cars.

He flipped up the hood of his sweatshirt, his blue eyes peering at Vee from the shelter within. "Ready?"

She nodded and hopped out, Zeus following her. Luke reached into the bed of the truck and pulled out a six-pack.

They crossed the beach, following the sound of music until they reached a small crowd scattered near two large canvas tarps spread across the sand. They passed a cluster of picnic tables and Luke paused to add the beer to the ones already in a cooler.

A buttery scent hung in the air, making Vee's mouth water. She leaned toward Luke. "What's that smell?"

"Heaven." He reached down and put a hand on the small of her back, steering her toward the man closest to the tarps.

Zeus beat them there and gave the man an enthusiastic greeting before heading toward the crowd to make his rounds.

Luke held out his hand. "Hector."

The man clasped it, a wide smile spreading across his face. "Isa said you were coming, but I can't believe it. It's good to see you." He turned his gaze on Vee. "And you brought a friend."

"This is Vee. Vee, this is Hector. He's about to feed you the best food you've had in your life."

Hector rubbed his hands together. "Let's hope so. Want to see?"

"Sure." Vee stepped forward as he bent to lift the edge of a tarp. Underneath, he used a long poker to shift a layer of seaweed and expose a variety of shellfish spread across a bed of hot coals.

He repositioned the seaweed and let the tarp drop. "Almost done."

"It looks amazing." Vee stepped back, bumping into Luke. His hand wrapped around to steady her, then didn't move from where it rested on her shoulder.

Hector's gaze grazed her shoulder and his eyes sparkled when they returned to Vee's. He looked down at the tarps, nodding. "It's going to be a good batch. Go, have fun. I'll call when it's ready."

On the outskirts of the party, Zeus took turns with a husky chasing sticks a woman hurled through the air. Luke's hand dropped as they walked, leaving a cold patch where it had been. "Come with me."

When they reached the woman, her face lit up and her arms wrapped around Luke for a hug. "I'm so glad you came." The fading sunlight had her bronze skin glowing as she pulled back and brushed dark curls from her face. "This must be Vee."

Luke took a step closer to Vee as the dogs thundered toward them. "Vee, this is Isa. She's been Zeus's vet since he was a puppy."

"One of my favorite patients." Isa lobbed another stick down the beach and both dogs took off. She wiped her hands on the front of her pants. "I'm so glad you guys could make it. Let's get a drink."

The last rays of sun were almost gone and a few of the guests went around, lighting the tiki torches that circled the party. Luke and Vee found a spot to sit on a cluster of driftwood and Isa brought three ice-cold beers. It took extra focus to keep her mind on the conversation each time Luke shifted, managing to brush against her with each movement. By the time they'd finished the beer, Vee felt like she'd known Isa for years, and the food was ready. Hector doled out plates piled high with clams, mussels, lobster, and corn on the cob.

Luke carried their food while putting Vee in charge of a large metal bowl full of napkins and an assortment of utensils. He led her to an empty table at the farthest edge of the party and flipped down his hood when he sank into the seat next to Vee.

Isa followed behind with a bowl of melted butter. She made short work of handing out the utensils, finishing by handing Vee a thin sheet of plastic. “Your bib.”

Hector joined them, passing out fresh beers and setting down his plate.

Vee tied the bib around her neck. “You guys don’t mess around.”

“We don’t.” Isa put the claw of her lobster in a nutcracker and squeezed until it cracked.

Vee copied her, but instead of cracking, the lobster shot off her plate. She couldn’t stop herself from laughing. “Sorry. First timer.”

Next to her, Luke grinned and set the lobster back on her plate. He kept one hand on it and raised an eyebrow. “Try two hands for more force.”

She laughed when she succeeded and the claw broke open.

Luke handed her a tiny fork. “Have at it.”

Mirroring Isa, she speared a piece of the soft meat inside, dipping it in butter. Her tastebuds sang with the first bite, and it only got better with the richness of the mussels and the sweetness of the corn.

Luke tossed the last of his clam shells into the metal bowl, sucking a drip of butter off his thumb before picking up one of the lemon-scented towels to clean his hands. “I’ve missed this. Hector, you’re an artist.”

Isa grinned at her husband. “That’s why I married him.”

Hector tossed his empty plate in the bowl. "The trick is the seaweed. A layer over the coals, then a layer on top of the food to help steam it from all sides." He took a sip of beer and looked at Luke. "Come on. I'll show you in case you want to recreate it up in Nova Scotia."

Luke flipped his hood up and stood, picking up the bowl. His face hid in shadows except for the reflection of the tiki torch in his eyes. "I'll be right back."

Vee bit her lip, fighting the panic that threatened to break out at the thought of Luke returning to Canada and disappearing from her life.

Isa studied her. "I'm glad Luke brought you. It's nice to see him happy."

Vee traced a track of condensation down the side of her bottle. A question surfaced that she wasn't sure she wanted the answer to. "He's not usually happy with the girls he's dated?"

"More like you're the first one he's mentioned by name, let alone brought here."

Behind her, Luke approached, letting the hood drop. He tucked his hands into his pockets and met Vee's eyes with an intensity that made it impossible to look away. Isa glanced over her shoulder to him and turned back, grinning.

Luke reached them and tilted his chin toward Vee. "Want to go for a walk before we head out?"

Vee cleared her throat and stood. "Sure."

"Take your time. I'll watch the boys." Isa nodded to where Zeus and his friend had settled under the table. "And if you want to bring him by for a check-up tomorrow, I have an opening at five."

Luke nodded. "Thanks."

They set off down the beach, the light of the party fading behind them.

Vee tilted her head up. "Living in Boston, I forgot there were so many stars."

"Boston? I thought you were from Seattle?"

"I am, but I relocated years ago for school, then stayed for the job I just threw away." A frigid breeze blew off the water, cutting through the warmth of the night like a knife. She crossed her arms against an involuntary shiver.

Luke stopped, pulled off his sweatshirt in one motion, and passed it to her. "Here. Add it to your collection."

"Ha ha." She slipped it over her head. "To be fair, I've tried to give the other one back more than once."

He watched her push the sleeves up and smirked. "They look better on you anyway."

Vee laughed as the material fell halfway to her knees, swallowing her up. "I bet."

Another breeze wound through her hair, and she raised a hand to brush it out of her face at the same time Luke did. The moonlight washed all color from his face, leaving the sharp angles and scars in shades of gray that faded to black. Rough fingers wound through hers. Keeping the clasp, he brought their hands to her lower back and pulled her toward him. Millions of stars surrounded his silhouette and her breath caught when he leaned down. His firm lips met hers while his free hand cupped her face.

The sounds from the party faded as they fell into a moment out of time.

When the kiss ended, he rested his forehead on hers, his chest rising and falling as fast as hers. "I'm so glad you walked into the ocean that night."

Her voice shook. "My best accident so far."

He chuckled. Stepping back, he unwound their arms from behind her but kept a hold of her hand. "We should get back."

They said their goodbyes and followed Zeus to the truck.

The ride home may as well have been on a cloud. Luke's strong fingers wrapped around hers as soon as she settled in the front seat, and through the windshield more stars seemed to exist each time she blinked. The short path from the driveway to the cottage stood out easily from the use it was getting and both Zeus and Luke walked with her.

The leaves rustled as they stepped from the tree line into the small yard. Vee reached into her pocket for her key. "I had a great time tonight. Thanks for think—"

Luke's hand clasped her arm, stopping her in her tracks. Laser focused on the cottage, his voice rumbled. "Did you leave your door open?"

Ahead, the front door swung open with the breeze. Goosebumps trailed down her arms. "No." She rubbed them away. She'd left in such a rush… *Did I?* "I don't know. I don't think so."

His eyes bore into hers and he let out a long breath through his nose. "Don't move. I'll check it out." He raised his eyebrows at Zeus. "Stay with her."

Zeus licked his lips and took a step closer to her before sitting.

Vee watched as the windows lit up one by one, marking Luke's progress through the house. A few minutes later, his shadow filled the door frame. "It's empty."

Both Vee and Zeus crossed the lawn and stepped inside. "Thanks. At least it wasn't that much to search."

Luke rubbed a hand over his face. "It wasn't, but I don't like the idea it needs to be searched at all. Do you really think you left it open?"

"I'm sure that's what it was." In the warm glow of the lights, confidence came easy, but in a minute both Luke and Zeus's massive presence would be gone. She bit her lip.

Luke studied her face and nodded. "Okay. Well, either way, you'll be safe tonight." Instead of stepping back outside, he turned to the living room and stretched out on the couch, facing the front door. "Zeus, come."

The dog obeyed, pacing a circle on the floor before settling down and resting his head on his huge paws.

She cocked her head and bit her lip, trying not to smile at the sight of Luke's broad shoulders barely fitting on the small couch and both his legs dangling mid-calf over the arm. "You're sleeping here?"

He closed his eyes and draped an arm across them. "It's getting late to drive."

"You live two seconds away."

"Most accidents happen within a mile of home. Turn off the lights on your way upstairs."

"It looks a little small for you."

"It's cozy."

She turned, hiding an irrepressible grin and flipped off the light switch. "Okay, I just thought you may be more comfortable upstairs with me, but if you're sure, good night."

The springs squeaked as he stood, and she froze on the bottom step of the stairs, butterflies rocketing through her stomach.

Strong arms wrapped around her waist and she leaned back against his solid chest. His low voice vibrated through her when he spoke. “Are you sure?”

She turned to face him, her arms encircling his neck, and she stared into his eyes, happy to be lost in their depths. “Completely.”

His normally confident voice shook as he commanded, “Zeus, stay,” before letting her pull him upstairs.

The next morning, he was still sprawled across the bed, his face relaxed in sleep when Vee tiptoed downstairs. It wasn’t until the coffee had brewed that he joined her in the kitchen. Vee caught her breath. Tousled clothes and hair wild, he was still more attractive than anyone she’d been within ten feet of.

He wrapped his arms around her, giving her a kiss that reached the deepest parts of her. His voice was rough from sleep. “That smells great.”

She handed him a mug and opened the fridge to get out the milk. “Did you sleep well?”

“Like a baby. Thanks.” He reached for the jug she offered and poured a splash into his coffee. He took a sip and his face went slack with surprise. “This is perfect.”

She beamed. “Secret ingredient…”

His voice joined hers. “Cinnamon.”

He took another drink. “It’s just the right amount.”

She closed the fridge and pulled down cereal and bowls from the cabinets. “Years of practice.”

He waved away the bowl she offered. “I’ve got to get Zeus home for his breakfast. When can I see you again?”

"I work late tonight, but I'm out early the rest of the week."

He took a gulp of coffee and stood. It only took two steps to close the distance between them in the small kitchen and his thumb made slow circles on her jaw as he kissed her. Pulling back, his hand drifted away. "Tomorrow."

He reached into his pocket and pulled out his keys, handing them to her and backing up. "Until then."

She wrapped her fingers around the cool metal. "Your keys?"

"They're yours for now. With no phone you at least need a quick way up the hill." Zeus padded out to the yard and Luke pulled the door shut behind them.

She took a deep breath. Up, not down the hill. A shockwave of understanding went through her. She shook her head. He was just a guy. *A perfect one who wants you to run to him if you're in trouble.*

She set down her coffee and shoved her feet in the sandals closest to the door. She needed a distraction or she'd be following him up the hill now, insane family or not.

The town was quiet and morning dew still glistened on the flowers Ema was tending in front of Bound. She stood at Vee's approach. "You're up early. Here for more of Mercy's story?"

"Yes, please."

Ema handed Vee a watering can. "You water. I'll talk."

Chapter Sixteen

Mercy

Mercy woke, nestled deep in an unfamiliar bed. She rolled over to see Thomas still asleep, walled-in by pillows, next to her. Yawning, she stretched her arms overhead and squinted against the sunlight streaming through the windows. This was the second inn they'd stayed at along their journey. It was the nicer of the two, and hopefully the last. Jonathan had assured her they would reach her new home before nightfall.

A gentle knock at the door was followed by a short blonde woman peeking around the corner as it opened. "Pardon, Miss. I have breakfast here, if you're ready."

Mercy bade her to enter with a smile. "Thank you." She fought the urge to get up and help. Being waited on was a novelty Mercy couldn't imagine getting used to.

The woman retreated to the hall only to return moments later carrying an armful of exquisite fabric. "The seamstress did the best she could with only a few days' notice, but I think it turned out quite lovely." She lay the dress across the foot of the bed and looked down at it, her hands on her hips.

Mercy stared at the flawless sewing. "I'm to wear that?"

The pleased look faded from the chambermaid's face. "Why, yes. As I said, it wasn't much notice, but if you don't fancy it, I'm sure you could have it altered."

"No. It's not that." Mercy couldn't look away from the light blue cloth that seemed too beautiful to touch. She'd been making do with the dress she'd been wearing the night of her escape, cleaning any stains as best she could each night. "I've never seen a dress so nice. It can't be meant for me."

Thomas stirred on the bed and the woman walked over. "Aw, now. I've found it's best not to question good fortune. Be thankful." Thomas cooed up at her kind face and she straightened up. "I'll leave you to your breakfast, but I'll come back to help you dress in a bit."

Mercy ate and fed Thomas, emerging from her room shortly after with a new confidence in the perfectly fitted dress. Jonathan hadn't told her he sent a rider ahead to arrange this surprise. How had this humble and generous man taken an interest in her?

She let the chambermaid tend to Thomas while she made her way downstairs, eager to reassure herself Jonathan was indeed real. In the entryway, his sturdy shoulders were easy to spot where he stood facing away from her, deep in conversation with Roderick. Roderick noticed her first with a quick glance that was followed by a second, longer look.

She stood a little taller as Jonathan turned, his face lighting up at the sight of her. Roderick stalked off without so much as a greeting, and Jonathan stepped forward to take her hand.

"My dear. You look even lovelier than I imagined." He kissed the back of her hand.

"Thank you." Heat rose to her cheeks. "And thank you for the dress. It's truly the most beautiful thing I've ever owned."

His smile faltered. "I'm sorry that for now, it's the only thing you own." He'd already broken the news that nothing had been salvaged from the fire.

"It's not the only thing." She reached into the small matching pouch that had accompanied the dress and pulled out its only content for the time being.

Jonathan's eyes widened while gazing at the tiny white ball glistening in her palm. "The pearl. You kept it on you?"

"Every day since you gave it to me." Her chest felt ready to burst and she slid the pearl back into the pouch so it wouldn't be lost.

He stepped forward and took her hand in his, lowering his voice. "I knew from the moment I met you, that you were meant to be mine." He looked into her eyes and trailed a finger down the side of her face. "And from here on, I will provide you with all the possessions you could ever want or need."

Her breath caught, sure he was about to kiss her, when a door to their side opened. One of Jonathan's coachmen strode through. "Pardon the interruption, sir. Your horse is ready and the carriage is being brought around."

Jonathan stepped back but didn't drop her hand. "Excellent. Thank you, Smith." He looked at Mercy. "I'm riding ahead to make sure everything is prepared for your arrival. But I will see you before nightfall. Until then, my beautiful Mercy."

He placed a lingering kiss on the back of her hand and walked, tall and proud, out the front door. As soon as he left, she gathered her dress up to keep from tripping on the lovely hem as she raced up the stairs.

The sooner she left, the sooner they'd be together again.

****

Cradling Thomas, Mercy entered the carriage a short time later and found Roderick inside.

She paused and took a quick breath. "Oh. Hello."

So far, she'd ridden alone, barring the times Jonathan joined her and Thomas. Roderick, who'd oscillated from cold to downright rude since they met, didn't make a welcome addition.

The imposing man crossed his arms in front of his chest, not offering her a hand as she stepped inside. "My horse went lame."

She kept her voice even, not wanting to convey her displeasure at the ride ahead in his disagreeable company. "That's a shame. Is there not one you could borrow?" She sat and placed Thomas in the bassinet fastened to the seat next to her.

"There wasn't." His quick response implied he wasn't any more eager than she was for the travel arrangement.

The door closed, and they began to move, the rhythm soon lulling Thomas to sleep. It was harder than she'd expected to sit in silence with a man she was so aware of. Every shift he made or clearing of his throat seemed like a direct antagonism.

When he stretched his feet out across the space between them and one of his boots hit her ankle in the process, she couldn't hold back. "Do you mind?"

"Do you?" he said, with equal irritation.

"I'm sure one of the other riders would be willing to trade places with you."

He leaned his head back and closed his eyes. "Jonathan wouldn't allow it. He's only allowing me in here since we're family."

"Family?"

His eyes opened to catch hers before closing again. "Brothers."

Brothers. Her interest perked. "I didn't realize you were brothers."

"He doesn't brag." A small laugh almost escaped her lips before he continued. "Besides, I'm a bastard, so I don't count."

A small tug pulled at her heart with his words. She knew exactly what it felt like to be less-than. "That shouldn't matter." She looked down and smoothed her skirt.

"What should matter rarely does." He opened his eyes and straightened up, pulling his feet back to his own side in the process. "And what about you?"

"What about me?"

"Are you what they say you are?" His crystal blue eyes cut into her own.

Not looking away, a fight brewed within her. "And what do they say I am?"

He answered with no hesitation. "A witch."

Her anger welled up. "No one cried *witch* when I healed fevers or mended injuries." She shook her head as a memory of Siobhan's confident hands harvesting herbs in the garden drifted through her mind. Mercy blinked back tears. "I wouldn't have thought people capable of such cruelty for the sake of a word had I not endured it myself." She wiped away a single rogue tear and glanced down at Thomas, grateful for the hundredth time in the past few days that they remained together.

Roderick observed her in silence long enough that

when he did speak, she startled. “Everyone is capable of cruelty.”

His words did little to comfort her, and they rode the rest of the way in silence, aside from the occasional quiet snore from his side.

Sooner than she expected, the coachman called back that they were approaching the Dryer Manor. Roderick sat up. His face, softened by the haze of sleep, didn’t have its usual scowl. In a rougher, less intentional way, he was as handsome as Jonathan.

He caught her staring and the scowl returned, erasing the sentiment.

She took a deep breath. “The air is different here.”

“It’s the sea.” Roderick pointed out the window.

The houses they’d been passing gave way to a stretch of the whitest sand Mercy had ever seen. Beyond that, gray-blue water rose and fell all the way to the horizon.

She gasped and whipped her head toward him, unable to contain her joy. “It’s incredible.”

Roderick smiled for the first time since she’d met him. “Aye. It is.”

The carriage turned, and they started to ascend a steep incline. Mercy couldn’t help herself. She leaned forward, pushing her head out the open window to try and catch the first glimpse of her new home.

The road began to flatten, and a mansion rose up in the distance. Sandwiched between a vast lawn that was so green it didn’t seem real and the deep blue sky, its tower beckoned to her. Tears of happiness sprang to her eyes. It was a fortress, and she was so close to being inside its safe walls.

Abruptly, the carriage made a sharp turn to the

right and started down a smaller driveway. They hit a bump and she lost her balance. Roderick reached out, catching her before she could fall. Their faces were only inches apart, and his strong hands clasped her waist longer than the situation demanded.

She pushed away, ignoring the surge of electricity that shot through her when they touched. Flustered, she took her seat and smoothed her hair back into place. “Was that not the house? Where are we going?”

His brows knit together. “What exactly did Jonathan tell you the arrangement would be?”

Dread crept up her spine. “He didn’t tell me anything.”

Roderick opened his mouth, closed it, and shook his head. “I’m sorry.”

Ice crept though her veins at the pity behind his stare. The carriage came to a stop and the door opened to Jonathan’s beaming smile. “You’re finally here. Come, I’ll show you your new home.”

Taking his hand, she stepped down and glanced back at Thomas.

Roderick kept his gaze on his shoes, but his deep voice rumbled. “I’ll stay with him.”

She looked past Jonathan toward a small cottage set in a clearing. “You live here?”

“No, I live up at the main house. This is where you and Thomas will live. Only a few minutes’ walk from me.” He reached for her hand and entwined their fingers.

Looking from the cottage back to him, Mercy frowned, then relaxed. “I’m to stay here until we are wed.”

“Wed? No, Mercy. We cannot wed. I’m already

married."

The fragile future Mercy had created in her mind crumbled, and she jerked her hand away, heat flooding her cheeks.

Jonathan was quick to respond, his eyes imploring her to understand his side. "Mercy, it is a marriage of convenience."

"But it is a marriage." Mercy surprised herself at the force of her own words.

"Only because her father is a lucrative business partner." His eyes bore into hers, pleading without words. "I no longer feel for her the way I do for you."

She bit the inside of her lip and looked away. "I cannot stay here."

"You can. I will give you a wonderful life. Come, see the cottage."

"I don't need to." She turned and got back into the carriage, purposefully keeping her gaze down. How could she have been so foolish?

She leaned over to pick up Thomas and found the bassinet empty. Her head snapped up with a surge of panic, but Roderick was already shifting toward her, Thomas asleep in his arms. "He was fussing." He handed him over with a gentleness she hadn't thought possible from such a brute of a man.

"Thank you," she whispered, intentionally avoiding looking at him in case any sympathy waited there to embarrass her further.

She sank onto the seat, not sure where to ask to be taken.

Jonathan opened the door to the carriage. "Mercy, hear me out."

"I don't want to hear another word. Please, have

them take me anywhere but here."

His eyes narrowed. "You can sit here all night. But this carriage will not move until you're settled inside the cottage."

Mercy stayed silent, head down.

Jonathan's voice rose. "Get out this minute, or I'll have you dragged out."

Roderick shifted forward and barked out, "Jonathan!" Glancing over to her, he added more softly, "Give her a moment to adjust."

"Stay out of it, *brother.*"

Mercy let her eyes lift to Roderick, who'd positioned himself between her and the door. He angled his head toward her with a purposeful look as he responded to Jonathan. "She'll realize she has no other options." He went to the door and jumped down, pushing it shut behind him and leaving Mercy alone with Thomas.

Her head spun and tears spilled from her eyes.

This world doesn't owe you fairness.

Siobhan's final words of wisdom came out of nowhere and echoed through her mind. Mercy looked down at her baby's innocent face. He'd done nothing to deserve any of the hardships that would come if Mercy set out on her own now. Roderick was right. She had no choice.

She dried her eyes and set her shoulders back. Exiting the carriage with Thomas in her arms, she walked toward the cottage.

Roderick and Jonathan were a few paces away, deep in conversation. Jonathan broke away and approached her with a look of relief. "Mercy…"

She stepped back, keeping an arm's length between

them. “Please don’t.”

He stopped and sighed. “I promise, you’ll want for nothing here.”

Her gaze rested on the stone cottage to avoid looking at him. “I want nothing but to be away from you.”

His voice lowered. “I look forward to the day you change your mind.” With that, he walked away, mounted his horse, and rode up the driveway.

Mercy ignored the coachman and Roderick but felt their eyes on her as she took Thomas into the cottage and shut the door behind her. She closed her eyes and leaned against it until the sound of the carriage departing faded away. Only then did she face her new reality and, with Thomas, explored their new home.

It was comfortable. More comfortable than even her parents’ home a lifetime ago. She found clothes for herself, a small nursery with everything she’d need to care for Thomas, and food in the kitchen. Under the stairs, a built-in cabinet contained rows of jars of the ingredients needed to make the tea Jonathan was so desperate for.

Later that night, Mercy found herself smiling, sitting on a blanket she’d spread over the soft rug in the living room. She celebrated with Thomas each time he succeeded in rolling over, pride radiating from his tiny face. They retreated upstairs and she left him sleeping soundly in a cradle fit for a prince. A war raged within her as she walked down the stairs, anger boomeranging through joy. She needed air.

She stepped out her front door and startled. Sitting on a bench near the edge of the woods was Roderick, biding his time by whittling in the fading light.

Steeling herself, Mercy walked up to him. "So, I'm truly a prisoner then?"

He glanced up at her, then returned to whittling. "It would seem that way."

"And how long will I have a guard for?"

He nodded to the towered house looming above them. "Until our majesty up there is sure you're not going to try to escape, I'd imagine."

Mercy sank onto the bench next to him. She reached into the pouch of her dress and pulled out the pearl. Holding it up between two fingers, she turned to face Roderick. "Jonathan gave me this months ago."

Roderick's gaze flicked up to it, then back down. "Aye. And?"

"And has he given away a lot of these in your travels?"

"A few." He roughly shaved off a chunk of wood. "None to anyone he'd risk bringing here."

The last flicker of the burning flame she'd felt in Jonathan's presence died at Roderick's words and she slid the pearl back into its pouch. "Yes. Well, I imagine none of them had the power to save a child." She stared at Roderick's profile. "His child, I'm to assume."

"Aye." Roderick leaned his back against the bench. "His boy. He has a daughter, but that will be all. His wife has been unable to carry any more."

Mercy looked up. Angry red streaks spread across the clouds that filled the sky, the sun's dying attempt to keep its grasp on the day. She pitched herself forward and stood, ready to go back inside, until his warm hand on her arm stopped her.

"You are not powerless in this situation. He needs you. Figure out what you need." His hand dropped, but he held her gaze.

Know your value to others.

Her heart fluttered at the strength his words echoing Siobhan's ignited in her, but she kept her voice neutral. "I'll consider that." She broke the eye contact. "Are you to stay out here all night?"

"You won't be alone for the foreseeable future." His sharp eyes bore into hers.

She nodded curtly. "Let's hope it doesn't rain then. Good night."

He laughed and hunched forward, returning to his project. "Good night, yourself, Miss Falls."

His words stuck with her, and she thought long and hard through most of the night. When she woke in the morning, Roderick was still outside. He'd moved from the bench to sit against a nearby tree, where he'd stretched his legs out, crossed his arms, and let his head fall back to rest on the trunk.

Mercy approached quietly, ready to turn back when she was close enough to tell if his eyes were shut.

Without opening them, his deep voice rumbled. "Yes?"

She cleared her throat. "I'd like to talk to Jonathan."

He didn't move. "I'll get word to him."

She rubbed one of her fingers over a chip on her thumbnail, picking at the rough edge. "I'd like you to be near when he comes."

Again, no sign of movement except for his mouth. "Then I'll be near."

A slight warmth spread in her chest at his easy acceptance, and she turned to go.

Behind her, he called, "There's a welcoming gift

for your son on the bench."

She picked up a perfectly carved owl that rested where Roderick had sat the night before. Each feather was etched with precision and the edges were as smooth as a river rock. She glanced back, swallowing the lump that formed in her throat. "Thank you."

A nod was his only response before he pulled his hat down over his eyes. She left him to his rest.

****

Mercy sat at the kitchen table in the cottage when Jonathan arrived a few hours later. He let himself in, followed by Roderick.

Jonathan turned to him. "You can wait outside."

"I'm fine here." Without giving Jonathan time to respond, Roderick went to the living room. He took a seat on the rocking chair next to where Thomas cooed in his cradle, gripping his new toy.

Mercy didn't stand and Jonathan took the seat across from her, reaching for her hands. "My dear Mercy. I'm so happy you've come around. I promise you'll be happy here."

She pulled her hands away. "No one can be happy in a cage, no matter how beautiful the bars."

Jonathan's smile faded. "So, why did you ask to speak with me if not to reconcile?"

"I would like an arrangement. If I am to be in your employ, I want to secure a fair wage for myself and a future for my son."

"Go on." Jonathan narrowed his eyes.

"The payment arrangement you agreed to with Siobhan shall continue. I will provide weekly batches of the tea along with any other medicinal help your family needs."

"Done," he said immediately.

"Furthermore, I want a document signed, witnessed, and filed with the town stating that Thomas will inherit this cottage and its land when he comes of age, provided that your child is still living." Mercy's eyes threatened tears as she remembered the day she and Siobhan had signed similar papers to ensure Mercy would inherit her home upon Siobhan's death. Those papers didn't matter now, but hopefully, these would.

Jonathan leaned his elbows on the table and tented his fingers. "And if I don't agree?"

"Then I will not help your boy." Out of the corner of her eye, Roderick's rocking stilled.

Jonathan glared at her, ice in his eyes and his words. "Even if that meant you and your child would die as a result?"

Roderick stood with the blatant threat. "Jonathan."

"Stay out of this." Jonathan barked, his cold gaze not wavering from Mercy.

She nodded.

He paused for a moment, frowning. "Fine. I agree to your terms. Anything else?"

"I don't want to be guarded. I want to be able to move freely throughout town. I have no reason to run."

Jonathan stood and held out his hand to shake. "Deal."

Mercy got up and clasped his hand, shaking it. She leaned in. "And this will be the last time you ever touch me." She pulled her hand away and turned to the dishes in the sink. "As soon as we sign the papers, I'll start on the tea." She held her breath, waiting for him to take back his agreement.

Behind her, Jonathan moved and she stole a glance

over her shoulder to watch as he pulled open her front door. "Start now. I'll have the papers ready tomorrow." He left and Roderick followed him with a rare smile in Mercy's direction.

She let out her breath in a sigh and went to Thomas. His face radiated pure joy, the owl in one hand and an equally well-crafted bear in the other.

****

Jonathan followed through on his promise, and Mercy handed off a week's worth of tea as soon as a copy of the paperwork had been filed with the town's magistrate and another rested in her hands. There wasn't more than a sentence or two exchanged between herself and Jonathan, making the experience better than she'd hoped.

He'd stormed out before the ink was dry. Mercy followed, slowed down by Thomas's pram when she reached the heavy door. She reached for the handle as the door opened. She stepped through and looked up at Roderick.

"Thank you." She paused once on the cobbled sidewalk. "And thank you for the gifts. Thomas hasn't put them down."

"It was no trouble." He let the door close. "If you're not busy, I told the jeweler's wife, Mrs. Hawthorne, that you may stop by." He nodded toward the point. "At the end of the lane to the left. I think you two may get on, and you could do to have another friend here."

He tipped his hat to her, then Thomas, and began to walk in the opposite direction.

The corners of Mercy's mouth turned up. "Are we friends then?"

Angling his head over one shoulder, he called back his one-word reply. "Aye."

Warmth spread through her chest and she turned Thomas in the direction of the point, bumping over cobblestones until they reached the jeweler's store. A hand-scrawled note stuck to the front door with an arrow: *Come round the back.*

Mercy followed the instructions and eased Thomas's carriage onto soft grass, rounding the house to find a gorgeous willow tree swaying against the backdrop of the bay.

A voice behind her rang out. "Hello. You must be Mercy."

Mercy turned to find the kind gaze of a woman who looked to be about the age of her mother. "Hello, yes. And you are Mrs. Hawthorne, I presume?"

"I am." The woman's face broke into a welcoming grin. "Would you like to come in for a cup of tea?"

Chapter Seventeen

Vee

Vee had settled onto the front steps of Bound, the watering can still in her hands. "So, she stayed."

Ema stood from the flower bed with a handful of weeds. "She stayed. But unfortunately, I have to go and the rest of her story will have to wait."

"Of course." Vee set the watering can down and stood. "Thanks for the distraction. I needed it this morning."

"No problem. It's what I'm here for."

The restless energy stayed with Vee through the morning. After breakfast, she sat in her makeshift art studio in front of a blank canvas, tapping her foot. Her mind replayed Mercy's story and she picked up a brush only to set it back down. She closed her eyes and rolled her head in a slow circle. Inspiration wasn't usually a problem and the lack of it prickled under her skin, a dam waiting to burst.

Opening her eyes, her gaze traveled over the canvases that lined the room. Varied colors and intricacies of the design didn't hide that they were essentially all the same.

What's wrong with me?

Above the canvases, the shelves along the back wall were bathed in the early afternoon light. Her mouth went dry. The figurines. She shot out of her chair, her eyes darted from one to the next. A rabbit, dove, deer, frog, crow…her hand shot to her cover her open mouth…*and an owl and a bear.*

She stepped back, stumbling when she knocked into her easel. Mercy's cottage at the foot of the Dryer property. This had to be the same one. *Her prison.*

Vee took a deep breath and looked around the room. It didn't feel like a prison. It felt like…*home.* The feeling of belonging surrounded her as much as it came from within. This had to have been Thomas's room. Her eyes darted back to the figurines. *A prison with good memories.*

The hair on the back of her neck raised and she whipped around, sure Mercy would be there.

Nothing.

She laughed to the empty room and rubbed her forehead. Barely two weeks with no internet or phone and she was already losing it. She needed to clear her head.

Crossing the hall to her room, she changed and slipped into running shoes. This time, she paced herself through town. A sign for the Dryer Nature Preserve peeked out through the trees and she paused at the map hanging beneath it. A couple paths joined to circle back to the entrance. *Perfect.*

Twenty minutes in, she cursed under her breath, pretty sure she'd missed the turnoff that would loop her back toward town. She was about to backtrack when she caught sight of a ranger hut. It didn't look open, but there was another map posted on its side.

She jogged to it and pulled out her phone to take a picture. Her finger traced the route she'd taken, looking for her mistake. There. The turn she wanted should be around the next bend.

About to set back out on the trail, a whirring noise made her pause. A few seconds later, an ATV roared down the trail, passed by, then reversed, rolling to a stop next to her.

The man set his dark brown eyes on her and flashed a smile. “You look a little lost.”

“No. I’m good. Thanks.” She started jogging purposefully in the direction away from where he’d been headed.

He reversed the four-wheeler to block her path. “You sure you’re okay out here all on your own? I can give you a lift back to town. Or to my place.” A cocky grin spread across his face as he looked her up and down.

If he wasn’t on the ATV, she would’ve considered a kick to the balls. “No. Really. I’m all set.” She pointed toward the trail he was blocking. “Do you mind?”

He raised his eyebrows and shook his head. “Your loss. But maybe we’ll run into each other again. Be safe out here.” The well-defined, tan muscles in his arms rippled as he gunned the engine and shot forward.

Vee jogged away, breaking into a full run the second she found the turnoff. Her ears stayed perked for the sound of his engine until she finally emerged from the woods onto pavement. She slowed to a walk, giving the tearing cramp under her ribs the break it wanted.

Prison or not, the cottage felt like a safe haven when she stepped through and locked the door.

The sensation that she needed to look over her shoulder melted away during a long, hot shower. She’d just finished getting dressed when a knock on her door revived the raw vulnerability from earlier in the day.

Nervous butterflies morphed into excited ones when she peeked out the window and caught a glimpse of a thumping tail. She pulled open the door and Luke's glacial eyes met her own.

He gave her a crooked smile. "I was taking Zeus for his vet appointment and thought we'd stop by to say hi."

She stepped forward and leaned against his solid chest. His arms wrapped around her and she relaxed fully for the first time since that morning. "Hi."

He tilted his head down. "Is everything okay?"

"Yeah. It's been a weird day and I have to get to work, so I don't have time to even start to tell you how weird." She pulled away and gave Zeus a pat.

"Want a ride?"

"Oh yeah. You're going to need your truck to get to the vet." She took a step back, about to run upstairs and get the keys.

He grabbed her hand and lifted it, kissing the back. "Nah. I took my dick-head brother's ride. Hopefully he needed it. Come on."

In her driveway, Luke opened the passenger door of the shiny black Range Rover but stopped her from getting in. He leaned down and plucked out an empty bottle of bourbon from under the seat. Shaking his head, he tossed it in the back seat, followed by a second one. "Fucking Blake."

He sighed and helped Vee in. A moment later, he settled into the driver's seat and started the engine. "So what made today so weird?"

She settled into the unfamiliar seat. "Probably the

strangest thing was learning the cottage I'm staying in has a connection to a witch."

The car jolted as Luke's head snapped toward her and they hit a pothole head-on. "What?"

Her stomach clenched, remembering too late how sensitive the topic was to his family. "It's nothing. Probably a coincidence. Someone was telling me about a woman who used to live in town. She described some figurines that sound identical to ones I found in the cottage."

Luke's face was a mask of concentration on the road as they turned from the driveway toward the inn. "That's not much of a connection."

"Yeah. My overactive imagination just took off." Saying it out loud, it did sound ridiculous. "The figurines would have survived two hundred years if it was true. I'm sure they'd be dust."

He pulled into a parking spot at the back of the inn's lot and turned to her. "Who was it telling you this?"

"A shop owner in town."

He leaned closer, his fingers grazing her jaw before he cupped her face and kissed her. When their lips broke apart, he whispered, "People in this town talk too much. Have a good night at work. I'll stop by tomorrow."

She hopped down and waved from the porch as he drove away. The inn's front door slammed shut behind her, but before she could turn a shoulder slammed into hers and JJ stomped down the stairs not slowing.

"JJ?" Vee called to her back, but she didn't give any indication she heard.

Shaking her head, Vee went inside, ready for the

day to be over.

****

Waiting tables through the dinner shift kept Vee too busy to think, and it wasn't until she left for the night that the first trickle of apprehension crept back in. She set her bag down on the inn's front porch and fished inside for her flashlight. The cold metal in her hand gave a solid reassurance, but she still jumped when the door swung open behind her.

Becca bounced out. "You coming to the beach? Damon's lighting a bonfire now."

Vee glanced at the dark driveway, then to the beach, where a warm glow grew larger by the second. She let the light drop back into her bag. "Sure."

Becca linked an arm through hers and pulled them forward. "Good. It'll be fun."

Vee fell into step with her. "You're allowed to light fires there?"

"Technically, no. But JJ's dad is the chief of police. He turns a blind eye, as long as we don't overdo it."

At the beach, most of the younger staff were surrounding what Vee would already consider "overdoing it," with flames leaping well over their heads.

Vee glanced around the crowd. "Where is JJ?"

Becca sighed. "I don't know if she's going to come. Apparently, someone saw Blake ripping through town on a four-wheeler today and thought it was a good idea to tell her he's back."

"A four-wheeler?" *Of course.* Vee shook her head. "I ran into an aggressive jerk on one today in the nature preserve. It had to be him."

"Probably. When he's in town, it seems like he's everywhere. Hopefully, he doesn't stay long." Becca dropped Vee's arm and peered around the fire. "Oh, wow. I think that's JJ coming now. I'm going to go check on her."

Becca had barely walked away when Damon called out. "Hey, Vee. Get over here for a game of Never-Have-I-Ever. There's no better way to get to know your coworkers than admitting your most embarrassing secrets in a public forum."

Laughing, Vee made her way around the raging fire and joined the group.

After a couple rounds, the wind shifted and Vee turned her back to the fire to keep the smoke from drifting into her eyes. She backed away, exiting the ring of light that the flames cast. A flicker of movement at the edge of the woods caught her attention. Two flickers actually, one taking quick strides, head down, the other keeping pace on four legs.

She crossed the beach quickly, trying to reach them before they got to the path and disappeared.

Rushing up the steps, she whispered, "Luke?"

He turned and paused. "Hey." His stormy eyes were calm and his mouth relaxed into a lopsided grin when he looked at her.

She crossed the road and stopped in front of him. Zeus shoved his head into her palm for an ear scratch. Her gaze traveled over Luke's sweatpants and T-shirt. "You out for a run?"

"Yeah. The party was a surprise." He nodded toward the beach.

"I've been told it's a rare occurrence. Any interest in joining?" She pulled her bottom lip in between her teeth.

He looked toward the fire. “Not even a little. But you go back, have fun.”

She nodded and ran the charm on her necklace back and forth. Seeing his old friends-turned-enemies, facing a party head-on, showing up with her like they were together…*Why’d I even ask?*

She turned to leave and his hand grabbed hers, gently pulling her back. He leaned down and met her lips with his for a slow kiss. When it ended, the look in his eyes sent a surge of desire all the way to Vee’s toes, leaving her light-headed. “You look so beautiful in the moonlight, by the way.”

Before she could respond, Damon’s voice raised above the general party noise that filtered toward them. “Vee! Where’d you go?”

Luke’s fingers relaxed and his hand slipped from hers. He took a step back so he was fully hidden in the shadows the forest provided. “Go. I’ll see you tomorrow.”

Vee turned back toward the beach. Damon was halfway between her and the water. He cupped his hands over his mouth and called, “Party’s not over, Ms. Disappearing Act.”

She glanced over her shoulder. There was no trace of Luke or Zeus.

Damon’s voice cut through the night again. “Paging Verity. Verity, you’re needed at the party.”

She jogged down the steps, shushing him as she went. “You’re going to wake the whole town.”

Damon clutched his chest. “Thank God, I really didn’t want to walk up that hill to get you if you’d gone home. Come on.”

She laughed and walked back to the fire with one last glance at the empty road.

Chapter Eighteen

Luke

In the dark cover of the forest, the ground tilted beneath Luke's feet and he braced himself against a tree. His lungs couldn't get enough air and he fought the urge to explode out of the woods.

Verity.

Her laughter trickled back to him, and his stomach clenched. He steadied himself and concentrated on taking deep breaths. His heart ached, at war with his brain. Vee could not be Verity Falls. Gail had kept track of her all these years. She'd just told him; Verity Falls was in…Boston. *Boston. Shit.*

Taking one last look at her silhouette, backlit by the bonfire, he turned and thundered up the hill at a breakneck pace. He exited the woods onto the lawn of her cottage and told Zeus to sit. The dog obeyed, panting while Luke jogged to the front door, ready to break a window if it was locked.

The knob turned easily and a soul-crushing panic descended on him. If she was Verity Falls, she'd been right here, under his father's nose, *with her door unlocked.* His vision clouded and he blinked his eyes, glancing around the dark interior. *Keep it together.*

Not sure where to start, he rifled through the kitchen drawers before making his way to her bedroom.

Invading her privacy felt wrong on every level, but he couldn't stop himself. He had to know.

Moonlight shone on her wallet, next to his car keys on the dresser. Swallowing, he flipped it open and slid out her ID, tossing the wallet to the side.

Verity Taylor. He almost sank to the floor with relief. *Not Falls.*

He ran a hand through his hair. The irrational fear had gotten his pulse racing faster than his run.

Picking up the wallet, he shifted his grip on the ID to put it back in its place. Her birthday stared up at him from the spot his thumb had been covering. His heart dropped to his stomach like a lead balloon. June fourteenth. Almost twenty-five years ago. The same day Verity Falls was born.

He set the wallet down where he'd found it with a shaking hand and backed out of the room.

No.

The part of him that had been so ready to believe only moments ago now tried to rationalize away the truth. Another coincidence. The odds of Verity Falls returning to Cliffside had to be a billion to one. It wasn't her.

Zeus fell into step with him when he strode through the front door. They took a slower pace up the hill. At the house, Zeus padded up to Luke's room while Luke continued through the maze of hallways to Eli's War Room.

Empty. *Thank God.*

He sank onto a chair and flipped open his laptop.

His fingers flew over the keys as he searched for Verity Taylor in Seattle, Washington and clicked through the links that came up until he found the one he was looking for. The site had basic info, name, phone number, approximate age, but it also listed other people who lived at the same address.

And there was only one, Rose Taylor.

He relaxed. Her Aunt Rose. And her last name was also Taylor, not Falls.

Be sure.

He typed the aunt's name into a search engine, ready to tie up the last thread. A people-finder website came up and he opened it, scrolling through a short list of the Rose Taylors who lived in Seattle. Clicking on the only one who fit the right age bracket to be Vee's aunt, he glanced at previous addresses and his jaw clenched. She only had one. Cliffside, Maine, almost twenty-five years ago.

The site offered an extensive background check for a one-time fee, but Luke buried his head in his hands. He didn't need any more information. It was her.

Verity.

Anger flooded through him and he hurled the laptop against the wall. It crashed to the floor in pieces. His breath, already coming fast, grew ragged.

The walls started to close in and he couldn't take being in the confined space as the worst memory of his life raked its claws over his skin. He fled from the room, through the winding halls, and out the front door. Rounding the side of the house, he kept running, right up until he reached the rail separating the edge of the cliff from the devastating drop. He let himself hit the railing hard, but it didn't give as the old one had.

With both hands on the cold metal, a sob escaped his throat and he squeezed his eyes shut, fighting against the memory that tore its way to the surface.

Oh, God. The thunder.

Vee's terror that night in the storm. She was right; it had been raining the night her mom died, but there'd been no car accident.

Luke squeezed his eyes shut, thrust back to the night that haunted him.

****

The storm threw angry tendrils of rain, lashing the window in ropes. Luke wasn't supposed to be home, but he'd backed out of plans to stay over at a friend's house with Blake at the last minute after they'd gotten in a fight. He didn't care. He was almost eleven. Too old to be hanging out with a couple of eight-year-olds anyway.

Luke had been watching TV when the power flickered and the cable went out. He made his way through the house toward the kitchen. The lights flickered again, then extinguished completely, plunging him into darkness.

A scream sounded from the front of the house.

Goose bumps ran down his arms and Luke changed his course, his walk turning into a jog. Flashes of lightning provided strobes of illumination every few seconds. He came upon the shadowed scene playing out in the entrance hall and froze. His father held a woman and a girl, who couldn't be more than four or five, at gunpoint next to the open front door. Gail stood off to the side, pleading with him to put the gun down.

Surprise overtook any chance to think, and Luke stepped toward Eli. "Dad, what are you doing?"

Eli swung toward the interruption, pointing the gun directly at Luke's chest. The wild look on his face had Luke lift his hands, sure he was going to shoot. But before Eli had time to do anything, the woman took advantage of the distraction, scooped up the child, and ran into the storm.

Pure fire and hatred filled Eli's eyes when his head swiveled to the open front door then back to Luke. "What the fuck is wrong with you? I had them."

"Had who? Who are they?" *Burglars?* It didn't make sense. Who would bring a child to a robbery?

Eli's words roared over a crash of thunder. "They're the end of us."

He took off after them, gun still in his hand, and Luke's head snapped toward Gail.

She was a ghostly wisp in the brief flashes of lightning, her face frozen in shock. "I didn't know…didn't think he really meant to…" She shook her head, and her eyes cleared. "Call the police."

"And tell them what?" His heart was pounding in time to the unrelenting rain.

"Tell them someone's hurt." Gail ran out the open front door, glancing over her shoulder to where Luke stood, immobile. "Luke, now," she yelled.

Her voice jolted him out of his stupor and he ran to the closest phone to dial 911.

Seconds later, a calm voice came through the line. "This is 911. What's your emergency?"

"I-I…we need the police and an ambulance."

"Okay. Can you tell me your name?"

"Luke."

"Hi, Luke. Do you know the address where you are right now?"

"The Dryer Manor."

Any response she had was cut off by another booming clap of thunder, and the line went dead. Luke dropped the phone and ran outside.

He raced across the yard, searching for any trace of them through the rain. A flash of lightning tore across the sky to illuminate the side of the house and Luke's stomach clenched into a cold fist. The woman and girl were backed against the flimsy wooden railing that marked the cliff's edge.

Gail grabbed Eli's arm as he raised the gun. A thunderous clap sounded at the same time lightning hit a tree on the edge of the property.

Startled, either from the thunder or mistaking it for a gunshot, the woman slipped. Her features twisted in terror. In her arms, the girl cried as they both fell backward, landing hard against the fence.

Luke blinked against the rain. It had to be a dream. *A nightmare.*

For a breathtaking pause, the thin strips of aged wood held their weight, but with a crack, it broke, tilting them both at a precarious angle over the edge.

Luke took a step toward them, but Eli's barking voice cut through the storm. "Don't you dare."

Luke paused, and in the stupidest second of his life, he believed his dad was protecting him from danger and about to help the woman and girl himself. When his gaze swung to Eli, the gravity of his mistake landed on his shoulders full force. Eli hadn't moved. Instead of even a hint of the horror the situation deserved, his expression was one of pure joy.

Another crack sounded as the fence gave way. The mother yelped, she and the girl both starting to slide.

Without hesitation this time, Luke sprinted, never taking his eyes off the pair. He'd almost reached them when they disappeared over the edge. He dove, arms flailing for anything to grab onto. His hand clasped warm skin that wrenched him downward.

Jagged pieces of the broken fence raked across his face and body as he fell. It slowed his descent enough that he was able to use his free arm to brace against one of the bent supports, stopping him from tumbling any farther. Luke lay face first on the remnants of the fence as it tilted precariously down toward the sharp rocks waiting below. The only thing still touching the solid ground above were the tops of his feet. But all that mattered in the moment was that his other hand clasped the little girl's. The mother was gone.

Luke gasped for breath, focused only on not letting go.

Behind him, thin fingers wrapped around his ankles with surprising strength. Gail's panicked voice rang out over the sound of the raging storm. "Pull her up."

Luke kept his eyes on the little girl's. "You're okay. I'm not letting go. But you have to climb."

Tears welled, but she nodded with the determination of a child given a very important task. She used her feet against the cliff to boost herself up, never letting go of Luke's hand. His shoulder muscles screamed, but he pulled as hard as he could, until she was close enough that she could wrap her small arms around his neck. Using the hand that had been holding hers, he nudged her farther. "Climb up my back. There's a lady at the top who'll help you."

Her tiny heartbeat pounded in his ears, even after she'd scrambled over him. Gail tugged on his ankles, shouting for him to push himself up.

Another clash of thunder broke through the night

and his arms began to shake. He inched himself backward, the jagged boards biting into his skin as he shifted position. Once he got far enough that his stomach was touching the cold earth at the top, Gail let go, and he rolled to his side. She ushered the child farther back from the cliff's edge and Luke crawled over to where the two of them sat.

Gail looked the girl over, panic in her voice. "There's so much blood. I can't find where it's coming from."

Luke tilted his head up. Cool rain stung his face, doing nothing to ease the fiery pain that came in waves.

Gail's gaze left the child and landed on him. "Oh my God."

The shock on her face confirmed the injury looked as bad as it felt. Gail reached a hand toward Luke's cheek but pulled it back before touching him.

Over her shoulder, Eli lay prone on the muddy ground.

Luke stared. "Did he slip?"

"That's what I'm going to tell him." Gail's hands shook and Luke followed her gaze to a bloody rock a few feet away from where Eli lay.

She stood, still holding the child, and approached Eli. She picked up the gun next to him and hurled it over the edge of the cliff. From the town below, the faint sound of sirens rang out over the quieting storm.

Returning to Luke's side, Gail knelt down and looked him in the eyes. "The police will be here any moment. I need to take the girl away before they arrive. Eli cannot know she survived. Do you understand?"

Luke turned to his unconscious father. "He was going to kill them both?"

"I don't know." She took a deep breath. "But if he was, then he will try again whether he's in jail or not."

"He can't actually want to kill her. She's harmless…"

Gail's answer was sharp. "Not to him." She stood. "I'll be back as soon as I can."

Her car had barely disappeared down the service driveway when the police and EMS pulled through the main gate. The house was still dark, but the rain had slowed to a drizzle, and moonlight peeked through the thinning clouds.

The officers started toward the darkened house, paramedics following. Luke stood and winced as razors shot through the right side of his ribs. He called out to get their attention and doubled over when the pain tripled from the effort. It worked, and the small group of police and paramedics changed course to rush toward them.

Two paramedics went straight to Eli, and the first person to reach Luke was the father of his classmate, JJ. The officer took one look at Luke and called over his shoulder, "I need a medic over here." Turning back to Luke, he put a hand on his arm. "Sit down, son."

Luke didn't move. His thoughts crashed together until an image swam through the storm. The terror in the woman's eyes right before she fell. He shrugged off the officer's touch and thrust a finger in the direction of the cliff. "A woman went over the edge. She may still be alive."

The officer's gaze flicked over Luke's shoulder to the broken fence. "Oh, Jesus."

He unclipped his radio and started to relay the message when Luke remembered what Gail had said.

"And a little girl. She was holding a girl when…she fell."

The officer's eyes widened. A swirl of dizziness hit Luke and he sank to the ground. The officer's voice faded away as he called again for a medic.

Luke woke the next morning in a hospital bed. Eli sat on the edge of the one next to him with his head bandaged, putting on his shoes.

Luke turned his face toward the window. Gail jumped up from her chair at the movement and went to his side.

She reached for his hand and squeezed it. "You're awake. Don't try to talk yet. Do you remember anything?"

He nodded. "Did they find her?"

She squeezed his hand again, hard, and shook her head.

"They didn't find either of them."

Eli's gruff voice cut across the room. "And they won't. The current probably carried them miles away. We can finally move on with our lives." He strode to the foot of Luke's bed and met his eye. "As long as you don't say anything stupid."

Luke glared at him.

"Don't give me that look. Before I tripped, I saw you try to save them. Tried to undo everything I've been working toward for years." His eyes were bloodshot and he gripped the foot of the bed. "If you'd messed this up, we might not have gotten a second chance."

Eli paused and took a deep breath. "There's a lawyer waiting outside for when the police come to ask you what happened. You say exactly what he tells you to. I'll see you at home after they release you."

Eli walked to the door but paused and turned back before opening it. "You're going to thank me for this one day. Every day until then, you can live with the scars to remind you of where your loyalty should lie." He pulled open the door and strode out.

Luke reached up and gently touched the bandages covering most of the right side of his face. He peered toward Gail. "How bad is it?"

"It's just cuts and you cracked a rib. You lost consciousness from shock. Physically, you'll be fine, and Eli will come around about the scars."

She held a glass of water toward him, and he shook his head.

Quietly, he asked, "And the girl?" Luke turned his gaze down, afraid of her answer.

Gail's soft voice soothed his broken soul. "She's safe."

****

Luke's knuckles were white where they clenched the rail.

He could never go back and change what happened. It had been a miracle he'd been able to save himself and the girl. But, if he hadn't hesitated…hadn't looked to Eli for guidance, could he have saved her mom? *Vee's mom.*

Every muscle in his upper body tightened from the strength of his grip.

All these years, wearing scars to remind him of his failure, the only thing that made it worth it was knowing the girl survived. And now, somehow, she'd made her way straight back to the lion's den.

A scream threatened to rip from his throat but died

with a terrifying thought.

Does Vee know?

Was she getting close to him, biding her time to take revenge? If she was somehow part of this, he couldn't bear it. Another person he cared about, using him, lying to him… Luke pushed off the railing and walked back to the house, head down.

Up in the tower, he stared out the window at the beach. Shadows shifted in the dancing flames. Any of them could have been her.

He rested his forehead on the cold glass.

Why did one of them have to be her?

Chapter Nineteen

Vee

Over a week. That's how long it had been since she'd found the note from Luke taped to her front door.

Something's come up. I can't see you tonight.

She slammed the door of the inn's linen closet as Becca came up beside her. "Whoa. What did the towels do to you?"

Vee pushed loose strands of hair from her face. "Nothing. Sorry. I'm in a bad mood."

"I may have something to cheer you up." Becca's eyes sparkled. "I'm having a little get-together at my place tonight. It's going to be incredible."

"Thanks. But I'm really not in the mood."

"Come on. It's Saturday. You have to come."

"I'll think about it."

Becca opened her mouth, then closed it again. "Okay. Think about it."

Vee managed to spend the rest of her shift avoiding people by folding laundry. When it was time to clock out, she finally emerged from the laundry room, almost running into Damon.

"Just the lady I was looking for."

"What's up?" She pushed the door to the laundry room shut and leaned against it.

"Becca asked if I could try to convince you to

come to her party tonight."

She cringed. "I don't think so. I'm not in the best mood."

"Something going on?"

"More like not going on. I think I'm being ghosted by flashlight guy."

"Ugh. I'm sorry." He raised an eyebrow. "Maybe a night hanging out with friends would help?"

She started to decline again, but he cut her off.

"Becca swore me to secrecy, but the reason she wants you to come so bad is that she happened to peek at the calendar in Meredith's office…"

"And?"

"And it has all the employees' birthdays on it."

"Oh." Vee tilted her head back. "And she saw mine is this week."

He put a finger on his nose. "Bingo. She thought a surprise party would be more fun on the weekend instead of waiting until Monday."

A small smile broke through Vee's bad mood. "That's really sweet of her. I'll go. What time?"

"Eight thirty."

She glanced at her watch. Just past five. Plenty of time for a nap to reset her mood. "I'll see you there."

On the way up the hill, her mind replayed her last few interactions with Luke. It still made no sense for him to just disappear on her. *Unless he's an asshole like his brother.*

To make things worse, Bound had been closed the whole week, taking her only hope of a distraction along with Ema wherever she'd gone on vacation.

Vee entered the cottage and trudged up the stairs. Flopping on her bed, she turned her back to the dresser so she didn't have to see his keys, the lone reminder that he'd seemed to care. She squeezed her eyes shut, but it was no use. If he wanted to end things with her, then she at least deserved to know it was over instead of being left to perpetually wonder.

Her feet landed heavy on the rug next to her bed and she snatched the keys up on her way by. She'd return them and make sure there was no question that they were done. It wasn't until halfway up the trail to his house that she swore under her breath. *I should have driven the truck.*

Even the idea of being home and hearing its engine signal Luke was nearby set an unwanted pang of longing through her veins. She paused, her chest heaving. Turning around risked the chance that she'd lose her grip on the anger and tip into sadness before she confronted him. Determined, she kept going up until she reached the side of his yard and slowed. The kitchen door was straight ahead and movement through the window caught her eye.

She forced her feet to take confident steps to the door and raised her hand to knock.

Before her hand connected with the wood, the door was roughly pulled halfway open and Luke's body filled the space, blocking her from seeing inside.

His brow was furrowed and his words were sharp. "You can't be here. Go, now." He looked disheveled in bare feet and a wrinkled T-shirt over equally wrinkled jeans.

Vee stepped backward off the stairs. Waves of apprehension turned into a tsunami of despair at the anger in his eyes. A sudden urge to cry washed over her and she bit the inside of her cheek, losing all her nerve.

He's done.

Before she could turn, the door whipped all the way open. Luke's hand shot out across the empty space, bracing himself in the frame. An older, heavier man stepped into view, blocked from going any farther by Luke's arm.

"Well, well. Who do we have here?" The booming voice wasn't any more welcoming than the scowling, red face it belonged to. "Move aside, Luke."

The muscles in Luke's jaw clenched. "No."

"Move," the man barked. *Eli.*

Luke met Vee's gaze with something worse behind the anger, fear. He dropped his arm and took a small step back.

Eli's watery brown eyes squinted in Vee's direction. "Can we help you?"

"Um, no thanks. Sorry. I made a mistake." She turned to go, heart pounding.

"Not so fast. This is private property. Accident or not, I report all trespassers to the police. What's your name?"

Eli started to step forward, only to be stopped by Luke, who clenched his teeth as he spoke. "She's not trespassing. I know her."

A look of shock crossed Eli's face and his eyebrows shot toward his combed-over hairline. He cleared his throat, recovering with a twisted smile. "My, my. A friend of Luke's. Please come in." He gestured for Vee to step forward.

Luke spoke through gritted teeth and his gaze bore into Vee's. "No. I'll see you later."

Eli snapped, "Don't be rude. Step aside for your *guest.*" His eyes sparkled when they turned back to

Vee.

Not sure what to do, she looked at Luke.

He glared at Eli but stepped back, making room for her to enter.

Eli looked down at her appraisingly as she walked past him and entered the kitchen. He held out a hand. "Eli Dryer. And you are?"

She grasped his clammy hand and fought the urge to pull away. Before she could answer, Luke cut in. "Her name's Vee. And I'm sure she can't stay."

"Nonsense. She came all the way up here. Can I offer you a drink, Vee?"

She tried to inconspicuously wipe the lingering feeling of Eli's skin on her palm away on her skirt. "No, thank you."

Luke glanced from her to his father. "She helped Zeus the other day. I told her she could stop by and see how he was doing." He gestured to where Zeus sat near the stairs to the tower, then stared pointedly at Vee. "As you can see, he's fine and you're free to leave."

Eli clapped his hands together. "Ah, but we must repay you for helping Luke's faithful companion. We were just about to sit down for dinner. Won't you join us, Vee?"

She was about to decline, but the smells coming from deeper in the house were intoxicating and her stomach let out an audible growl.

A smug look of triumph set on Eli's face. "It's settled then. Join me in the dining room when you two are ready, Luke." He strode out of the room, picking up a half-full glass of scotch on his way past the island.

Luke let out a huge breath and ran a hand through his hair. "I'm sorry. It's been a rough couple days. I needed some time to think."

"I'll just go."

She started to turn, but his sharp word stopped her. "No." He ran both hands over his face and stared at her. Shaking his head, he moved around her and closed the door. "If I try to hide you now, it's going to make it worse."

Hide me?

"The less reaction we give him, the quicker he'll lose interest. You leaving now would be a reaction." He paused, pleading with his eyes. "We'll eat fast."

His keys weighed heavy in her pocket, but all her desire to throw them at him had evaporated.

"Please." The tenderness in that one word sealed it.

She nodded and crossed her arms, following him deeper into the house.

They wound through the maze of halls until they passed a larger, more industrial kitchen that was the source of the delicious aroma. Luke paused and took a deep breath before stepping into the next room.

Inside, huge windows looked out over the ocean. Eli stood at one end of a table set for three but large enough to seat at least twelve. He uncorked a bottle of red wine and handed a glass to each of them.

"There we are. Vee, why don't you take the seat with the view?" He pulled out a chair facing the windows.

She sat and Luke started to pull out the chair next to her but Eli stepped forward, blocking him from sitting, and pointed to the chair across from her. "Now Luke, no need to be shy. I'm sure Vee's noticed the scars. Haven't you, my dear?"

Luke's knuckles turned white where he gripped the

back of the chair, his eyes locked on Eli's in a silent challenge.

Vee cleared her throat and picked up her wine glass. "I've certainly noticed the view. It's breathtaking." Truthfully, looking out over the water gave her the sensation they were floating and it was making her queasy.

Luke let go of the chair and took the long way around, avoiding crossing Eli's path.

Eli took his place between them at the head of the table and raised his glass. "To new friends." He clinked his glass lightly against Vee's. Luke took a seat, not touching the wine.

Eli spread his napkin across his lap. "So, Vee, do you live nearby?"

Luke responded for her. "She's only here for a summer job."

"A job where?" Eli took another long drink of wine.

"I'm working at The Cliffside Inn."

Eli scoffed. "I can't imagine that's worth traveling for." He started to say something else but was interrupted as a discretely concealed door opened in the corner.

An older woman entered from the kitchen, carrying a basket of rolls. Vee turned toward her and the woman startled, dropping the basket, all color draining from her face.

She stared at Vee, sending a chill down her spine until the woman's head snapped in Luke's direction, breaking the trance.

He shot up out of his chair. "Here. Let me help you."

The woman's gaze flicked toward Vee again and she bent to swoop up the basket. “Yes. Thank you. How very clumsy of me.”

“No bother, Gail,” Eli said, refilling his glass and emptying the bottle. “When you come back with fresh ones, could you bring another bottle as well?”

“Of course.” She stood and Luke placed the last of the rolls in the basket.

“I’ll get it,” Luke said, following her into the kitchen and pulling the door shut behind them.

Eli shook his head. “Poor thing’s getting up there in years. Still, she refuses to delegate when it’s just the family here.”

A vaguely familiar male voice came from behind Vee. “No one told me we were having company. Now, who do we have here?”

The man from the nature preserve strolled into the room.

Vee cringed when he approached. *Blake.*

Standing, he was tall but still a half foot shorter than Luke. He looked down at her, an initial expression of surprise turning into delight as he sank into the empty chair next to her.

The door to the kitchen opened and Luke emerged with an open bottle of wine while Eli made the introductions. “Vee, this is my other son, Blake.” He raised his eyebrows at Blake. “Vee is here as a guest of Luke’s.”

“Oh, is she?” He angled toward Vee in his chair and clasped his hands together. “So, tell me, Vee. Did my brother win you over with his charm, or was it his good looks?”

Luke took his seat and glared across the table.

"Blake thinks his bank account excuses the fact that he's a jackass."

Gail returned and set a wine glass down in front of Blake, followed by a plate and silverware.

"Thank you, Gail." He picked up the bottle and poured an oversized glass for himself as she disappeared back into the kitchen. After taking a long sip, his attention turned back to Vee. "I'm just saying, if you were looking for a rich boyfriend, you could have the more handsome model."

A laugh escaped Eli and Luke growled out, "It's not like that."

The conversation was momentarily halted by Gail coming back in with a steaming platter. "Roast haddock with a chorizo crust."

The dish she set down looked as amazing as it smelled, with a ring of vibrant asparagus and charred cherry tomatoes surrounding the portions of fish. Eli leaned forward and grabbed the serving spatula, gesturing for Vee's plate. "Ladies first."

Vee complied, handing him her plate.

Blake continued down the warpath with Luke. "If you're not dating her, you won't care if I ask her out?" He smirked at Vee, then looked to his father. "That is unless she's on the payroll. You trying that one again, Dad?"

"Enough." Luke slammed his fist on the table and stood, knocking his chair over. "Come on, Vee. I'll take you back to the inn."

He stormed out of the room and she stood to follow but Blake grabbed her arm. "If you want a less volatile companion, you don't have to leave." His thumb caressed the inside of her wrist as he spoke.

She yanked her hand away. "I'm ready to go, now. Thanks."

Outside the room, Luke waited just outside the door. "This was a mistake. Let's get you out of here."

Before she could answer, he took off down the hall, head down.

He didn't slow when they got to the front door or when leading her across the driveway toward the Range Rover.

When he reached it, he yanked open the passenger door but didn't wait for her to get in before circling around to get in the driver's seat. He already had the engine going by the time she climbed up and the second she pulled her door shut, he took off.

Tension radiated off him, but they both stayed silent until they reached the end of her driveway and he shifted into park next to his truck. He rubbed a hand across his chin then turned to look at her with a frown. "I'm sorry about that."

"I'm sorry for you. What a nightmare of a family."

"That's an accurate assessment." His eyebrows knit together. "Blake seemed to recognize you."

"We ran into each other a few days ago in the nature preserve. I didn't know who he was. I was more focused on getting away from him than exchanging names at the time."

Luke sighed. "It wasn't a pleasant encounter I take it?"

Vee let out a single laugh. "No. It wasn't."

He stared through the windshield at the trees. "I'm sorry about that too, then."

The gentleness behind the pain in his voice had her wishing she could read his mind. She ran her charm back and forth on her necklace. "What's going on, Luke? It's been over a week since you left me that note. Is it you're done with this?" *With me?*

"It's a complicated situation…my dad's completely lost his grip on reality—"

"Because of the curse?" She broke in.

He flinched. "Yes. Because of the curse. But it's going to end soon. The date will pass in a few days and it will be over."

She dropped the charm back to her neck. "Then?"

"Then we'll talk."

Hurt settled in her stomach like a stone. No point in drawing it out. "Talk now. If you're ending this, then end it. I don't want to go back to playing games with you."

"It's not that simple."

Her voice raised. "It is. God. The signals you send are so mixed." She huffed out a breath. "I should never have gone up to your house tonight."

"No. You shouldn't have," he snapped. "You shouldn't even be here. You should've never left Boston."

The words cut worse than anything she'd feared, momentarily taking her breath away. "Good to finally know where you stand. Goodbye, Luke." She dug the keys to his truck out of her purse and tossed them onto the seat.

"Vee, wait. I—"

She slammed the door only to hear his open seconds later. He jogged ahead, blocking her way. "Please. I didn't mean it to come out like that. I don't want to lose you." His hands clenched into fists at his side. "But I don't have a choice."

Tears threatened to break through her anger, but her voice didn't waver. "Then you don't have a choice. Move, please."

His voice lowered. "If you could just give me time to figure out how to explain…"

"I'm good." She crossed her arms and nodded toward the path he was blocking. "I have a party to get to, if you don't mind."

His eyes cut into hers, but he stepped aside.

She'd already reached the cottage's yard when his final words trickled through the trees. "I'm sorry."

The depth of sadness almost made her pause. Instead, she turned downhill and headed toward town, praying Ema's vacation had ended. If Mercy's story could distract her for a while, it would be late enough to make an appearance at Becca's party and go home. This day had to end.

A cool breeze warmed as Vee got closer to Bound. When she found Ema sitting under the willow tree, the air stilled.

Vee's shoulders relaxed and she took a deep breath. "You're back."

Ema looked up from a book. "Hello, Vee. Time for a little more of Mercy's story?"

"I'd love that."

Ema patted the ground next to her and set her book down.

Vee settled onto the soft grass, facing the water as Ema began.

"We left off with Mercy deciding to stay and finding a friend in Roderick. Over the next two years, that friendship would grow into much more…"

Chapter Twenty

Mercy

Mercy woke to a frantic pounding on the door downstairs. Her heart hammered in her chest almost as loud. Beside her, Roderick was already getting out of bed.

"Stay here," he said, slipping on pants before he left his bedroom.

Mercy wrapped a blanket around herself and crossed quietly to the door, cracking it open to hear what was happening.

Below, Roderick opened the front door. "Yes?"

A man cleared his throat. "Sir. You're needed at once. Miss Falls has gone missing and must be found immediately."

"For what reason?"

"The young Miss Dryer is very ill. Mr. Dryer is going mad with worry and has ordered a house-to-house search until Miss Falls is located. His daughter is unconscious at the manor."

Roderick swore under his breath. "Call off the search. She'll be right there."

The man's gaze flicked toward the second floor before he nodded. "I'll let him know her presence is imminent."

Mercy was racing around the room to get dressed

when Roderick returned to the bedroom. Jonathan's daughter, Julia, was still a child at fourteen. Time could not be wasted.

Mercy glanced at him as he pulled on his boots. They'd kept their relationship a secret since it began. Only on the rarest occasion did she stay at his house. But last night, the governess that Jonathan provided for Thomas had offered to stay with a knowing grin when Mercy mentioned she may be out late. It was a special night—the following day Roderick was leaving for a trip to Boston, and the morning would mark one year since their relationship began. Since they'd be apart by day's end, they wanted to begin it together.

She snatched up her bag, her thoughts trailing from her own concerns to the sweet girl who was suffering every moment she was delayed. "I need to get there quickly."

"I'll take you," Roderick answered.

Mercy's heart faltered. "You can't. He'll know."

He crossed to her and used his thumb and forefinger to tilt her chin up. "Word that you were here will precede us. He'll already know by the time we get there." He placed a calming kiss on her lips. "It had to happen. Now, let's go."

As the hoofbeats thundered up the hill, the solidness of Roderick in front of her was reassuring. Their protective bubble of secrecy may have burst, but surely Jonathan wouldn't be as possessive of her as Roderick feared. She squeezed him tighter and one of his hands left the reins to cover hers with a comforting warmth. It would be okay.

Jonathan's wife, Elizabeth, paced on the front porch when they arrived. Her presence did not bode well for what they would find in the house. She generally avoided Mercy at all costs. Mercy had once tried to convince her that she wasn't a threat, but Elizabeth had shown no interest in hearing her out.

As soon as Mercy's feet touched the ground, the woman ushered them into the house. Avoiding direct eye contact, she led them with brisk steps.

The anonymity of misplaced hatred would have been welcome compared to the look on Jonathan's face when she met him at the door to his daughter's room. The intensity of his gaze burned as she approached him.

Mercy cleared her throat. "What's happened?"

Jonathan didn't answer. He'd gone rigid watching Roderick round the banister at the top of the stairs and come up behind Mercy. "Get out."

"I'm not leaving her here." The sureness in Roderick's voice washed over Mercy, a cooling rain.

"She'll be fine," Jonathan said.

"Aye. That she will." Roderick took a step closer to her.

Jonathan opened his mouth, but Mercy cut in before he could speak. "Your daughter…What's happened?"

Jonathan glanced toward the open door behind him, then turned back, his rage dampened. "Julia." He took a deep breath. "I have a business associate and his son staying with us. She felt ill at the start of dinner and retired to her room. Almost an hour ago, the son found her in the kitchen and witnessed her collapse. We brought her up here, but no one's been able to rouse her since." He ran a hand over his face. "Any chance of him as a possible suitor in a few years is probably ruined after this spectacle."

Ignoring the callous remark, Mercy stepped past Jonathan and approached Julia. The girl's mother sat bedside, smoothing her hair. She left wordlessly upon Mercy's entrance and disappeared into the hallway. Mercy took her place and set down her bag.

After examining the girl, she was perplexed. There was nothing visibly wrong. No fever, her chest rose and fell at a normal rate, no visible injuries, and the pale complexion wasn't out of the ordinary for her.

Jonathan and Roderick had entered the room and stood on opposite ends from each other, watching Mercy silently.

Mercy lifted Julia's arm and let go, where it dropped heavily back to the mattress. "Is anyone else ill?"

"No. No one." Jonathan turned to the darkened window and slammed a fist down on the frame. "This makes utterly no sense. She was fine all afternoon."

Mercy would have likely voiced her agreement with his frustration had she not glanced down at Julia and caught the briefest opening of her eyes as they flicked toward her father. Mercy swallowed the comment and focused her energy on not reacting. Julia's eyes had closed so fast it was possible that it had been a trick of the light, but Mercy wasn't imagining the increased rate Julia's chest rose and fell as her breaths came faster in the aftermath of Jonathan's outburst.

Mercy stood and looked to each man in turn. "Both of you, out. I'll need to do a more thorough exam."

Roderick was closer to the door but didn't move until Jonathan conceded and stormed out first. With a nod to Mercy, he followed, pulling the door shut behind him.

Mercy sank back into the chair and leaned forward, propping her elbows on the bed. Keeping her voice low, she asked, “What is so bad about tonight that you’d choose unconsciousness over facing it?”

The girl didn’t make any indication she’d heard, and Mercy sighed. “I’m sure your father has already sent for the doctor in Proctor. It’s a thirty-minute ride, so he should be here momentarily and his method of assisting patients to regain consciousness is quite unpleasant, if not brutal.”

Still, nothing. Mercy sat up straight and slapped her palms on the top of her thighs. “Fine. I’ll let your father know there’s nothing more I can do here. Good luck.”

She stood and picked up her bag, only to stop when the girl’s meek voice reached her. “It’s Robert.”

Mercy sat and met the gaze of the miraculously recovered girl. “Who is Robert?”

Julia cringed. “The *suitor* my father mentioned. He’s disgusting.” She shuddered. “He hasn’t stopped sweating since he arrived, and he smells like onions.”

Mercy couldn’t help the smile that spread across her face. “That does sound bad.”

Julia’s look of misery changed into one of panic and she grabbed Mercy’s arm. “Please, you can’t tell my father. I was only going to feign a headache, but I got so hungry. I thought everyone had gone to bed and when Robert walked into the kitchen, I didn’t know what else to do.”

“So, you pretended to faint?”

Julia nodded and pressed her head back into the pillow.

Mercy took a deep breath. "All right then. Here's what we're going to do. I'm going to tell your father that your condition is most likely from being exposed to something environmental and that you will recover fully."

Julia frowned and swallowed but nodded.

Mercy tilted her head to the side and smiled at the girl. "I will add that you should stay on strict bedrest for the next two days and your visitors should be limited. That should keep Robert at a safe distance in case he mistook your faint for a swoon and doubles his attention."

Julia's eyes opened wide. "Thank you, Miss Falls."

Mercy patted her hand, then stood and turned to leave.

"Miss Falls?" Julia whispered, which made Mercy pause and look back. "If it's true that you are a witch, you are certainly a good one."

The hint of a smile crossed Mercy's lips. "Look drowsy when they come back in," she advised. Jonathan's wife pushed past Mercy as soon as she informed them that Julia had woken. Jonathan followed and Julia played her part perfectly, smiling while keeping her eyelids heavy.

Mercy placed a satchel of her own favorite blend of calming herbs on the foot of the bed. "Give her a cup of this tea tonight, and again tomorrow night. After that, the following day she should be fine to start with a gradual return to her normal duties."

Jonathan's wife made no indication that she heard her, other than a sharp nod of her head and Mercy left the two with their daughter.

Mercy and Roderick wasted no time leaving the

house. Roderick mounted his horse in the driveway and reached a hand down to pull Mercy up. Before she had a chance to take it, the loud slam of the front door made her turn.

Jonathan came toward them with long, angry strides.

His eyes were pools of fire when they landed on Mercy. “Since you’ve taken to sleeping *anywhere*, you’ll be staying here until I’m sure Julia’s well.” He grabbed her arm and turned, pulling her back toward the house.

Roderick jumped down and caught up to them in an instant, placing a firm hand on his brother’s arm. “Unhand her.”

Jonathan let her go and spun around to face him, his eyes wild. “You’re in no position to ask anything of me. After everything I’ve done.” Spit flicked from his lips with the words. “Everything I’ve given you. You have the nerve to take what’s mine?”

Roderick took a step toward him, his voice a low growl. “She’s not property to be taken.”

“The hell she isn’t. Do I not provide her a home? Pay her wages? Provide her son with the same governess who raised my own children?”

Roderick shook his head. “All the money in the world and you still have no sense. Having the decency to fulfill your end of the bargain you struck with her doesn’t make her yours. You have a business arrangement, nothing more.”

“Oh, that’s what you think? Have you forgotten, *brother,* that it was her love for *me* that convinced her to come here in the first place? You’re nothing but a conciliation.”

Roderick took a step closer to him, making them almost toe to toe. “Conciliation or not, I have her heart now and I didn’t have to pay to get it.”

Mercy stepped toward them, exhaustion weighing on her. “Stop. Now. Both of you. Let this night end.” She turned to Jonathan. “I will be at the cottage should you need me through the night, but I can assure you, Julia is in no danger.”

She put a hand on Roderick’s arm, and he allowed her to lead him away after only a moment’s hesitation. Jonathan didn’t argue any further, but his scalding gaze burned Mercy’s skin as they rode away.

The first hint of dawn was barely breaking through Mercy’s window when her eyelids fluttered open. Not sure what woke her at first, she rolled to her side and looked at Roderick, still asleep. He’d never stayed at her house before, both wary about Thomas inadvertently disclosing the nature of their relationship in one of his three-year-old rambling recaps of his life that he provided to anyone who’d listen. But after last night, there was no reason to hide anymore. The thought brought a warm smile to Mercy’s lips. It didn’t last long.

A quiet whistle sounded from outside, followed by a laugh.

“Brother,” Jonathan called from the front yard.

Roderick grunted as he sat up and joined Mercy at the window.

Jonathan stood in the front yard, a bottle in one hand and a sword in the other. His voice took on a sing-song quality of a child’s. “Dear brother. Come out, come out.” Jonathan took a drink from the bottle, threw it to the ground, and crossed to where Roderick’s horse was tied. His sword rose along with his voice. "Let's see if the scent of fresh blood draws your attention."

"Blazes. He's off his head." Roderick pushed back from the window and, for the second time that night, dressed in a hurry.

Mercy followed suit, stopping only to peer into Thomas's room and make sure he was still asleep. Both he and his governess slept soundly in side-by-side twin beds. She shut his door securely and followed Roderick outside in time to see Jonathan slice through the horse's reins. He slapped the freed horse firmly on his flank and laughed as the untethered animal took off toward the driveway, fresh rays of sunlight streaking through the trees lighting its path.

Roderick approached Jonathan with unhurried strides. He paused a few feet from him and tilted his head to the side. "You done?"

"I hope not, but we'll see. Won't we?" Jonathan threw the sword at Roderick, who caught it in one hand.

Roderick pointed the tip of the blade downward. "You're talking in riddles. It's time you go home."

"Not yet." Jonathan stepped to the side and picked up a second sword from where it lay in the grass. "I propose a tussle."

"I don't want to fight you." Roderick's voice stayed level.

"Why not? Because you're afraid I'll beat you here like in every other aspect of life?"

Roderick's answer boomed across the yard. "No, because I've already won."

Jonathan glared at him and he lifted his sword, tossing it from hand to hand. "Come on, *brother.* You win and I'll leave you two alone. I'll even give you a wedding gift."

"And if you win?"

"There's a ship leaving for England tomorrow morning. If you lose, I want you on it."

"No." Mercy's sharp yell cut across the yard from where she'd been watching the scene unfold. She stepped toward them, and Roderick turned to face her. Glancing past him to Jonathan, Mercy frowned. The excited glint in his eye caused goosebumps to raise on her arms. She turned her face toward Roderick. "I don't like this. You can't."

"There's really no risk. The worst thing is I take a trip at his expense, I'll be on a ship home the second my feet touch the other shore." One of his rough hands cupped her face and he tilted her head up to meet his eyes. "Besides, he's never bested me in a fight. Never."

Staring into the eyes that had provided her more comfort in the past year than she'd found in her whole life, she shook her head. "No." It was too much to risk.

He sighed and brushed his thumb across her cheek before he turned back to his brother. "Sorry. You'll have to keep hating us just the way things are for now. Go home, Jonathan."

Jonathan dropped his head and laughed. "You really don't get it?" He turned his eyes from the grass to meet Roderick's. "I always get what I want."

"What great news. Try to want to go home, will you?"

The fire in Jonathan's eyes turned to ice. "I knew she'd never come here. The old woman."

Mercy's breath hitched as a breeze blew through the yard.

"What?" Roderick squinted.

"The witch. I didn't even bother trying to convince her. Once I was sure of what they were"—Jonathan nodded toward Mercy—"I knew I could use it."

Siobhan. The ache radiated from Mercy's chest.

Overhead, thin gray clouds blew across the sun, dulling the morning light.

Roderick had frozen in place. "What do you mean?"

"I mean, that once the illness arrived, it wasn't hard to point the finger. As soon as I heard whispers of people falling ill there, I made a special trip and put the thought in the magistrate's mind." He looked past Roderick to Mercy. "To your credit, they were fiercely loyal at first. It wasn't until I returned a few weeks later that enough death had come to make them more suggestible."

The lone rider. The image flashed through Mercy's mind. From her view on the hill, she'd been so sure it had been Jonathan riding into town, then so sure she'd been mistaken when he didn't come to see her for weeks. It had been him. Come to plant the seeds that would hasten Siobhan's death.

"You didn't," Roderick said.

"You can be sure I did. It should serve as an example to you of how far I will go to get my way." Jonathan spun his sword in a slow circle. "At least, in this case, I'm offering you a chance. Fight me, *brother.*"

Roderick went from stone-still to lashing forward in a blur of movement. Jonathan barely side-stepped in time for Roderick's blade to catch the hem of his untucked shirt and not his flesh. A menacing grin spread across his face as he continued the movement to circle Roderick. A cold gust of wind blew through the trees as Roderick turned, keeping his eyes and blade trained on his brother. Jonathan lashed out, but the blow was easily deflected by a swift move of Roderick's sword.

Mercy brought her hands to her mouth, unable to cover her eyes, and unable to make herself scream for an end.

Round and round they went, Roderick clearly with the upper hand for the whole fight until he feigned a strike only to lash out with his foot, sending Jonathan crashing to the earth. Roderick pinned him with a boot on his heaving chest, tip of his blade at his throat.

Do it.

Mercy caught her breath at the thought, horrified by herself.

Roderick's face was a mask of fury, and she was sure he had the same terrible wish in that moment.

But instead, he spoke through gritted teeth, "You will leave us be. From this day forward, I don't want to see you so much as glance in Mercy's direction." A breath passed and he speared his sword into the ground next to Jonathan's head, then offered a hand to help him up.

Not saying a word, Jonathan glared at him but took it and stood.

Roderick turned to Mercy and their eyes locked, the ghost of a smile pulling his mouth up. Before she'd even taken a step toward him, it faded into a look of shock. The blade of a sword stuck out of his abdomen.

Behind him, Jonathan yanked it out and speared him again. He pulled it out one last time and stepped back, watching as Roderick took a tentative step, coughed up a mouthful of blood, and fell to the ground beneath an elm tree.

No.

Mercy's voice had left her. She ran across the lawn, collapsing next to him and rolled him onto his back. Her hands frantically pressed against his abdomen and chest, but she couldn't tell where the wounds were. There was so much blood.

"No. No. No," she whispered, panicking as she tried to remember anything that may save him.

Roderick's hand pressed against hers and she tore her gaze from his chest to his crystal blue eyes. He squeezed her hand, an impossible reassurance in the most devastating of moments.

"You can't go," she begged him. "A year wasn't enough."

Another squeeze as he choked on a breath. "It was everything."

His eyelids closed and his chest fell but did not rise again.

A wall of sadness descended over Mercy. She put her hands on his chest and focused all her energy on willing him back to life. Nothing. Every bit of power flowing from her hands poured useless on the ground.

Jonathan's cold voice came from behind her. "He's gone."

She froze in place, oblivious to the rising wind. Her hair whipped around her face as she stood and turned to face Jonathan.

He took a step back. "You so much as harm a hair on my head and I'll make sure your child suffers the same fate." He glanced toward the cottage, then at her. His words were hard, but there was an edge of fear behind them and it soothed Mercy like a calming balm.

The turmoil and instability raging in her veins drew inward, a snake coiling tightly before a strike. The last gust of wind blew past her, lifting her hair off her neck as gentle as a kiss and she narrowed her eyes. “I won’t kill you, Jonathan.” *But you will suffer.*

He cleared his throat, a semblance of confidence returning to his posture. “Good, right. I’m glad we’ve struck an understanding.” His gaze flicked to the ground behind Mercy, where Roderick’s lifeless body lay. Shaking his head, he walked away.

Mercy waited until he’d disappeared up the driveway before she pushed her anger deep down where it wouldn’t muddle with her rising sorrow. Slowly, she turned and sank to her knees beside the man who would never be replaced. The finest of rain began to fall, blanketing Mercy in a light mist. She stayed in the same position, head down, clasping Roderick’s hand to her chest, until the clouds finally burst. They poured out a lifetime of sadness in thick ropes of rain that fell straight down like arrows. When there was nothing left, Mercy rose a different person.

Ready for what would come next.

Chapter Twenty-One

Vee

Vee's mouth dropped open and she stared at Ema, pain for a woman long gone searing through her. "No."

Ema's mouth twitched, pity behind her gaze.

Hope surged. "He can't really be dead. Was it a mistake?"

Ema shook her head. "No mistake. Roderick died that day."

Vee looked out over the ocean. Gray reflected in the water from the clouds that had thickened across the sky as Ema talked.

A few moments passed before Ema broke the silence. "Are you okay?"

"Yeah. It's just been a long day." Vee wiped her eyes and checked the time. "I have to go."

Ema handed her a tissue. "The story's almost over. Come back soon."

Vee stood and brushed grass from her legs. "Thanks."

Twilight had fully claimed the day and tears blurred her vision. She stepped carefully down the cobblestone lane that led to the main road.

Mercy's sadness bled into her own and her next breath caught before it could fill her lungs. Roderick, Luke…how did it feel like she lost them both in a day?

Her pace slowed as she fought down a sob.

Above, the clouds shifted, spilling moonlight on the road and her head turned to face the clifftop house. Her gaze trailed down the hill, where somewhere her cottage waited. A certainty washed over her as a warm breeze caressed her skin, drying her tears. With or without Luke, this was where she was supposed to be.

She turned back to the road, her sure steps only faltering for a moment. *Please let it be with him.*

Chapter Twenty-Two

Luke

Luke stood in Vee's driveway long after she disappeared down the hill to town. The part of him that wanted to tell her everything lost to the half that couldn't bear the thought of how much the truth would make her hate him, and he stayed rooted to the spot.

Fucking coward.

It wasn't until the shadows lengthened in the setting sunlight that he strode back to the Range Rover and retrieved the truck keys from the front seat where she'd left them. Their sharp edges dug into his clenched fist. He deserved to bleed. His chest tightened, each breath coming on top of the last one. He had to tell her.

You lose her either way.

He flung open the door to the truck and hurled the keys in. Covering his face with both hands, he tried to regain control of his ragged breathing. When the threat of hyperventilating passed, he dropped his arms and bent to pick up the keys from under the gas pedal. Setting them in plain sight, he made sure the truck's door was unlocked before closing it and driving the Range Rover back up the hill.

Over a week he'd spent agonizing on what to do, and each sleepless night hadn't brought him any closer to an answer. With the curse date only two days away, things had gotten bad enough at his house that he'd sent Zeus to stay with Isa, far from Eli's unpredictable temper.

Everything was spiraling into chaos, but what little he could control to keep Vee safe, he'd keep doing. Knowing that Eli had set eyes on her, been close enough to touch her, had fire ants crawling under his skin. It took everything he had to not turn around and figure out what to say to Vee to get her to disappear. The only thing driving him in the other direction was that Gail would still be at the house. Her face when she saw Vee burned behind Luke's eyelids each time he blinked.

She'd recognized her.

Through all their conversations, she'd never hinted that she knew who Vee had become as an adult. And he'd asked her point blank. Hadn't he?

His feet continued to propel him forward as his mind replayed the last time Gail had visited him in Nova Scotia. It had been only a few months ago, well before Eli showed up and Luke agreed to come home.

****

A light drizzle from the morning had turned into a soaking downpour. Luke didn't wait for Gail to take off her jacket before he hugged her and he stepped back damp.

"I missed you too." She looked around his small cabin. "This is cozy."

He grinned. "It fits me."

She eyed the top of the door frame where it came just short of grazing his head. "Barely."

"Come in. Have a seat. Can I get you a drink? Coffee, tea, whiskey?"

She shrugged out of her coat and hung it on the back of her chair. "Tea, please." She raised an eyebrow. "With a drop of whiskey."

"Coming up." He made a cup for himself as well and joined her at the kitchen table.

She reached for her mug and slid it close. "Thanks. We need to talk about your father."

Luke rubbed his eyes and took a deep breath. "You know, when I was a kid, you never waited until 'three' before you'd rip off the bandage either." He picked up his tea, wishing he'd made it more whiskey than water. "Let's hear it."

She tilted her head and gave him a small smile. "Over the past few months, he's convinced himself there's a living Falls descendant."

"He knows the girl survived?"

Gail shook her head and stared into her mug. "No. Thank God." Returning her gaze to meet his, she said, "But he's sure there's *someone*, so he's resumed his search."

"Why now?"

"A major deal fell apart last June fourteenth and it got him all stirred up. Apparently, it should have been iron-clad, but it unraveled overnight and cost him a small fortune in time and expenses. He started looking at the past twenty years and found a few other unfortunate events occurring on that date each year."

Luke sighed. "So, he thinks the curse is still happening, which, in his twisted mind, means a relative of Mercy Falls must still live."

"Exactly."

Apprehension prickled under Luke's skin. "How close is he to finding the girl?"

"Not close, for now. He's combing through the genealogy. He's sure there's a cousin or an undeclared child somewhere in the line. It's going to take a while for him to come up empty-handed, and that buys us time." Gail sipped her tea.

"Time for what? Once he finds nothing, who knows where his mind will go? He may figure it out." Luke ran a hand through his hair.

"He may. But we have the chance to get ahead of him and redirect his efforts."

"How do we know where to redirect his attention if we don't know where she is?"

Gail looked down. "I know where she is."

"I'm sorry, what?" He coughed on his sip of tea. "I thought she went into the foster care system as a Jane Doe."

"That's not technically what ended up happening." Gail stared at her cup, twisting it on the table. "I wanted to make sure she stayed safe."

The thought that she could've been put into a worse situation hadn't crossed Luke's mind. Afraid of the answer, he asked, "And did she?"

The corners of Gail's mouth turned up. "From what I've gathered, she's had a wonderful life."

"So, you know her?" The crazy notion of meeting her struck like a bullet.

Gail shook her head and picked up her tea. "No. But I know enough that we can point Eli in a different direction. We just need an idea on how to do it."

Starting to warm from the tea and whiskey, Luke shrugged. "That's easy. I can start a breadcrumb trail that makes it look like fake Verity Falls is living somewhere far from wherever the real Verity ended up."

"We may need a better long-term solution."

"I don't think so. His drive is mostly based on the idea that something huge is going to happen in a couple months on the two-hundredth anniversary. Once that passes, he'll see he's nuts, or if it's as bad as he believes, we'll all be dead. Either way, she'll be safe." Luke glanced up from his mug, smirking, but Gail wasn't laughing.

He tilted his head. "Come on, Gail. You can't believe—"

"Of course I don't." She leaned back, cradling her mug in her hands.

"Good. Because that girl's life depends on it."

****

Nothing she'd said during that visit implied she knew Vee, but tonight, she'd recognized her. Not in the hey-you-look-vaguely-familiar way he'd expect for someone confronted with a grown-up version of a person they hadn't seen since they were five. The look on Gail's face when she saw her held an unflinching certainty she knew who Vee was.

When Luke followed Gail into the kitchen under the guise of helping her get the wine, the question she spat at him confirmed his thought.

What have you done?

It stung to remember the look in her eyes. Like he'd knowingly do anything to hurt Vee. Verity. *Dammit.*

Luke cleared the edge of the forest and parked. His dad's car was gone, but more importantly, Gail's was there.

He wasn't the only one that had to answer some

questions.

Luke jogged through the house, calling her name until her soft voice responded, guiding him to Eli's War Room. His steps slowed as he approached the open door, suddenly not wanting the reality this conversation would bring.

She was facing the timeline drawn on the wall, arms crossed and her back to Luke when he entered. She didn't turn, but her quiet voice broke the silence. "Did you know?"

No point in lying. "Not at first."

She let out an angry sigh and turned to face him, her eyebrows furrowed. "But you did know last night. You knew and you brought her here. Why? After everything we've done, everything we're *doing*...how could you?"

Luke cringed at the tears in her eyes. "I'd only just figured it out and I didn't know she'd come up here. Are Dad and Blake home?"

"No. Blake couldn't find his keys, but your dad's dropping him off somewhere."

Luke reached into his pocket, brushing Blake's keys. *Good. I hope he wasted a ton of time looking.*

Gail leaned against a desk and crossed her arms." "Does she know?"

"No. I was going to tell her…" Luke paused and cocked his head. "How did you know it was her?"

Gail pinched her lips together so tight they became thin white lines. When they parted, her face showed no emotion. "Because the woman who raised her is my daughter."

Luke sank onto a chair. "Your daughter?"

"Yes. Rose. She tried for years before finding out

she couldn't have kids. Her marriage ended over it and she'd given up. And then that night…things happened so fast."

"How?"

She sank into a chair and tented her fingers in front of her face. "I drove Vee to a hospital a few towns away to be sure we wouldn't cross paths with you and Eli. I didn't have a plan beyond making sure she was okay. The pain meds they gave her had her half asleep, and between that and the shock, she hardly said a word. She certainly didn't argue when I claimed to be her grandmother. It made me think about Rose."

She took a deep breath then continued. "Vee was asleep when they were getting ready to send us home and by then I'd settled on a plan. If she went into the foster system, she'd be too easy for Eli to find. She had to disappear. Back then, all the records were on actual paper, and I slipped her chart into my bag on my way out. We drove to Rose's and by the time I convinced my daughter there was no safer choice, Vee had curled up on the couch next to her and fallen asleep with her head in Rose's lap. There was no going back. She truly believes Rose is her aunt and, from what Rose has told me, she never regained her full memory of that night."

"So what? You've known her all this time?" An irrational wave of jealousy swept over Luke.

"From afar. I never visited; I couldn't risk the chance. Rose uprooted her whole life to move Vee away…I was content with the letters and pictures she sent." Gail's face softened and she looked at Luke with unbridled fear. "How did she get here?"

"I honestly don't know. She came for the job at the inn. It doesn't look like Eli had anything to do with it.

Then I was jogging and saw her fall into the ocean…" He shook his head. The absurdity was almost enough to make him laugh. "I didn't know who she was until a week ago and I've been trying to figure out what to do since then."

"Well, this can't continue. As long as Eli's here, she's not safe. We need her to leave. Rose's unreachable for the rest of the week, but I can try to get a message to her. She can make up an emergency that makes Vee go home."

"No." The firmness in his voice made it louder than he planned. "She can't leave. I can keep her safe here. It's the last place he'd look."

"Luke, that's insane."

"It's not." The thought of letting her disappear somewhere beyond his reach had his heart racing, but it also wasn't his choice to make. "I'm going to tell her the truth and she can decide."

"You can't. She'll realize her whole life was a lie. Depending on what happens, there could be legal ramifications for Rose." Gail bit her lip and shook her head. "You can't, Luke."

"I can't keep it from her."

"Then let me try to reach Rose. We can tell her, once she's far from this place."

"No. She's not leaving until she knows. You tried it your way, and she still ended up here."

The front door slammed, and Eli's voice rang out. "Gail?"

Her voice dropped to a whisper as Eli's footsteps echoed in the hall. "Luke, please."

"Gail?" Eli called, pausing in the open door. "There you are. Could you whip something up? I'm starving." His gaze landed on his son. "Why hello there, Luke. Expecting any more unannounced visitors tonight?"

Luke forced all emotion off his face, doing his best not to take any bait. "No. I think it's safe to say you scared the poor girl off."

Eli took off his jacket and folded it over an arm. "If she scares that easily, she's not worth your time. The last thing you want is someone who runs for the hills at the first sign of trouble."

"Good point." The lie burned on its way out.

"Plus, from what Blake said, that girl was all over him when you weren't around."

He knew it wasn't true, but even the thought stirred a swirl of panic in his chest. He gritted his teeth. "Good riddance then."

Eli smiled like a poker player who'd just bluffed his way to a win. "Glad you feel that way. Blake's hoping to run into her at some birthday party right now."

Any chance of keeping up the ruse that he didn't care evaporated. Luke was out the door and running toward the Range Rover, keys already in his hand.

Chapter Twenty-Three

Vee

Becca's house was easy to find on the edge of town. Music and laughter led the way as Vee walked up her street. When she got close, the small group on the porch rushed inside and the music cut. Vee couldn't help but smile.

Subtle.

She climbed the porch stairs and opened the front door. "Hello—"

"Surprise!"

Even though she'd been expecting it, the force of the greeting made her jump.

Becca cut through the crowd and flung her arms around Vee. "Happy almost-birthday. I'm so glad you came."

"Thanks, Becca, this is so thoughtful of you."

"You're one of us now. Drinks are over here." She pulled Vee to the kitchen.

Steering clear of shots and a huge bucket labeled "Punch," Vee opted for a beer and Becca pointed her toward the back door.

Outside, Damon stood next to the keg, filling his cup. "Beer for the birthday girl?"

"Yes, please." She glanced around, recognizing a few faces in the glow from the strings of twinkling lights that were hung around the yard.

"Here you go." He held her beer out and she took a drink as JJ stepped out the back door.

Her eyes locked on Vee. There was even more menace in her glare than usual before she whipped around to re-enter the house.

Vee took a deep breath. "I don't know what happened. She seemed to be starting to like me, but today, she hates me more than ever."

Damon focused his attention on the ground and stayed uncharacteristically quiet.

"Damon? Do you know why she's mad at me?"

He looked up toward the sky. "I mean…can we really ever know anything?"

"Come on. What is it?"

"All right, well, you know she's hung up on Blake. She thought when he came back, they'd get back together. Why she wants to waste time with that piece of crap is the real mystery." He glanced at the door she'd disappeared through.

"So? What does that have to do with me?"

He tilted his head toward her. "You're kidding, right? She told me she saw you two together at work today."

"What?" Vee exclaimed. "Never. No way."

"Vee, we all know his car."

"The Range Rover." It clicked and her pulse shot up. "That wasn't him."

Damon cocked his head. "His vanity plate is unmistakable." He pinched the bridge of his nose like he had a headache coming on. "I mean, WINNER? It's not even creative."

"It was his car, yes. But not him."

"Come on. Blake's not the sharing type." He took a gulp of his beer. "Look, I don't want to be in the middle of this, but I'll tell you, lying isn't going to help you make friends here."

He started to turn away and Vee took a deep breath. "It was his brother, Luke," she said quietly.

Damon froze and stared at her. "Luke? Dead Luke?"

"Yeah, but he's not dead. It's a stupid lie Blake made up. Luke didn't even know about it until I told him."

Damon grabbed her arm and pulled her to the side of the yard. "Are you fucking kidding me?"

"No. He's alive."

He ran a hand through his hair. "JJ's been beating herself up for years thinking she drove him to *kill himself.* What kind of twisted fuck makes something like that up?"

The worst kind. "I have no idea why he did it. But I know Luke hasn't been rushing to correct the mistake."

Damon's cheeks puffed out as he blew out a huge breath. "I need to tell her. She's mad at herself for nothing. She's mad at you for nothing."

"If I see him again, I'll let him know he's not a ghost anymore." Vee glanced at the barely drunk beer in her hand and set it down on a folding table. "I might as well go now. I'm not really in the mood for a party."

"I know the feeling," Damon said, following her into the house and out the front door.

She stopped in her tracks as soon as her feet hit the porch.

Blake jogged up the steps from the driveway and took a swig from the open bottle of tequila in his hand.

He flashed a smile at Vee. “Hey, just the girl I was hoping to run into.”

At the other end of the porch, JJ flicked a cigarette over the edge. She walked to the stairs, head down, and pushed past Blake.

Damon stared daggers at Blake. “You’re a real piece of shit, man.”

Blake clutched his chest. “Wow. That hurts coming from you. Who the fuck are you again? Wait…” He looked up and put one finger on his chin like he was thinking. He shook his head and smiled. “Nope, I still don’t care.”

Damon stepped toward him, and Vee broke in, pointing in the direction JJ had gone. “Damon, go catch her.”

He glared at Blake, then glanced at Vee. “This is so fucked up.” He turned away, shaking his head and jogged down the stairs, chasing JJ’s shrinking silhouette.

Vee crossed her arms. “What do you want, Blake?”

He came up the last of the steps and set the bottle on the railing. Next to them, the door flung open with a group of laughing, drunk people stumbling through. He put a hand on her arm to steer her to the side.

She yanked her arm away from his touch, and he smirked. “I thought it was time we got to know each other a little better.” He leaned one hand on the wall next to her head.

Her skin crawled from the energy between them. “Thanks. But I’m good.”

She started to walk away, but he slid his arm lower on the wall, blocking her path. “Hold on now. Don’t listen to everything you hear about me.” His gaze trailed over her body before coming to rest on her eyes. "I'm not all bad."

The heavy scent of alcohol on his breath turned her stomach. "I'm dating your brother. Does that mean nothing to you?"

"With the way you look, it means your standards are too low."

Vee glared at him, the fire of her feelings for Luke flaring. "You aren't half the man he is."

She started to step to the side, but his other arm shot out, pinning her in place. "Big words. But you can't be sure unless you give us both a chance, can you?"

Behind him, the sharp sound of tires screeching to a halt on the road cut through the night, but she kept her eyes on Blake's. "Move. Your. Arm."

Instead of listening, he stepped closer and leaned in with a lowered voice. "You can't seriously want him over me."

She shifted her weight, about to slam a heel down on his foot, when a hooded figure stormed across the driveway. The hood slipped down as he took the porch steps two at a time. Her heart betrayed her mind with the excited rhythm it jolted into. *Luke.*

Blake followed her gaze, and the smirk fell off his face as quickly as he backed away from her. "Hey, bro. Decided to join the land of the living?"

Luke positioned himself between Vee and Blake, his voice a low growl. "You touch her again, and you'll be leaving it."

"Easy. I'm on your side. I was testing her…making sure she's loyal."

Vee scowled, and Luke's hand clenched into a fist

at his side.

She reached for his arm, and he flinched under her touch. “Don’t, Luke. Let’s just go.”

Vee counted two more breaths by the rise and fall of Luke’s shoulders before he started to walk away.

Blake’s smug voice pulled him right back. “You should know she didn’t pass the test. She was two seconds from going upstairs with m—”

Luke’s fist connected with Blake’s face, sending him straight to the ground.

“You never know when to stop.” Luke shook out his hand and turned his back on his brother. His cold blue gaze landed on Vee. “Ready?”

She nodded, and he put a hand on the small of her back, gently guiding her through the group of people who’d come outside to watch the commotion. Aside from the music drifting from the house and a few whispers, the party had gone silent, with every face turned toward Luke.

In the middle of the street, the Range Rover was still running. Vee slid into the passenger seat while Luke rounded the car to where his door had been left open. She glanced out the window toward the house. Someone tried to hand Blake what looked like a towel while he leaned against the porch railing. He shoved it away, his eyes locked on Vee as the Range Rover shot forward.

Luke stared through the windshield with a clenched jaw. Not sure what to say, Vee let the silence stretch the whole way back to the cottage. He pulled into her driveway next to his truck and cut the engine.

Her heart pounded as he got out and strode around the front of the car to her door. He pulled it open, and she turned to him, uneasy. "Luke, I wasn't going to go anywhere with him."

He held his hand out to help her down, then wrapped both his arms around her, tilting his head down so his chin rested on the top of her head. "I know. I'm sorry that happened." He pulled back to look at her face. "Are you okay?"

"I'm fine." She reached for his hand and looked at the knuckles. They'd started to swell. "Are you?"

"I wish I hit him harder."

A breeze ruffled her hair, and she pushed it off her face before reaching for his uninjured hand. "Come inside."

His fingers wrapped around hers, sending their warmth up her arm.

How can something this hard feel so right?

Inside, Vee flicked on the lights and crossed to the freezer to get something for his hand. She pulled out a bag of frozen peas and turned to him, getting her first real look at his face. His brows were knit together in a frown and dark circles hung beneath his eyes.

She walked back, holding out the bag. "Are you ready to talk?"

He turned his gaze down but took the bag. "Yes. We should sit."

The scratch of branches on the window accompanied them into the living room as a gust of wind wrapped around the house. Vee tucked one leg underneath her on the couch so she could face him. Her other knee bounced from nervous energy trying to escape through the ball of her foot.

He slapped the bag of peas on the back of his hand and winced. "It's about what my family's doing." His voice dropped along with his head. "And what they've done."

Vee reached up and clasped the charm on her necklace. "Okay."

"You already know the rumors about there being a curse." His gaze flicked to her, then back to his hands.

"Yes."

"It's a story passed down in my family for generations, but my dad believes it. Like wholeheartedly is convinced that it exists." He flexed his hand and tossed the peas onto an end table. "He believes that a witch cursed his ancestor, and since then, the date of his death marks a tragedy in our family, every year. This year will be the two-hundredth anniversary, and he thinks it's going to bring something catastrophic."

She rolled the charm back and forth between her fingers as she thought. "And Blake believes it too?"

Luke let out a half laugh, half sigh. "I know he believes in staying in my dad's good graces until he gets his inheritance."

"That's why your dad does all the local research? He's looking for a way to break it?"

"Not exactly." Luke ran both hands over his face, then turned to look directly at her. "He thinks the curse will continue until all the descendants from the witch's bloodline are dead."

"His research…" A chill ran down Vee's spine and her stomach dropped. "He's looking for her family?"

Luke's eyes met hers, steel blue and sharp. "Yes."

Electricity between them prickled up the hair on the back of her neck. She swallowed even though her mouth was dry. "You said he asked you to come here to help with a project. Is this the project?"

He leaned forward, resting his elbows on his knees. "It is. But I'm not helping him." He turned his head to face her, his eyes shining. "I'm doing everything I humanly can to stop him."

She leaned toward him, resting her head on his shoulder. "How did you get born into the same family as them?"

He tensed. "I'm not that different from them."

"Stop." She nudged his ribs with her elbow. "I may only have my aunt, but she would never treat me the way they treat you."

He shifted to look at her. "She was good to you?"

"The best." A pang of guilt ricocheted against her ribs. "I hate that I lied to her to come here."

His voice lowered. "She would have stopped you?"

"I'd bet my life on it. All she ever wanted was a secure future for me, and now I've thrown it away."

"She really loves you." His face relaxed into a less pained expression.

"That goes both ways." Vee looked away as a horrible thought broke to the surface. "The woman who fell off the cliff years ago…was it an accident?"

Luke didn't answer until she turned her head to face him. His lips were parted, but his teeth were clenched and his eyes shone, two pools of pain as a single word fell flat. "No."

Leaves battered the window as sorrow rose from a forgotten place in her heart. "He killed her?"

Luke swallowed, his voice still rough when he spoke. "She fell, but it was his fault."

The sureness in his answer triggered another terrible revelation. "You were there? Your scars—"

He cut her off as his face crumbled. “I tried…I tried to save her. I just couldn’t…I didn’t get there fast enough…I’m sorry…I’m so sorry.”

He buried his face in his hands, and Vee launched herself toward him, pulling him close. “It’s okay, Luke. It wasn’t your fault. Shhhhh. It wasn’t your fault.”

Her eyes squeezed shut, each wave of his grief crashing over her as it poured out. She held tight, determined to be the anchor in this storm. When the calm finally came, she took his face in both of her hands and raised up on her knees to put herself at eye level with him.

“Every scar you have is proof that you have nothing to be sorry about. Don’t doubt that.” She used one thumb to wipe away the trail of the last tear.

His breath caught and he grimaced. “I don’t think I can bear it if I lose you.”

“You won’t lose me.” The invisible tether between them snapped tight, and she couldn’t close the distance between them fast enough.

The salt from his tears mingled with mint on his breath as her lips crashed into his. His chest rumbled with a low moan and his arms wrapped around her like a steel band.

Outside, the wind howled, and her lips trailed to his ear, gasping out a lone word. “Upstairs.”

In a seemingly effortless movement, Luke slid her onto his lap and lifted her with him as he stood. His mouth caught hers and they didn’t break the connection until he lowered her onto her bed and paused, hovering over her. “Vee, I really don’t want to hurt you.”

One of her hands lifted and she traced the longest of his scars, her heart fluttering when his eyes closed and he pressed his face into her hand. No one had the potential to hurt her more, but the certainty that he'd do everything in his power not to settled into her heart like it belonged there. Her answer came as the air stilled around the cottage. "You won't."

His eyes shot open, and she fell into them as they crashed together.

****

The next morning, Vee extracted herself from the tangle of sheets in her bed and showered before heading to the kitchen. She was about to pour a cup of coffee when he came up behind her, wrapped his arms around her waist, and nuzzled into her neck.

She smiled and leaned back into him. "I have cereal if you're hungry."

His voice was low. "Just coffee." He stepped back as she poured. "I poked my head into your art studio on my way down. You have a really specific style."

She turned and handed him a mug. "Not usually. Since I've been here, that pattern is all I seem to be able to paint."

"They're beautiful." He stared at the steam rising from his mug. "Haunting really, when you see them all together like that. What are you going to do with them?"

"I have no idea. I thought I'd paint a bunch of landscapes over the summer and try to see if a local shop would sell some. I don't know where to even start trying to find a market for these."

"Consider your first sale done. I'll take the big black and white one near the window. Just name your price."

"It's yours." He'd done more than just poke his

head in. That one was one of the first ones she'd done and it was buried behind at least two others. To find it, he must have really looked. Tears brimmed and she turned her gaze down. "Last night, I thought you were trying to end things with me. I had no idea what you were going through with your family being back."

He ran a hand over his face. "It'll be over soon. The date will pass tomorrow and Eli will see there's nothing to it." One eyebrow raised. "Or we'll all be dead and won't care anymore."

Vee's hand shot to her neck, gripping the charm. "That's what he thinks will happen, all three of you will die?"

Luke shrugged. "It's one of his theories."

Her mind circled back to a detail she'd almost missed. "Tomorrow? He thinks the curse date is June fourteenth?" *My birthday.*

Luke stared at his coffee and nodded.

She glanced around the kitchen. The same kitchen Mercy Falls stood in two hundred years ago. Her blood ran cold. "What if he's right? What if there is a curse?"

Luke shrugged and took a sip. "Then I guess I really will be a ghost."

"I'm not kidding. The woman in town who's been telling me the story of the curse, so far it all sounds very real. First, the figurines, now I'm almost sure this cottage used to be Mercy's."

Luke froze, color draining from his face. "She knows the witch's name?"

"Mercy Falls."

The lines of his face deepened with worry. "What else has she told you?"

Vee leaned against the counter and took a deep

breath. She started at the beginning and told him the whole story Ema had relayed so far.

When she finished, Luke rubbed his chin. “And this all started when she saw your necklace?”

Vee nodded. “She specializes in the same design.”

“I want to talk to her.” He crossed to the sink and set his empty mug inside.

“Now?”

“Yes. Now.” He pulled on his hoody.

“There’s no way the store is open now.”

The angles of his face hardened as he turned to her. “We’ll see.”

She grabbed a sweater off the back of a chair and followed him down the path.

The whole way through town, they didn’t pass a soul and when they arrived at Bound, it was dark with a sign in the window declaring it closed.

Luke peeked through the front windows then tried the knob, which turned in his palm.

“Luke,” Vee whisper-yelled, coming up behind him. “You can’t break in.”

“It’s not breaking in if the doors open.”

“The girl who works here is a little strange. She probably just forgot to lock it. We can come back,” she said to his back as he shoved the door open and stepped inside.

“Hello?” he called out.

“Luke,” Vee hissed, “this is trespassing for real.”

Ema’s voice floated out from the back of the building. “Vee? Is that you?”

Vee looked from Luke’s triumphant smile to the darkened interior and rolled her eyes. She led the way. “Yes. Sorry to bother you.”

In the back room, Ema opened the French doors to the view of the bay and turned. "No bother at all." She narrowed her eyes at Luke. "And you brought a friend."

Vee stepped close to him and took a deep breath. "Luke, this is Ema. Ema, this is Luke Dryer."

Ema's sharp eyes trailed from Luke to Vee, then back again before they crinkled into a warm smile. "Well then, I imagine you have a special interest in hearing the end of Mercy's story."

"I do," Luke said.

"And do you already know the rest of the story?" One of Ema's eyebrows twitched up.

Luke stared at her for a moment. "All but the end. I want to know how it ends."

A breeze blew from the ocean, lifting the willow's branches and a chill ran down Vee's spine as Ema's smile faded. "Even if there is no happy ending?"

Luke didn't hesitate. "I need to know. Sometimes endings change."

"Or they repeat themselves." Ema broke eye contact with Luke and her smile was back when she turned to Vee. "Shall we then?" She gestured to the table.

Vee took a step forward, but Luke caught her hand in his, stopping her. His eyes met hers as he entwined their fingers together then lifted her hand, placing a kiss on the back.

Vee smiled and crossed the room with him, unnerved by the fear and longing in his deep blue stare.

Through the open doors, dark clouds gathered over the cliff.

Chapter Twenty-Four

Mercy

Mercy stared from the edge of the yard as men loaded Roderick's body into a cart. Her tears spent, she felt nothing. He was gone. And she had things to do.

She made her way down the hill and through town, ignoring the thick fog that wound through the streets. She arrived at the silversmith's as Mr. Hawthorne was stepping out.

"Why hello there, Mercy. The missus is just putting some bread in the oven." Turning his head toward the kitchen, he called, "Dear, you have a visitor."

Moments later, his wife appeared, pulling off her apron. "Mercy, hi." As she approached, her eyebrows knit together in concern. "Is everything okay?"

Mercy nodded quickly. "Yes, quite. Thank you. I found myself with a couple free hours and thought I'd see if you had a few minutes to spare."

"I do. Why don't we pick up where we left off last time?"

It was exactly what Mercy had hoped for and she followed her out the back door as her husband excused himself to run an errand. They sat at the small table beneath the willow tree and her friend set down a basket of knotting cord. "Well, Miss Mercy-nothing's-wrong. Resuming our lesson should take your mind off whatever brought on that faraway look you're doing a terrible job of hiding."

Mercy gave her a halfhearted smile and picked up a length of cord. "Last time, you were showing me a binding knot."

"Ah, yes. Complicated piece of work." Fishing out two marbles from the bottom of the basket, she handed one to Mercy. "The trick is in being precise. Each time you circle the object you are trying to bind, the cord will cross itself and set a new axis. These intersections are where you focus your intention."

She leaned over to watch Mercy's work. "Good, but be careful. See where you've run your latest wrap parallel with one of the earlier ones?" She pointed at the mistake. "Single strands only. No two paths of the cord can overlap. Here, watch again." She repeated the process as many times as it took for Mercy to be able to do it on her own.

As they worked, Mercy let the conversation drift from one menial topic to the next until enough normalcy had passed that the questions she had wouldn't be suspicious. Mercy covered her mouth and exaggerated a yawn. "Pardon me. I was up late. Julia Dryer was ill in the night."

"Nothing serious, I hope."

"I don't think so, but it was odd. There seemed to be no reason for her affliction." Mercy lowered her voice. "I think I was called to help because her parents suspected a hex of some kind."

Mrs. Hawthorne's hands stilled. "That would be a very big accusation."

"Indeed. They were convinced otherwise by the

time I left, and the girl is now fine."

Mercy's friend exhaled and went back to crafting the knot in her hand. "That's a relief. Times have changed, but not so much that it's wise to let down one's guard. Accusations can lead to tragedy." Her eyes met Mercy's over the table. "As you well know."

Mercy knew. She focused her attention on the knot as she worked, to not appear too eager. "Siobhan never spoke of hexes to me."

"It's the darkest of energies. She was right not to speak on it."

Undeterred, Mercy cocked her head to the side. "But if I know nothing of it, how will I know if I encounter one?"

"It can be tricky. Depending on how recently the hex was cast, you may notice a deep feeling of wrongness when close to the person suffering, or you may only have a vague sense of unease if it's close to wearing off."

Mercy frowned. "How fast do hexes wear off?"

Mrs. Hawthorne raised her eyebrows, intent on her work. "Could be days or even weeks depending on how strong the intention of the one who cast it."

Deflated, Mercy's shoulders slumped. Weeks of suffering would not serve justice. "That's not very long."

"Not as long as a curse. Those can last years. Lifetimes in some cases."

Mercy held her breath, silently willing her friend to continue.

Across from her, Mrs. Hawthorne lowered her voice. "Now, if you come across a curse, that will be easy to recognize. You'll feel it in your bones as soon as you come across someone afflicted. Unless, of course, the curse is sealed in an object. Then you wouldn't know it was there unless it touches your skin."

Mercy's heart thundered with excitement, but she kept her voice calm. "In that case, wouldn't the object be cursed, not the person?"

"No. It acts as a conduit and a container."

"Why would someone want to put it in an object versus cursing a person directly?"

Mrs. Hawthorne undid her completed knot and held up the marble. "Like everything, a curse is simply energy. If it's directed and focused on a person, it joins their energy. When they die, the curse dies." She spun the marble in her fingertips. "Focus that energy into an object and it becomes immortal as well as much harder to detect."

Mercy faked a shiver. "That's it? You just focus the malintent on an object and it's done? That seems terrifyingly easy."

"It is and it isn't. Yes. The curse itself is created from only an intent, but there are other necessities depending on how bad the intention is."

The thrill of walking a tightrope flooded through Mercy. "What sort of necessities?"

Mrs. Hawthorne studied the knot she was working on and frowned, undoing it and starting over. "For a simple hex, intuition will usually guide." She glanced at Mercy. "Or so I've heard."

Mercy nodded, keeping her focus on her own work, each knot forming easier and more secure than the last. "And what about a curse? Something really harmful wouldn't come from simple intuition, I'd imagine."

"To cast the worst curses, and I mean something that would be truly devastating," Mrs. Hawthorne lowered her voice, "it needs to be born in blood. You see, this type of magic only follows the footsteps of death."

"So, someone needs to die for the curse to have life?"

"Exactly. The blood needs to touch the person or object directly."

Both women's eyes were drawn from their work to the door as sounds of Mr. Hawthorne returning came from the hall. A few moments later, he entered the room, his face grim. "Bad news from town. One of Jonathan's men passed in an accident this morning."

"Oh, no." Mrs. Hawthorne set down her cord.

"The big lad, Roderick."

Mrs. Hawthorne's face fell. "That is dreadful news. He was so kind." Her eyes fell on Mercy across the table. "Remember, just last week, he followed us halfway across town to return the toy Thomas dropped at the market."

"Aye," Mercy said, remembering him approaching them and gifting Thomas with a perfectly carved dove. One that certainly had not already belonged to his growing menagerie. Mercy cleared her throat. "I should head up to the manor. No doubt they are probably distraught with the loss." The words fell off her tongue like lead, but no one seemed to notice.

"Of course, of course." Mr. Hawthorne held out a hand to help her to her feet.

She thanked him, then added, "Once things settle down, I was wondering if I could beg a favor of you?"

"Name it."

"I have an idea for a charm, and I'd be ever so grateful to have you make one when the time is right."

"I'd love to, provided it's not too intricate. My old eyes aren't the same as they used to be, and I've had to start turning down some of the more delicate work I'm known for."

Intricate didn't do justice to what Mercy had in mind. "What if you teach me? In exchange, I'll help you with the work that requires a keen sight."

A wide smile broke out. "An apprentice," he exclaimed. "Why I'd be happy for the company."

Mrs. Hawthorne rolled her eyes and smiled at Mercy. "You've made his day. He's been hard-pressed to find someone with the patience it takes to craft in silver."

"Patience will not be an issue." *How could it be when time has stopped?*

Mercy bid them farewell and stepped back into the lane. In her palm, she clutched a perfectly constructed binding knot. Wound around a uselessly benign marble. Whips of the lingering fog swirled around her ankles as she walked, each step surer than the last.

****

After leaving the Hawthorne's, Mercy raced back to the cottage, praying that the drenching rain that morning hadn't washed the earth clean. She flew up the stairs to her dresser and dug through the top drawer until her fingers clasped the cold, white pearl Jonathan had gifted her years ago.

Planning on throwing it into the ocean after finding out about Jonathan's deception, she'd placed it on the dresser the night she first arrived at the cottage. A vague memory surfaced during her conversation with

Mrs. Hawthorne of it rolling into the top drawer where it had gotten lost in the garments waiting for her. She'd forgotten of its existence entirely. Until today.

Holding it in her fist, she rushed back to the yard and found the spot Roderick had last lain. She clawed at the soft earth, digging until her fingertips came up stained red. Her heart lurched and a miserable wail threatened to escape, but she focused on the task. Tossing the pearl into the hole, she buried it and pressed down the soil with both hands. Every ounce of focus she possessed homed in on the pearl, visualizing it in her mind.

The fog that persisted throughout the morning thickened and rolled across the lawn, swallowing her in an unrelenting wave. No longer able to see her hands on the ground in front of her, Mercy closed her eyes. Her lips moved in silence as she willed life into the curse.

The cold blanket of fog pressed in from all sides and gave texture to each of her inhales, nearly choking her on the earthy scent. She opened her eyes to a wall of gray, seeing nothing, feeling nothing except the cold dirt beneath her palms. Gently pressing her hand into the soil, her fingers found the pearl and she plucked it out.

The fog pulled back, the same way it had arrived, a tsunami receding now that its propelling force had crested. Mercy stared at the small iridescent pearl in her hand, no longer pure white but now as black as the darkest of nights.

In the cottage, she rinsed her hands until the water ran clear. She had to make herself presentable. The Dryers had suffered a loss, and she would go up the hill to pay her condolences. After straightening her hair and changing into a fresh gown, Mercy stepped outside into the sun, the dark pearl heavy in her pocket.

****

One Year Later

The Dryer's housekeeper led Mercy down the hall to the study where Jonathan spent most of his time since falling ill months prior.

The housekeeper looked back at Mercy over her shoulder. "Today's a good day. He's almost like his old self again."

"Good. Although, from the course so far, I imagine this is more of a glimpse of the past rather than a hint at a turn for the better." She could voice the prediction with confidence. The dose of belladonna she'd give him shortly would see that whatever lucidity was there today would be gone by morning.

The housekeeper gave her a sad smile as they arrived and gestured for Mercy to enter. "I'll bring his meal."

Mercy thanked her and stepped across the threshold. Jonathan sat in his wheelchair, a book in his lap, but his gaze out the window to where the sun was breaking over the horizon.

He didn't turn. "It's spectacular."

"It is." Mercy stood next to him and watched as deep red trails crept like fingers from the horizon, stretching toward the house and setting the morning alight in a fiery glow.

Quietly, Jonathan said, "Red skies at night, sailors' delight…"

"…Red skies in the morning, sailors take warning," Mercy finished the rhyme that Roderick had taught her.

Neither spoke again until the housekeeper returned

and set down a tray with tea and breakfast.

Surveying the tray, Mercy smiled when she saw Jonathan's meal included the porridge he favored. The cinnamon mixed in was perfect for masking the taste of the belladonna that she'd been slipping in his food and drinks for the past six months. It had taken an immeasurable amount of self-control to not start right after Roderick's death. But she'd taken the time to convince him that she'd finally accepted that her power didn't match his. And it didn't. Her power far exceeded anything he was capable of. He'd find that out today.

She stirred in a few drops of the poison and brought the tray to him, setting it across his lap.

He picked up the spoon immediately and began to eat. "Seems I have my appetite back today. You may have to ring the girl and ask for a second helping."

Mercy didn't respond and sat in a chair, watching him eat. His appetite certainly was back, his speech coherent, and the spastic movements that had plagued his arms and legs were nonexistent. Mercy exhaled. She'd tapered his dose a few times over the past weeks, experimenting to make sure he'd be able to comprehend what was going on when she wanted him to.

He set down his spoon in the empty bowl and picked up his tea with a steady hand. "Yes, I think call her. Tell her I'd like more. And maybe some bread with preserves. I'm famished."

"We should talk first. We don't have that much time." Less than fifteen minutes if everything went according to plan.

"What are you getting on about?" He put down the tea and used his finger to scrape the edge of the bowl for the last bit of porridge.

"Soon, the poison I added to your breakfast will start to take effect and your symptoms will return."

Jonathan cocked his head to the side and his eyebrows knit together in confusion. "What?"

"Don't fret. It won't be the worst day you've had. I kept the dose low today, so you'll be at least semi-aware of what happens."

He sat up straighter, staring at his empty bowl, then at her. "You didn't…you couldn't…"

She stood and leaned over him to remove the tray, her eyes inches from his. "Couldn't I?" She lifted the tray and set it on a side table.

He shook his head. "Impossible. If you were capable of it, why not just kill me outright?"

Mercy crouched down in front of him. "Because I want you to live. To live and see what I've set into motion."

He snorted. "And what is that?"

"I've cursed you, Jonathan. And your entire line."

A laugh burst out. "Okay, great. I was worried for a minute that you were serious." His left leg began to shake, and he placed both hands on top of his knee, trying to steady it and failing. His laughter ceased and he leaned forward in the chair. "Get the girl back in here, now."

"I'll call her in a minute. It seems like there's not much time left, and I'd like you to know everything. Even when your stupor returns, it will bring me comfort to know that somewhere in there"—she tapped one finger on his forehead—"you're aware of what's happening."

Jonathan clenched his teeth as a twitch jerked his head to the side. "Call her."

Ignoring him, Mercy asked, "Do you know what today is?"

"Tuesday?" he said with a sarcastic edge.

It fell flat since it was really Friday. A small reminder that she'd already robbed him of his basic faculties. That fact strengthened her. He was already nothing.

"It's June fourteenth. Exactly one year since you stole Roderick from me. One year of happiness, followed by a year of pain." The empty hole in her chest deepened momentarily and her breath caught. "I've gifted you the past year of bliss, not knowing what was coming, although I don't know how much you've enjoyed yourself." She paused and smiled as his pupils dilated. "Every year, on this date, you will suffer a tragedy. Unrelenting and unstoppable."

"I'll have you killed for this." Another spasm jerked his head to the side.

"You won't."

"Eventually, someone will enter this room and I'll tell them everything."

Mercy raised her eyebrows. "And you think they will believe you? Or care to believe you? After months of spouting paranoid delusions, incoherent ramblings, and outright abuse toward the people who've cared for you, tell me, who do you think is going to listen to the latest absurdity you wail on and on about?"

"I'll make them believe it." His jaw clenched again, allowing the words to escape through gritted teeth.

"You won't," she repeated, triumph welling at the first signs of fear in his eyes. "You're going to sit back and watch whatever tragedy unfolds today, helpless and weak. Then tomorrow, you can begin the nightmare of knowing worse things are coming."

"I'll refuse to eat or drink anything. I'll starve myself to death."

"Oh, please do. It won't matter. The curse will live on as long as blood of mine walks this earth with yours."

"I'll stop you."

The fire in his eyes did nothing except stoke the furnace already burning inside Mercy. "You can't."

Jonathan began to fumble with the cord around his waist, strapping him to the chair. One of Mercy's suggestions to keep him safe as the mysterious disease progressed. She walked around the back of the chair and slid it so that the clasp was behind him and out of his reach. A scream of frustration tore from him, his face red with a sheen of sweat developing on his brow.

Mercy walked across the room, looking back at him. "Count yourself lucky that I've been able to hold the doctor off from mistakenly treating you for syphilis. From what I've heard, the cure is worse than the disease." Mercy opened the door to the hallway, shutting it behind her to muffle his screams. She took a deep breath and strode down the hallway to the main dining room, where she found Jonathan's wife, sitting with her back to the door to face the massive windows overlooking the sea.

Opposite to Jonathan, the last six months had seen her well. Her usually gaunt frame had filled out and her skin had taken on color from spending more time outdoors.

Mercy paused after entering the dining room. "Mrs. Dryer?"

Elizabeth barely tilted her head toward Mercy. "Yes."

"I thought I should warn you that whatever reprieve Mr. Dryer's had from his symptoms has ended. He's working himself up into quite a state. He just began accusing you of poisoning him, I'm afraid."

"Me? Poison him?" The woman's shoulders rose and fell with a sigh. "Is that all?"

"Yes. I just thought you should be aware. I'll see if I can give him something to soothe his nerves and make sure he's looked after."

Elizabeth nodded but said nothing and went back to staring at the view on the other side of the glass.

Jonathan's tantrums raged throughout the morning. Mercy took no pleasure from them. He'd had similar fits since his symptoms first began, and they'd become mundane. By late afternoon, fear began to creep in that the curse had not worked. But then footsteps approached while Jonathan was in a lull between outbursts.

Elizabeth entered and went to his chair. "Jonathan." Her quiet voice roused him enough to lift his head from where it had been lolling on his chest. "There's someone here to see you."

She stepped next to him while Seamus, the man who'd replaced Roderick, stepped into the room. "Sir. I'm sorry to tell you, but there's been a fire at the dock. Both your ships were lost." He cleared his throat. "They were prepared to leave tomorrow morning. The loss of cargo…was great."

Seamus continued with the details, but Jonathan's gaze swung from him to Mercy. A strangled cry broke free from him, cutting the man off mid-sentence. "She's cursed us. Cursed us all." He yanked on his wife's grip, causing her to yelp as he pulled her closer. "She's poisoned me. Poisoned, and now cursed me."

Elizabeth tried to extract her hand from his with no success. "Jonathan, you're hurting me."

Seamus stepped forward, and Jonathan let go only to use his hands to brace himself and try to stand. Held in place by the belt, it was futile even if his weak legs would have found the strength from his rage to stand. Elizabeth stumbled backward, stopped from falling by Seamus' outstretched arm.

Across the room, Mercy stood alone, hands clasped together. Her breaths came quickly, and tears dampened her cheeks. *It worked.*

Seamus ushered Elizabeth out of the room, chased by a torrent of foul language as Jonathan's attempts to stand turned into angry thrashing. Mercy followed them.

Elizabeth had her arms crossed against her chest. "Just this morning, he accused me of poisoning him as well. Me, of all people."

Seamus took one look at Mercy's tears and shook his head. "Neither of you ladies should be subjected to this. I'll stay with him. Go call for the doctor," he directed Elizabeth and she nodded, quickly retreating into the house.

Mercy turned in the opposite direction and took fast strides toward the front door. A fresh wave of tears broke free as Jonathan's yells turned into screams behind her, and she covered her face to hide her smile until she burst out the front door. A laugh exploded from her as she lifted her skirts and started an unrestrained run down the driveway, her hair whipping in the wind behind her.

****

A full year of being Mr. Hawthorne's eyes had provided her with a key to his workshop, and after leaving the Dryers, that's where she went. Working through the night, the morning sun broke the horizon just as she finished cooling the final product of her efforts.

The door behind her opened and Mrs. Hawthorne stepped in, a shawl wrapped around her shoulders against the morning chill. "Mercy? I thought I heard someone down here. What's got you inspired so early?"

Mercy held the charm up to the light and her friend stepped up next to her.

Mrs. Hawthorne gasped and turned to her with wide eyes. "Is that a binding knot crafted from silver?"

"It is." Pride radiated from Mercy.

"Why, the silver's as thin as hair. This is incredible. May I?"

Mercy nodded and placed it in her outstretched palm.

Cool blue eyes immediately shot up to meet Mercy's. "What does it contain?"

Mercy grinned and took it back, fitting it on a chain and slipping it around her neck, then turning around. "Something that must be kept safe at all costs. Could you help me clasp it?"

Mrs. Hawthorne frowned but nodded and did the clasp as Mercy lifted her hair out of the way. "There. Would you like to stay for tea?"

"No. I think I'll be getting home. It looks like it's going to be a beautiful day." Mercy glanced to the open doors at the back of the workshop. Beyond them, the willow tree's branches swayed softly in the breeze as the sunrise erupted behind it, an explosion of orange and gold.

The woman smiled and pulled her shawl tighter around her shoulders as Mercy opened the front door to leave.

Pausing in the doorway, Mercy turned back to her friend before stepping through. "Thank you for everything, Emalina."

Chapter Twenty-Five

Vee

Goosebumps ran up along Vee's arms. Her fingers instinctively clasped the charm hanging from her necklace. The exact charm Ema had just described Mercy crafting in this very house hundreds of years ago.

Across the table, Ema sat with her legs crossed, hands folded in her lap, unnaturally calm for the story she'd just relayed.

Vee had told her the first day they met that her necklace held a black pearl. For Ema to take all this time…drawing out the story. Having a ridiculous palm reading would have been better. If this was a ruse, it went beyond elaborate.

Vee dropped the charm back to its place around her neck. "So, you're telling me my necklace is the same one Mercy cursed Luke's family with?" She glanced to where Luke slouched in his chair, one hand on the table toying with the edge of a napkin. *Is he buying this?*

When no one else spoke, Vee raised her eyebrows at Ema. "And let me guess…You have a cure or antidote to help restore my necklace to a non-cursed state."

Slowly, Ema shook her head. "No."

Vee frowned. "So, what was the point of the

story?"

"The point was to tell it. And now, I have."

Uncomfortable with the uncertainty of what was going on, Vee reclasped the charm between her fingers. "But what happened to Mercy? To Thomas?"

"Thomas lived a long and happy life. Mercy did not." Ema stared out the French doors at the willow tree. "Mercy's sole intention with the curse was to make Jonathan suffer. Even death wouldn't provide relief for him because he would die knowing the curse continued." Ema turned toward Vee. "She wasn't prepared for the toll it would take to watch the suffering his innocent loved ones would be subjected to. It wore on her, weakened her, and ate at her from inside until the day she died."

Vee could barely find her voice over the intensity of Ema's gaze. "Did she ever think of calling it off? Finding a way to stop the curse?"

"Almost immediately. The fire that tore through Jonathan's ships killed six men. The following year, Jonathan's daughter fell from a horse, crippling herself." Anger edged Ema's words and she paused to take a breath. "Mercy put herself in an impossible position. The curse would continue until Jonathan's bloodline ended, or hers did."

A sharp pang of regret coursed through Vee. She'd been so eager to have Mercy get revenge she hadn't considered the ramifications. "What about her friend? Mrs. Hawthorne. Couldn't she help?"

Ema's crystal blue eyes bore into Vee's. "If Mercy had told her what she was planning, she could have tried to talk her out of it. But once the curse was spoken, there was no going back. The only help she could provide Mercy at that point was the suggestion to use gloves when applying the belladonna topically once Jonathan began to refuse all food and drink."

"She kept poisoning him?" Vee's stomach churned at the thought of how much this must have weighed on Mercy.

"She'd given herself no choice. If anyone started to believe Jonathan's accusations, Thomas would have been in danger, along with herself. If it had been her alone, I'm quite certain she would have ended her life, stopping the curse in its tracks."

"But it wasn't just her." An image of Thomas giggling up at Roderick flashed through Vee's mind. The horror of having to choose your child's life over generations of innocent strangers filled Vee in a flood. A tear rolled down one of her cheeks, and Ema slid a napkin toward her. Vee wiped the tear away and quietly asked, "And Jonathan?"

Luke's low voice rumbled next to her. "He died ten years into the curse." He ran a hand over his face. "On June fourteenth."

Ema nodded. "His heart weakened from the belladonna."

Vee opened her mouth, then closed it again, not sure how to put what she was feeling into words.

Next to her, Luke tapped the table. "So how do we end it?"

A chill took the place of Ema's gaze as her attention left Vee and focused on Luke. "It won't end until it's fulfilled."

Luke's jaw clenched. "Bullshit. There has to be a way without my family all winding up dead."

"There is. Your father knows it, and you know it."

Ema's voice was devoid of emotion, but the hair on the back of Vee's neck stood up.

Luke stared across the table, matching Ema's intensity. His lips parted and a forced breath escaped. "Are you working for him?"

"No."

"But you just happen to know this story? All these details? Details that *he's* never even told me?"

Ema raised her chin slightly. "I'm a Hawthorne."

Luke laughed. "Of course you are. Let me guess, Ema's short for Emalina?"

Ema cocked her head to the side. "It's a family name."

Through the tension, a thought struck Vee. "Why don't we just give him the necklace?" She looked to Luke, who'd gone pale. "Your dad. We give him the necklace and he can destroy it?"

Ema shook her head. "It wouldn't change anything."

"So what?" Vee grabbed Luke's arm. "All we need is for him to think it could work. He destroys it, thinks the curse is over, and everyone moves on with their lives."

Ema leaned forward. "It won't work. The pearl is merely a vessel, a symbol of its existence. The curse would exist, contained or not. He would find it cannot be destroyed."

Luke slapped both hands onto the table and exploded at Ema. "So, what then? There's nothing we can do?"

Vee jumped at the sudden shock from his outburst, but Ema hadn't so much as blinked. The muscles in Luke's neck tightened along with his fists, but his agitation couldn't completely hide the fear in his eyes. A thick rope of dread tightened around Vee's chest. *He believes it's real.*

Across the table, Ema said softly, "I'm sorry. I can't change the past."

He leaned forward and growled, "But you think you can change the future?" He pointed back and forth between Ema and Vee. "Because otherwise, what's the point of this? Why are you telling her all this?"

"She has to know." Ema's gaze pierced Vee as it returned to her. "There will be a choice—"

Luke rocketed out of his chair. "There is no choice," he shouted.

Ema bit her bottom lip, eyes shining. "You'll see."

"Let's go," Luke said to Vee, then pointed at Ema. "She's insane."

Vee's legs trembled as she stood. Unnerved by the conversation, she noted that the walls and ceiling seemed closer than they had been moments ago. Luke disappeared out the French doors, but Ema sat still, staring at her hands.

"Ema, I'm sorry…"

The woman gave her a sad smile. "I'm the one who's sorry." She nodded to the door. "Go with him."

Vee gave her a last smile, then followed Luke's path to the door, tossing the napkin Ema had given her toward the trashcan on her way. She missed and stooped to pick it up, only then noticing a familiar logo. The coffee shop in Boston she'd been in when she found the flyer advertising the job at the inn.

Staring at it, she turned back, "Ema, when—"

Her voice trailed off, finding an empty table.

Behind her, Luke leaned into the door. "You

coming?"

Another chill ran up Vee's spine, but she balled up the napkin and tossed it a second time, not missing. "Yeah."

Outside, Luke flipped up his hood and tilted his face toward the ground.

He didn't say another word the whole walk back. That was just as well, Vee had no idea where to start.

When they reached her cottage, Luke faced her, misery pouring off him. "I have to go home, but can I come back? I have some things I need to tell you."

"I've got to get to work, but I'm off tonight at ten. Will that be too late?"

He shook his head and stuffed his hands into his pockets.

Before he could leave, she met his eyes, desperate to erase the fear that had settled there. "I just need you to know…none of this has me doubting my feelings for you."

The intensity of his stare was scalding. "It will." He broke the connection, thick eyelashes lowering.

She caught his hand, willing him to not give up.

He tensed, then his thumb traced a slow circle on her palm. "I'll wait for you here when you get off work. Don't go anywhere else."

She took a step toward him, but he turned and disappeared into the trees.

****

A couple hours later, Vee gnawed on her lip as she turned down the driveway to the inn. She'd showered and taken a cat nap, but the details of Mercy's story still felt raw.

At least it would all be over soon. Tomorrow was

her birthday. *The curse day.*

She shook her head to clear it and walked faster toward the inn. Luke's newfound belief had gotten under her skin. Maybe he'd come around to the idea of giving Eli the necklace. She clasped the charm. It felt wrong to even consider it, but at least it was something to try.

She spent the first part of her shift helping both the kitchen and the dining room, making sure lunch wrapped up smoothly. Half paying attention and half trying to keep her mind from replaying the morning, time passed too slowly. As the lunch crowd finally dwindled, Vee ladled out a bowl of soup and fought to keep her eyes open. Before she could sit, the swinging door to the kitchen slammed open and JJ stormed in.

She glared at Vee, not slowing as she passed. "You love the Dryers so much, then you wait on him. I'm taking a fucking break." She stomped out the side door to the kitchen's garden.

A pit of dread growing in Vee's stomach, she set the soup down. She stepped through the swinging door and froze. Blake sat at a table next to the windows, tapping the corner of his menu against the table.

Vee crossed the distance between them quickly. "What do you want?"

"A recommendation would be lovely. I was thinking the clam chowder, but I've heard rumors it's a bit thin."

Vee didn't react, and he put the menu down.

He held up his hands. "Fine. You caught me. I just wanted to stop in and apologize for last night. I would have never acted so boldly if I'd known the party was an early celebration for *your* birthday. I heard the actual date's tomorrow, right?"

"Yes. Apology noted. Please leave."

"And you're going to be what? Twenty-two? Twenty-three?"

She clenched her teeth. "Twenty-five. You need to leave, lunch is over."

"Interesting." He let out a short laugh, then pushed his chair back and stood. "That's fine."

She waited until he was halfway to the door before she picked up his discarded menu.

His voice calling across the room set her teeth on edge.

"And Verity?"

She glanced over her shoulder, one hand on the swinging door to the kitchen.

A look of triumph came over him. "Thanks for giving me what I came for."

She fought the urge to ask what he meant. Instead, she cleared the silverware and glasses from his table. Even if he didn't touch them, she wanted them washed.

Vee skipped her own lunch for a nap in an unoccupied guest room. Even with that, she trudged through the rest of her day, distracted and unfocused. It didn't help that one of the guests accidentally left their bathtub running and flooded both their own room and the one below. Vee stayed late to help with the clean-up and moving the guests to new rooms.

When she finally left, more than an hour after she was supposed to, the sun had long set behind the blanket of dark clouds that had hung overhead all day. She pulled her flashlight out of her bag as soon as she stepped off the front porch. Hopefully, Luke was still waiting.

Her heart sank when she reached the edge of her yard and saw the cottage was dark. The sorrow of Mercy's story hadn't left her all day, but now, standing here alone, she couldn't tear her gaze from the patch of lawn under the elm tree. A breeze crept through the leaves overhead and she shivered. In the distance, the slightest rumble of thunder echoed and her mind was made up. There was no way she could be here alone for another minute with the ghosts of Mercy and Roderick surrounding her and a storm on the way.

She made her way up the hill, each step coming quicker than the last as a second low rumble growled from the clouds. Fat raindrops had started to fall when Vee reached the Dryer house. Light spilled out from the kitchen to the garden, and Vee strode to the kitchen door. She raised her hand to knock, but a sudden gust blew past her, flinging the door open wide.

"Luke?" she called out. "Hello?"

Silence. She turned back to the open door and yelled for the dog in case he was back from Isa's and the reason it hadn't been latched all the way. "Zeus! Zeus, here boy," she called over the rising wind.

When he didn't appear, but a brief flash of lightning did, she ducked inside and shut the door tight. She called up the darkened staircase to the tower rooms, still with no answer.

The barn.

She stepped out of the kitchen and headed in the direction of the front door. She turned around once, then a second time when the halls she'd chosen dead-ended. She was lost.

A roar of thunder sent her already racing heart skyrocketing. She had to find Luke. Her mind tried to calm her. It was just a storm. She was safe inside. All she needed was to get to a window to the front yard. Even just seeing the lights on in the barn would bring comfort. And if the storm was as bad as it sounded like it was going to be, it would break whatever trance Luke was in while working. He'd come running and she'd be waiting inside the front door. If she ever found it.

Another turn into another unfamiliar hallway. She glanced out the window to her right as a streak of lightning illuminated the ocean. She groaned. Wrong side of the building. All she had to do was take the next left and she'd be going in the right direction.

She rushed down the hall, finally sure she was going the right way, but paused when the contents of an office caught her attention. Unlike the rest of the museum-like rooms in the house, this one was chaotic. Papers tacked up like wallpaper, boxes open with files piled wherever they fit. One wall was completely covered in a timeline scrawled in what looked like permanent marker. Stepping inside, she turned and froze.

Two side-by-side family trees stared back at her, written in the same thick black ink, almost all the names were crossed off. Except on one side, Luke, Blake, and Eli were intact, their respective birthdays written beneath the names. The second tree had only one name and birthday. Verity Falls. Circled over and over again.

A voice behind her made her jump. "You're not supposed to be in here."

Her heart pounding, she turned toward the door and pointed at the wall. "What is this?"

A massive clap of thunder struck, and Eli took a step into the room. “It’s your family tree, Verity.”

Chapter Twenty-Six

Luke

Raindrops splattered across Luke's windshield. He'd waited at the cottage until he thought he'd crawl out of his skin. Ten turned to ten thirty, one painful second at a time, then spiraled wildly into eleven o'clock while his mind raced through a million terrible scenarios for why Vee was so late.

Even if he was overreacting, now, with the promise of a storm, he could justify showing up at the inn as chivalry and offer her a ride home. Then he'd tell her to pack a bag and they'd leave. He'd made up his mind. He'd tell her everything, but far from here. She could hate him, as long as she was nowhere near Eli come tomorrow.

He eased the truck down the inn's driveway and pulled into an empty spot. The building glowed against the dark sky, warmth oozing from its windows. It wasn't enough to melt the block of ice that had settled in his chest.

The receptionist looked up when he plowed through the front door and the smile momentarily fell from her face.

Take it easy.

Between the stress and the scars, he probably looked like a serial killer. "Hi. I'm looking for Vee."

The girl's eyes flicked to a door propped open to a dining room and back to him. "Is she expecting you?"

A lunatic stalker who can't seem to take a full breath until he makes sure she's okay? "No. She's not expecting me, but..."

A vaguely familiar blonde came down the stairs with an armful of towels. "Luke?"

"Yeah. Hi. Becca, right?"

She beamed. "Yep. You looking for Vee?"

"I am. Is she still here?"

"I think so. I'll drop these off and go check for you."

A weight lifted off his shoulders, and he sank down into a leather armchair. The receptionist hadn't moved and she shifted from one foot to another. He glanced at her. "Is it okay if I wait here?"

She nodded more than was necessary. "Yes. Yes. Of course."

He tried to give her a reassuring smile. "Thanks." *Still don't need to waste money on a Halloween mask...*

"You're so much nicer than your brother."

"So I've heard. Sorry to hear you had a run-in with him."

"It's crazy. They told me Dryers never set foot here and now both of you on one night."

His heart lurched. "Blake was here tonight?"

Becca bounced back in. "Sorry. I was wrong. Vee left like twenty minutes ago. Time flies when you're cleaning—"

He was already out the door and running through the downpour to his car. His tires flung gravel in their wake as he floored it out of the parking lot and down the driveway. Panic clawed through his veins while his brain fought to rationalize the fear away.

He'd just missed her. She'd be safe and home, and they could laugh about his paranoia later. There were other reasons Blake could have gone to the inn besides to mess with Vee.

He glanced at the dashboard clock and he pressed harder on the gas. Almost eleven thirty. *Thirty minutes until June fourteenth.*

When he reached the turn-off that would take him to the cottage, dread weighed too heavily to check there again. If she was there, she was safe. But if she'd gone up the hill… He floored it, careening around the last bend to the Dryer Manor.

Slamming the truck into park, he jumped out and sprinted to the front door. Wind whipped the rain inside when he flung it open and raced down the hallway.

"Vee? Are you here? Vee?" His head swiveled side to side as he ran, peeking into each room that passed.

The faint echo of her voice reached him. "Luke!"

His feet hammered into the floor as he sprinted through the house. He flew around the corner and ground to a halt at the door of his father's War Room.

Thunder growled outside as his gaze landed first on Vee, then on his father.

Eli glared at him. "Why, Luke, how wonderful you could join us. You'll never guess what Verity and I were just discussing."

Luke's heart dropped at the casual use of her name and his head swung toward her. "Vee…" His words disappeared.

Her eyes brimmed with tears, and she pointed at the wall. "Is it true? You believe this is my family?"

His father's stare bore into him, but he didn't take

his eyes off her. *Think.* "I did at first. Because of your name, but I did a background check." He tore his gaze away to look at his dad. "It's not her. The name's a coincidence."

Eli pursed his lips and nodded. "And her birthday?"

Luke's mouth ran dry. "Another coincidence."

Eli's head tilted down and he laughed. "What a crazy world." He stepped toward Luke, forcing him to back up until he hit the stack of boxes behind him. Eli turned his rage-filled eyes up, lips curling into a snarl. His voice boomed in the small space. "And I suppose you're going to tell me that it's a coincidence she was raised by Gail's daughter?" He slammed a fist into the box next to Luke's head.

Vee jumped, and Luke met her terrified eyes as another crash of thunder broke overhead. Panic ripped through him, and he shoved his dad to the side, shouting, "Run!"

Eli pivoted and shoved Luke back against the boxes, pinning his neck with a forearm.

Next to them, Vee sprinted toward the door but skidded to a stop as Blake stepped in. "Leaving so soon?"

Luke struggled against his father's hold, but Eli pressed harder into his windpipe, cutting off his air. Darkness crept into the edges of Luke's vision, and he tore his attention away from where Blake had Vee trapped. Luke bent his knees. He exploded up, slamming an elbow into Eli's face and pushing him away as he ran for Blake.

A cold click came from behind, and he froze when a gasp escaped Vee.

Luke turned, stepping in front of her, his focus lasered in on the gun Eli pointed at him.

Blood dripped from Eli's nose and he pressed a handful of tissues to it with his free hand. "Enough. I want answers. Or I kill you both now."

Blake's normal bravado was gone as he stared at the gun in Eli's hand. "Dad, take it easy."

Eli's gaze barely flicked to Blake. "Shut up or leave." He turned to Luke. "Answers. Now. How is she alive?"

Luke's heart galloped in his chest, but Blake cut in, his gaze still on the gun. "Why don't we all go sit down and talk. She's not going to tell you how to end the curse if you're threatening her."

"She is the curse," Eli shouted, his face flaming red. He fired a shot into the wall behind them, and Vee screamed, clutching Luke from behind.

Luke reached a hand back to grab hers, making sure his body stayed between her and the gun. Trembling fingers found his and nausea from the sheer terror of what he had to lose rolled through his gut.

Luke held up the hand not gripping Vee's. "Okay. Okay. You only thought you killed both of them, but you—"

Spit flew from Eli's mouth and the gun shook in his hand. "They both went over the cliff. They should both be dead. How is she not?"

Out of the corner of his eye, Blake paled, but Vee rested her forehead against Luke's back and squeezed his hand. That small reassurance was all he needed to keep going, his voice cracking on the words. "I didn't get there fast enough to save them both." *Because of you.*

Eli wiped his nose again. "And that traitorous bitch sent her to live with her own daughter. When I find her…" He threw the bloodied tissues to the ground.

Luke stayed silent. There was no point denying Gail's involvement.

Eli steadied the gun. "Thanks for making this easy."

The slightest flicker of movement from Blake gave Luke the warning he needed, and he spun around, pulling Vee to the ground as Blake hurled Luke's broken laptop toward Eli.

The wild shot was deafening in the small room, and Luke's ears rang as he pulled Vee to her feet. He shoved her out the door as Eli dove to the floor to retrieve the gun.

Blake ran ahead of them, leading the way back to the front door. They raced out into the soaking downpour and the sky split open, a bolt of lightning striking the oak tree between them and Luke's truck. The tree exploded into flames, and Blake stumbled, falling to the ground and blocking their way.

Luke's head snapped toward Vee. The flames reflected in the wild panic of her eyes.

Another crack of thunder and she took off. She sprinted into the storm, headed directly for the cliff.

"Vee! Stop!" A gust of wind swallowed his words. He chased after her, lungs burning.

At the edge of the cliff, she stopped, facing the ocean, hair whipping in the wind.

She froze at its edge, turning slowly to face him with her eyes closed. Her lips were moving, but whatever they were saying was stolen by the wind. She paused and nodded, then opened her eyes. The calm there unnerved him worse than the terror it replaced.

She held up a hand. “Stay back.”

He slowed, panic ricocheting through his brain, making it impossible to figure out what to do. If she was thinking about jumping, he didn’t want to force her into a decision. “Vee, wait—”

Eli exploded out of the shadows of the house. He plowed into her, pulling her to him, and pressed the gun against her head. “This time, I want to see a body.”

“Vee!” Luke shot forward.

“It has to be this way.” Her eyes met his for the briefest second before she tilted her head up, rain running in rivers down her face.

The hair on Luke’s arms stood on end. His gaze swung from Vee to the sky, eyes widening.

No.

A scream tore through him over the roar of the storm as a shatteringly bright bolt of lightning hit Vee, sending Eli flying backward.

Luke charged across the lawn, catching her as she collapsed.

Cradling her in his arms, his heart fought to ignore what his mind already knew. There was a difference in lifting an unconscious body and a dead one, and Vee’s lifeless body hung, dead weight as he lowered her to the ground.

No. No. No.

He turned her face toward him, gently tapping her cheek. “Vee…wake up. Come on, wake up.”

Blake ran to them, stopping next to Luke. “Holy shit. Did that hit her?” He ran a hand through his hair, his words tumbling into one another. “It looked like it hit her. Is she okay? Holy shit. Is she okay?”

Luke pressed his head to her chest. His own heart threatened to stop. "She's not breathing." He used both hands to press into her chest, over and over. "Please, Vee…"

Blake fumbled in his pocket. "I'm calling 911."

Luke leaned down, breathing for her, begging her to return.

Blake's rambling into his phone was nothing but static. All that existed was Vee and the overwhelming desire for her to live. Each compression of her chest, every breath from his lips into hers, every tear falling from his eyes were a prayer.

The distant whirl of a siren echoed up the hill as the storm receded.

The piercing bullets of rain had gone. Now, soft drops fell, kissing her face while he searched for any sign she was coming back.

He leaned down to check for breath and a pulse.

There was nothing. Just his unanswered prayers, drifting away with the storm.

Chapter Twenty-Seven

Vee

Shouldn't it hurt to burn?

Vee swam through darkness without moving. She'd been running, terrified of Eli, terrified of the storm, terrified for what Luke would do to stop his father…then Ema's voice echoed through her mind.

There will be a choice…

The fear left, bringing a calm acceptance in its wake. Mercy's presence was in every drop of rain. Each breath of wind that caressed her skin was an apology. For the curse to end, she had to die.

In the moment the choice had to be made, her eyes landed on Luke and his scars. *He saved me first; now it's my turn.* The suffering her blood had unknowingly carried for generations melted away as Vee whispered the acceptance of her fate. "Take me and end this."

There'd been no pain when the bolt struck, just a white glow, lifting her out of her body and into the dark.

Then, Luke's voice. A guiding light through the storm.

She followed his calls and sensation came back to her as the storm faded away, nothing left but a gentle mist.

Her eyes fluttered open and landed on Luke. Dark

hair hung in damp strands as he leaned over her, brow furrowed. His piercing blue eyes went wide, and he placed his palms on each side of her face. "Vee, can you hear me?"

She nodded, her throat scratchy. "Yes."

"Oh my God. Oh my God." He clutched her to him. "Are you hurt?"

His arms were shaking, but they were solid and warm beneath his soaked shirt as she clung to him. "I don't think so."

Over his shoulder, Blake waved his arms, signaling the arriving paramedics. Vee turned to where she'd been standing before the bolt hit. There was nothing but singed grass. "Where's your dad?"

Luke's head snapped up. He crawled to the cliff's edge and looked down. Sitting back on his heels, he shook his head. "I don't know."

****

Vee's eyes opened to sun streaming through her hospital room's blinds. Luke sat in the chair next to her, his long legs stretched out in front of him and head resting on the wall. She rolled to her side and let her gaze trail over every line on his face.

Last night had been a whirlwind of paramedics, doctors, blood work, and machines. Luke had been by her side through it all, demanding they run every test the hospital had at its disposal. There hadn't been a minute alone to talk before they'd given her a sedative and she slipped into a dreamless sleep.

His eyes opened, the crystal blue tearing through her with their intensity.

He pitched forward and ran a hand over his face. Resting his elbows on his knees, he clasped his hands.

"How do you feel?"

"I feel fine."

He frowned. "I'm so sorry. I should have told you." He stood. "I just wanted to make sure you were okay…I'll go."

She sat up and grabbed his arm. Gently, she turned his palm up and placed her hand in his. The scar running down his arm met hers and continued on her skin, one line from him to her. She turned her gaze up and met his. "You saved me."

His voice was barely above a whisper. "Yes. But I couldn't save—"

Vee rocked onto her knees and pulled his face down to hers. "No more apologies. You've done nothing that needs to be forgiven."

A sigh escaped him as their lips met and his arms swooped around her back, pressing her to him. Her heart pounded as the world around them faded away.

He broke the kiss by cupping her face, his lips trailing across her cheek to her ear. "I don't want you to leave me again."

She pulled back enough to stare into his eyes. "I won't."

His gaze swept over her. "There's something you need to see. He pulled out his phone and handed it to her with the camera open, her face filling the screen.

A gasp escaped her, and her hand flew to the neck of her hospital gown, pulling it down and angling the camera lower, goosebumps breaking out from the chill that shot down her spine. "What is that?"

Blossoming out from her ear, a fern-like pattern spread down her jaw to her neck, then fanned out in deep red tendrils across her chest and stomach before trailing down her left arm.

"The doctor said they happen after a lightning strike. He called them Lichtenberg figures."

She reached up and ran a finger along one of the trails, the movement familiar. The radiating paths burned into her skin were the same ones she'd painted over and over since she arrived.

Luke cleared his throat. "They should fade, possibly even in a few days."

She passed him back his phone. "I hope they don't." *They were meant for me.*

Luke's mouth spread into a wide grin, and he leaned down to kiss her again.

A cheerful nurse opened the door. "Good morning. Oh…" She cleared her throat. "Well, good to see you're…up. You have another visitor."

Behind her, Blake stepped into view. Dark circles framed his bloodshot eyes. "Can I come in?"

Vee swallowed but nodded. He walked in with his head down and hands in his pockets.

Luke tensed. "What do you want?"

Blake frowned, his face haggard. "I want to say I'm sorry. To both of you. I never thought the old man was actually trying to hurt anyone. I knew he was crazy but capable of this…" He glanced toward the machines next to the hospital bed, then to Vee. "Are you okay?"

It was impossible to hate him when he looked so worried. "I'm fine. They've tested every inch of me at this point."

Blake let out a sigh. "Good. If you need anything…" His gaze flicked to Luke, and he shrugged.

He started to turn toward the door but stopped when Luke spoke. "Any word on Dad?"

"Not yet. The coast guard's out searching."

Vee bit the inside of her lip and leaned into Luke. No matter how awful Eli had been, part of her hoped he'd be found safe and sound. Death left no room to repair.

"Let me know if anything changes." Luke watched his brother as Blake took a step toward the door. He cleared his throat. "And thanks, Blake."

Blake glanced from Luke to Vee and nodded before slipping out of the room with his head down.

Luke's arm slid off Vee's shoulders. He sank onto the bed next to her, rubbing his forehead. "What a mess he made."

Vee raised her eyebrows. "Eli?"

"Yeah. I half believe Blake didn't know he'd take it this far." He snaked an arm behind her and pulled her close.

Vee used one hand to turn his face toward hers. "Can we go now, or do you have another battery of tests you're going to badger them into doing?"

The slightest crinkle of a smile tugged at the edges of his mouth. "You know you technically died, right? You're lucky I don't have them fit you for a protective bubble."

She pulled away, raising an eyebrow. "Go find whoever can discharge me, or I'm sneaking out the window."

****

They pulled up to the cottage and Luke jogged around the truck to open her door. He tried to help her down, but she pushed him away. "I'm really fine."

Shockingly, it wasn't a lie. A new energy coursed through her veins, her fingers itching for a paintbrush.

Finally.

On the bench in front of the cottage, Gail waited with Zeus at her feet.

Both stood as they approached. Gail smoothed her already smooth hair.

Vee slowed to a stop in front of her, her face softening. She had Rose's mouth. The enormity of what the woman had done for her welled up and she threw her arms around Gail's neck, whispering in her ear, "Thank you."

Gail pulled her close. "I'm so sorry. I didn't know what else to do. I spoke to Rose. She's going to be on the next flight." She cleared her throat and pulled away. "We both understand that there will be legal consequences for our choices."

"There won't." Vee shook her head, one hand scratching Zeus behind the ears. "You did everything you could to keep me safe, more than most would have done. I owe you both so much."

Gail's lips parted, taking in a hitching breath. She squeezed Vee's hand. "I look forward to getting to know you."

Luke wrapped an arm around Vee's shoulders but focused on Gail. "Any word on the search for my dad?"

"They found blood on the rocks at the edge of the cliff, but they haven't found him." Her voice dropped. "No one could survive that fall. It's turned into a recovery rather than a search. I'm sorry."

Luke shrugged. "I figured as much."

Gail pulled a small package from her pocket, handing it to Luke. "Here you go. I'll go start supper and have Blake bring some down when it's ready."

Vee jumped in, "You don't have to do that." Evil

or not, Gail had known Eli for decades. This news couldn't be easy to digest.

Gail waved her comment away. "Nonsense. It'll occupy my mind for a while."

Before she could leave, Luke hugged her, his arms enveloping her small frame. "Thank you for picking up Zeus and thank you for everything else."

Gail squeezed her eyes shut then pulled away, turning quickly and waving a hand toward the cottage. "Go, rest. I'll see you both later."

She disappeared into the trees as the clouds returned, covering the sun and dulling the day.

Luke held the package out to Vee. "Happy Birthday."

Vee gave him a half-hearted smile. "Hard to be happy with what happened to your dad."

Luke pulled her closer, resting his chin on the top of her head. "He did it to himself. If it weren't for him, none of us would have been up on that cliff. Either time."

Vee tilted her head. "Still, I thought since I technically died, the curse would have broken. Him dying means we can't be sure."

"We can't be sure it wasn't broken either." Luke nodded toward her gift. "Open it."

She unwrapped the plain brown paper. Inside, a picture-perfect carving of her cottage fit in the palm of her hand.

Luke pointed to a tiny latch. "It's a jewelry box. I thought it would be a way for you to remember this place, wherever you end up going next."

Light streamed from between the clouds, matching the warmth coming from within. "I can't picture myself anywhere else."

His voice rumbled. "That's because you haven't seen my place in Nova Scotia. Six hundred square feet of drafty heaven."

Vee grinned. "You really know how to sell it."

"You'll see." He started toward the cottage with Zeus, but she didn't follow.

Her gaze drew to the patch of earth under the elm tree. "I'll be there in a minute."

Luke nodded and followed Zeus in.

She walked to the tree and knelt on the ground next to the cold spot. Tentatively, she reached out a hand and placed it on the grass.

Nothing.

No chill, no goosebumps, no douse of cold. She ran her hand through the soft grass that covered the place Roderick had died, the place the curse was born.

Sitting back on her heels, she unclasped her necklace and held the charm in her palm.

A single beam of light cut through the clouds, shining on the metal.

Vee squinted, the pearl easier to make out than usual. Her breath caught and she closed her fist, unbelieving. Unwrapping her fingers, she peered down. The iridescent pearl peeked through the silver, no longer black but pure white.

Tears blurred her vision at the impossibility of such a tangible sign that the curse had died with her.

She shot to her feet. She had to tell Ema.

****

"You're supposed to be resting," Luke grumbled as they turned onto the cobblestone lane.

"I feel fine." Bound came into sight and Vee took

quicker steps.

She pushed through the front door. Amanda's eyes flicked up from her phone. "Need help?"

"No, thanks." Vee hurried through the rooms until she reached the last one.

She stepped through the curtained doorway and froze. It was the same…but not.

Beside her, Luke's face mirrored her confusion.

The French doors were there, overlooking the willow tree as its branches drifted on an unseen breeze. But, instead of a table for two, a workbench strewn with tools and half-finished projects took in the view.

A chill ran down her spine and she took a step back, bumping into the display case next to her. She reached out a hand to steady the stand of necklaces on top as a young woman stepped into the room.

She set down a bag and smiled at Vee with eyes that felt familiar. "Oh, hello. Are you interested in trying one on?"

Vee clasped the charm on her own necklace, sliding it along its chain. "No, thank you." She glanced at the worktable that looked like it had been there forever. "I was actually looking for Ema Hawthorne."

"I'm Ema Hawthorne. How can I help you?"

"No. I mean…is there another Ema?" Vee glanced at Luke then back to the unfamiliar woman.

"I'm sorry, but I'm the only Ema."

"My mistake—" Vee's apology was cut off as the chain around her neck snapped. She tightened her hold on the charm, keeping it from falling to the floor. "Oh, no."

New Ema held out a hand, a warm smile pulling up the corners of her mouth. "Maybe you do need me. Let me see."

Vee handed it over, clearing her throat while Ema studied the charm. "It's a binding knot."

"I know." Ema nodded toward the row of necklaces behind her. "I made those. This one is incredible, though. Where'd you get it?"

"It's been in my family for a long time."

Ema took it to her workbench, examining it under a magnifying light. "One of the links in the chain broke. I'll have it fixed in a sec."

Luke's phone rang with Blake's name coming up on the screen. Vee nudged him when he silenced it. "Go, take it. It may be about your dad."

He nodded and ducked through the door, answering the call.

A minute later, Ema stood. "There. Good as new." She dropped it into Vee's waiting hand.

Vee reclasped it around her neck. "What do I owe you?"

Ema waved a hand in the air. "Don't worry about it." She tilted her head. "You said you were looking for someone else named Ema?"

"I did. I thought she worked here, but maybe I was mistaken." Vee's cheeks flushed as her eyes darted around the unfamiliar room. *Or hallucinating.*

"Well, if you're going to be around for a while and are looking for friends, a couple of us meet here for tea on Wednesday afternoons." Her gaze flicked to Vee's charm, then trailed down the pattern the lightning had left on Vee's arm. "I think you'd fit right in."

"That would be great. My name's Vee, by the way."

"Nice to meet you, Vee. I hope to see you soon."

Vee thanked her again and made her way back through the shop. In the front room, Amanda caught her eye. "Want your books?"

"My books?" Vee approached the register.

"Vee, like the letter, right?"

"Yes." She pinched her arm as she crossed the room, half sure she would wake up at any second.

Amanda reached under the register and pulled out the stack of books Vee had left her first day in the shop. Amanda rang her up and slid them across the counter. She plucked a bookmark from a pile and handed it to Vee. "Here you go."

"Thanks," Vee said, tucking the books under one arm.

Outside, she flipped the bookmark over and found the store's logo on one side, the store's history on the other. *Bound has existed one way or another for the better part of two centuries. Starting as a simple jewelry store, it has grown over the years and become a fixture on Cliffside's point. Handed down through generations, it has stayed in the Hawthorne family since Emalina Hawthorne first opened its doors in 1832.*

Beneath the description, a hand-drawn portrait of Emalina stared back at Vee. She paused in the middle of the cobblestoned street as the familiarity of her friend's eyes bore into her.

Luke walked toward her, pocketing his phone. He glanced at the bookmark and wrapped an arm around her. "You okay?"

She nodded and leaned against him, relishing in his solidness. "Are you?"

He squeezed her closer and pressed his lips against

the top of her head. “I’m good. Let’s get you home.”

Vee glanced back toward the shop. In the window, Ema, who should have been dead for two centuries, stared back. She raised her hand in a wave and smiled through the glass. A warm breeze lifted Vee’s hair off her neck, and she blinked, brushing it out of her eyes. The window, now empty.

A word about the author...

Josie Grey comes from a long line of story tellers. She's carrying on the tradition with her own blend of suspense and romance. When Josie isn't writing, she can be found practicing yoga or spending time with her two young sons.

Thank you for purchasing
this publication of The Wild Rose Press, Inc.

For questions or more information
contact us at
info@thewildrosepress.com.

The Wild Rose Press, Inc.
www.thewildrosepress.com

Milton Keynes UK
Ingram Content Group UK Ltd.
UKHW022052110624
443988UK00015B/638

9 781509 254392